W9-BUF-671

FEB 13
FEB

A PERFECT
EXPLANATION

A PERFECT EXPLANATION

....

ELEANOR ANSTRUTHER

Houghton Mifflin Harcourt
Boston   New York
2020

To Pardy

. . . .

For information about permission to reproduce selections
from this book, write to trade.permissions@hmhco.com or to
Permissions, Houghton Mifflin Harcourt Publishing Company,
3 Park Avenue, 19th Floor, New York, New York 10016.

hmhco.com

First published in Great Britain by Salt Publishing Ltd.

Library of Congress Cataloging-in-Publication Data
Names: Anstruther, Eleanor, author.
Title: A perfect explanation / Eleanor Anstruther.
Description: Boston : Houghton Mifflin Harcourt, 2020.
Identifiers: LCCN 2019024925 (print) | LCCN 2019024926 (ebook) |
ISBN 9780358120858 (hardcover) | ISBN 9780358123040 (ebook) |
ISBN 9780358172277 | ISBN 9780358306733
Subjects: LCSH: Campbell, Enid, 1892–1964 — Fiction. | Argyllshire
(Scotland) — Fiction. | GSAFD: Biographical fiction.
Classification: LCC PR6101.N76 P47 2020 (print) |
LCC PR6101.N76 (ebook) | DDC 823/.92 — dc23
LC record available at https://lccn.loc.gov/2019024925
LC ebook record available at https://lccn.loc.gov/2019024926

Printed in the United States of America
DOC 10 9 8 7 6 5 4 3 2 1

"As Bad as a Mile" by Philip Larkin quoted with
kind permission of Faber & Faber

As Bad as a Mile

Watching the shied core
Striking the basket, skidding across the floor,
Shows less and less of luck, and more and more

Of failure spreading back up the arm
Earlier and earlier, the unraised hand calm,
The apple unbitten in the palm.

PHILIP LARKIN

1

.....

Finetta, 1964

WHAT IRRITATED FINETTA about her mother was not the lack of love but the obvious hatred. Lack of love was easy to explain — her mother had loved others more, her love was finite, there was only so much to go round. But her hatred was endless. Finetta had tried in myriad ways to understand it, but at forty-four, she was tired. It was inexplicable. She had to live with it.

For her own daughter she felt little either way. She neither loved nor hated her. She felt ambivalent towards her and the ways about her: her presence, how she did her hair or poured the tea. Her daughter was a stranger who moved with a stranger's mood; a thing that passed and left little trace, unlike her son, for whom she felt a love so crushing she could only watch him, constantly, whether he was there or not. She wondered, sometimes, if it mattered; this black and white way of her heart — but what could she do? There was either feeling, or there wasn't, and neither force — ambivalence nor adoration — had dissuaded her from duty. She'd fed and bathed them both, divorced their father and sent them away to school as soon as possible. They had grown up. Now she found herself back in the role for which she was made and in which she felt the least and most comfortable — that of looking after her mother. Her mother's nursing home was in Hampstead. It looked pretty from the outside, a large red brick house on a quiet street, but the inside had been stripped of beauty — it had unfortunate lighting and a lift that didn't work, Formica tables, single beds and nylon sheets. It was her mother's just deserts.

She looked at the letter again while the kettle boiled. *Coming Tuesday. No need to tell her, better not. I won't stay long. Shall we lunch beforehand? Say 1pm, usual place? Ian*

Better not to tell her for whom? Him? Her? Their mother? Obviously she'd had to tell the nurses — they liked to know the name of every visitor — but she'd made it clear. She'd made it absolutely clear that they weren't to say a word until she got there. She'd be the one to say, *Ian's here. He's come to see you.* Not the nurses with their incontinent nonsense, spilling it out as though it were something thrilling. No. Finetta would be the one to tell her — perhaps she'd have to make him wait outside the door, but it would be her who'd do the spilling, with care and consideration and just enough distance to duck. Her mother might think her a bloody nuisance, but she wasn't cruel or stupid. She knew what it all meant. She put the letter back in its envelope, propped it again on the shelf beside her notebook and got her cup and saucer from the cupboard.

Finetta was beautiful and tall. She had hooded blue eyes like a sculptor's Nemesis set in an angular face framed by thick dark hair that waved gently without curlers. She'd cut it to shoulder length and wore it clipped back like a schoolgirl. She was thin, as her mother was, with elegant hands that drew attention from her face when men were desperate to look somewhere else. She wore no rings — her failed marriage was discarded in the bottom drawer of her bureau.

The kettle boiled, the pot already warmed on the Rayburn. While the tea steeped she sat at her kitchen table, a quilt on her lap, and opened the sewing box. It was to have been a Christmas present for her mother but she'd almost finished it. One more patch to go. She could finish it this morning and give it to her this afternoon. It was probably better not to wait for such dates as Christmas or birthdays anymore — in the face of her mother's deterioration they had become arbitrary. Who knew if she'd live till then? It was better to finish the patch now and give it to her before death crept any closer.

It was pretty enough, pieces cut from old dresses and curtains, backed on to undyed linen. Her mother would hate it but the nurses would think her ungrateful and keep putting it back on her bed. It gave Finetta joy to think of the confusion, the kind prison her mother was in. She rearranged the quilt to stop it slipping from her knee.

Starting something was easy, she thought as she adjusted a pin.

It was the starting that was the joy when no mistakes had been made, when the world was free and open, when nothing was said that needed to be unsaid and there were no bad stitches. If life were nothing but beginnings with something else taking over the difficult middle and horrid end, how much simpler it would be. How much happier. People were not designed to change — God had not thought it through. They broke down instead, but what did God know? He who had made such a hash of it all. God was a trick made up by people too frightened to think of anything else. She spread the quilt over the table. It would do. Most of the mistakes were hidden under calico.

She poured her tea and arranged herself again at the kitchen table, the quilt on her knee. Her needle travelled back and forth through the patch of red silk dotted with white flowers and she kept her eyes upon it. She was used to the sharp sting of a misdirected point and though she'd done it — made patchworks, darned socks, mended skirts — a thousand times before, she still got pricked occasionally and it still stung.

She stopped for a moment, drank some tea and sniffed. Winter. What a bore. Freezing nights and her mother still not complaining. If only she would act normally, like all the others who crowded into that dreadful place, getting meat jammed in their teeth and holding hot water bottles to their stomachs, wiping their streaming eyes with the backs of their painful hands and chivvying each other along. But her mother refused to be drawn. She was silent, focused, upright except to turn slow watery eyes upon her daughter, fail to smile and look away. She never asked her how she was, never said thank you when Finetta drove halfway into town to fetch her new stockings, never said thank you at all.

With her ankles crossed, a cashmere thrown over her shoulders, an electric fire pulled to the middle of the kitchen floor emitting a three-bar heat, Finetta looked like a flower grown used to growing in the dark. Precision, that's what she cared about, a commanding order that gave her life outline. Tea before toast, a quilt before death, an annual lunch with her brother. She turned it over, tied the thread and snapped it with her teeth. The last patch was from a blanket the moths had got to. She hadn't liked it. It had reminded her of poverty.

The Rayburn poured slow heat over clean tiles, empty surfaces, polished sink. The cupboards, worktops and floor were all varying shades of tan. Tan, she'd discovered, was an easy colour to make look clean. She took a half-loaf of bread from the bread tin, a board from behind the sink, a knife from the drawer, and cut a slice. Tea, toast, precision, quilts, her mother, and occasionally she made fudge in the afternoon when she'd nothing better to do — she had tins of the stuff, she couldn't keep up — but these things kept her occupied. As a child she'd had her bird book.

It had been easier then — her thoughts had not developed the ragged edges they had now, the subtle insistence that there was more to realise if only she'd follow them up. When she was a child they had been single, isolated cut-outs which had been easily replaced with a picture of a robin. Now she had to look away sharply to avoid seeing what her thoughts dragged with them. But she was strong. She would not be drawn. It did no one any good.

She stood at the worktop and buttered her toast. Surely she was too old to feel angry. She wished the sensations would go away. There was no need for them, and it was rude of them, in her quiet kitchen, to think they could intrude when she was supposed to be getting dressed and getting ready for a normal day that had just one little bump in it. They had begun to intrude more and more, edging in until it seemed normal to see them inside the door, sitting on the kitchen floor, crouched at the foot of her chair. Soon they'd find their way into her bedroom. Then she'd have to take a sleeping draught to keep them away.

She'd spent her life believing things could be compartmentalised, kept apart by scissors and sticky tape, labelled and stuck down with no risk of one image sneaking over to another. She'd had her mother page, where she'd been Neat, Solemn, Quiet to the point of Piousness. On her aunt's page were Good Manners, Amusing Chatter and Gossip. With her father she was Pretty and Happy; with her brother, Un-minding and Stoic — it had all worked surprisingly well until she'd grown up and left home. But as an adult, the overlay of romances, children and divorce had smudged the cut-outs and she'd returned to the pages to find they had bled one into another. Who could she be to her brother now? Why did Neat no longer work with her mother? It was as if survival was a debt she must repay by ghastly examination. She didn't want to peel the images apart. She didn't want to look. She should tell her mother to stuff it, but was over-ruled by a small girl in pig tails with a bird book trying to pour tea without spillage. What about loyalty? Yet she returned, week after week to attend to that disappearing life as if it had offered her warmth. Her brother said she was a fool, yet the older she got, the younger she became. She'd got along perfectly well for forty-four years refusing to be affected by anything. Why start now? But, like everything else in the childhood that crept upon her, it felt beyond her control.

She rubbed her chest with the heel of her hand. She wanted to put the contents in the sink with her cup, wash them up, pour them away. Of course she couldn't. She had to clench her jaw, go upstairs and get dressed. She kept a firm grip on the knife as she ran the blade under hot water.

In the bathroom, she inspected her face. It will do, she thought, touching her lips with the tips of her fingers. She always thought that as she moved away from her reflection. It will do. She knew she'd been beautiful, as if it were a fact stored in a book at the London Library. Everyone said it and men, well, they'd ogled her, but what she saw was pointed and sharp. She saw her mother's eyes and her mother's mouth and wished she didn't.

As she ran her bath she thought she heard the telephone ringing. She turned off the taps and opened the bathroom door, but the house was as still and as quiet as ever. Nothing. She shut the door and turned on the taps again. She undressed, laying her cashmere over the back of the bathroom chair and her nightgown folded neatly on the seat. Gratefully, she stepped into the deep, warm water. Thank goodness the boiler had been mended. The water was piping. But just as she dropped her head back and let the water slop over her, the phone started ringing again.

Goddamn it, she thought, sloshing her legs and getting out. She wrapped a towel around her and padded downstairs, shoulders wet, the tips of her hair dripping.

2

.....

Enid, 1964

F ROM HER CHAIR by the window, Enid stared at the trees which bowed and swayed and threatened to dislodge the pigeons that clung there. Her reflection was ghost-like in the glass. The light picked out her crinkled skin, the sag of her cheeks, how thin her mouth had become. Her hands, folded in her lap, conveyed the essence of her bones; gnarled with a tremor that mislaid things.

She was trying not to think of her sister. She was trying very hard indeed. She'd mostly erased her, she'd almost got rid of her completely, but this morning, up she'd come, resurfacing like so much flotsam, as present as if she were in the room — the living, breathing Joan who perhaps still lived and breathed somewhere. Enid could almost smell the trail of Turkish tobacco, the slick of gin and hint of eau de lavender, could almost see the defiant bones that broadened that face, the globe eyes, the heavy lids open on blue islands with black at their heart. One of these days it wouldn't just be memories, it would be her in spirit, come to say sorry.

But today it was memories, and although she closed her eyes and opened them again, though she stared at the trees and counted the pigeons and made a bet with herself over which would fly off first, her sister reared before it all, blotting out everything like the ghost that she couldn't get rid of.

Her fingers played over a ring on her left hand; an emerald set amongst diamonds on a band of deep gold. Ageless and prominent as if washed up on driftwood, the jewels glinted above skin that had lost its fat and become the colour of mud-spattered sand. Once upon a time, even after Joan had got the knives out, Enid was young and beautiful; always more beautiful and younger than Joan, and perhaps that was the shallowest of causes. Just that. She even had a portrait by Augustus John to prove it — her head half-turned, her hand in mid gesture as if she were saying something. She had been, though she couldn't remember what. It had moved with her, from one corridor wall to another and finally to here, a bedside cupboard in Hawthorne Christian Science House.

She pushed her thumbs against the top bones of her eye sockets, making her forehead ache. She wished she could stop thinking of her. Like the television downstairs that fired pictures of American soldiers into the shabby lounge of the nursing home, Joan transformed a tired plain into a place of war. The anger that slept and the grief that haunted woke up and shouted, the hurt showed itself undimmed and Enid's thoughts became furies, a battlefield overrun with blood and trenches. On days like these it was impossible to traverse from one side of her mind to the other without falling in a hole, tripping on a jagged bone or snagging her skirts on barbed wire; her very own Vietnam or Gallipoli, alive with a carnage she couldn't stop.

There was a knock on her door.

"Enid?" It was Carol, one of the nurses. Fat Carol with the piggy eyes, come to brush her hair and clean her up, ready for her weekly visit from Finetta.

Her daughter always came on a Tuesday, and she was very particular about Enid's care, noticing the smallest things, like a ladder in her stockings or whether her nails had been done. Enid didn't know why she bothered. If it was inheritance she was after, there was none; Finetta should be the first person to know that. Enid played with the ring, moving it with slow, unconscious rhythm over her knuckle. There was nothing Finetta could possibly want that she wasn't going to get anyway: a wardrobe of tattered clothes, a few stoles lying about, a bit of jewellery, the Augustus John. She couldn't think that any of it was worth anything, apart from the ring. Enid pushed it down her finger again, back into its place, and tapped the emerald. She couldn't bear assumption. She had half a mind to be buried with it. But what on earth more did Finetta hope to gain? Some emblem of a parent, just because everyone else seemed to have one? Enid had done nothing to deserve such loyalty and she resented it. She wanted to be left alone. She didn't want to have it pointed out that she was still a mother. It was as if Finetta did it on purpose, shoving the reminder of her existence as a punishment from which Enid could not escape, a revenge dripped week by week, never letting the grass grow, making Enid re-tread the paths with every Tuesday view of her bloodline.

Enid brushed down her skirt and tried to see her mouth in the window. She scratched at each corner, her lips in an O, and then pressed them together as if she wore lipstick. She didn't. What would be the point? Finetta was still such a beauty she hadn't considered the possibility of her own lips growing thin. Or perhaps she had. A failed marriage, a son she doted on, a daughter she occasionally spoke of — the haunting of another generation. What did it matter if Enid's stockings were laddered? Who was going to see? Finetta had been like that since a little girl, particular about the slightest detail of her own dress or nails, her manners, her composure in the face of turmoil. Perhaps she was making up for the fact that until she grew up and left home, with that silent, breath-taking beauty of her own, no one had taken any notice of her at all.

Carol finished straightening the bed. "Have you had enough breakfast?" She picked up the tray of untouched porridge, the half-piece of toast, the empty tea cup and stainless steel pot.

"Enough," said Enid, her hand loosely in the air. It was too late for vanity now. Everyone in this nursing home was waiting to die and doing nothing about it.

Carol carried the tray to the door and put it on the trolley that she'd parked in the corridor. She came back in, closed the door behind her and walked heavily over to Enid. She placed her plump hand on Enid's shoulder.

"A little comb through, shall we?" Carol's cheeks were so large that when she smiled her face creased into an undulating mass and her pig eyes nearly disappeared completely. Joan had been fat too. Not as fat as Carol, but large enough to make every item of clothing look as if it were screaming. Last time she saw her, she'd been squeezed into a blue suit and squashed onto a bench in court, Pat clinging to her side. Lesbians. Enid would have used the word if she'd thought she'd have been believed, but she knew, she'd known then, that their mother would have deployed her favourite weapon of looking the other way.

She felt Carol's hand drop from her shoulder. In the reflection of the window she watched her fetch a comb from the sink and felt it softly tug through her hair. Enid tilted her head and rested it in Carol's hands, lifting her gaze to the pattern of the trees outside — limbs bare against a pallid grey — and then higher still to the edge of the window and the ceiling above her, white-painted and empty but for the strip light, flickering on low. Carol said, "Keep still," and untangled a knot.

She hadn't reckoned on being reminded, when it was all too late, that everything they'd done was based on grief.

"Perhaps you'd like to change into something clean?" said Carol.

I'll pay you £500 if you give him up. But she hadn't known that Joan meant: *and never see him again.* If she had known, no money on earth would have been worth it.

"I could look out your blue one with the collar."

Twenty-five years ago. He'd be in his forties by now.

"Enid?" Carol touched her arm.

Enid felt the light press on her sleeve but all she could see was her son in the back of her sister's Rolls Royce as it eased slowly down the narrow street, paused briefly at the end, turned left and accelerated out of sight. She'd pretended, for a while, that he'd come and see her. It had eased her mind. There'd been no reason why he shouldn't; she was still his mother. She gripped the arm of her chair. If Joan had been forced through the imprisonment of marriage and brutality of childbirth, perhaps she'd have done the same, but she hadn't and so how foolish to think she'd have understood.

"Enid?" Carol gently shook her arm, her face close. "Everything all right?"

"What?" Enid's voice was cracked from under-use.

"I asked if you wanted to change into something clean. You've been in that since Saturday."

"Oh. Yes, I suppose so."

"It's time we put that one in the wash." She held out her hand for Enid to stand up.

"Can't you do it later?" She couldn't just now, she was too tired.

Carol put the comb on the sink. Enid stared out of the window. Twenty-five years and nothing. Not a visit, a phone call, a note. His father had died, and of course she hadn't gone to the funeral — it would have been improper. There was no knowing who might have been there. Joan would have been there. A grave was no place for a reunion and anyway, she'd heard of it too late. She could have gone to her mother's funeral, she supposed. Ian would have been there, too. She'd wavered over that one. Despite everything, it would have been perfectly correct. That galleon ship, that empress of duty had done what mothers the world over did when an heir was lost — she'd drifted and grown old, become suggestible and weary of the load. But Joan would have been there too, slipping into their mother's shoes, and Finetta had talked Enid out of it. She'd said Scotland was a long way to go.

"You'll want something nice, won't you?" said Carol. She stood behind Enid, her hands lightly touching her shoulders.

Enid stared at her reflection. Their mother wouldn't have wanted her at her graveside anyway. She would have seen it as an offence, and Joan would have agreed absolutely. They'd been an army of two, allied in everything, and the thought of being shamed again, even after their mother was dead, had been too much. As she'd expected, no letter from the executors had arrived, no summons to hear the Will. Nothing but an aside from Finetta: that the funeral had been quite pleasant, although it had rained.

Carol patted a stray strand of Enid's hair into place. "I'll get you the mirror."

She'd had no one to fight for her, that was the thing. No one to hold her hand, talk her round or give her reason to think sensibly. Ian's father had cowered and done as he was told. He'd had no reason to defend her, but was there no such thing as compassion? The men she'd loved were dead — her brother, her father. Sometimes she was grateful that her father hadn't lived to see his family fall apart. Her mother had told her once that it was

Enid's marriage that had killed him. Some words, once uttered, could never be forgiven.

Carol held the mirror up for Enid to turn her head from side to side and admire what little was left. "All right?" She put it into Enid's hand and went to the cupboard. There was a jangle of metal hangers as the blue dress with the scalloped collar was removed. "I'll give it a quick iron."

Enid laid the mirror in her lap.

"Anything else you need?" Carol was beside her, the blue dress over her arm. She reached for her stick and took Carol's hand. No, she'd had no one. No one had held her in their arms and said, *I understand. You've been under a terrible strain. You mustn't worry. I'll take care of you. Everything's going to be all right.* No one had been there for her when she'd needed help. It was no wonder she'd panicked.

Carol led her into the middle of the room. "Do you want to sit somewhere else?"

She wasn't at all sure why she'd stood up. "I'll sit here." She pointed at the easy chair by the unlit grate.

Carol patted her on the shoulder. "I'll be off, then. I'll get this back in a jiff." She was smiling like a clown, a fool with something to say, tight-lipped and squeezed. "We'll be expecting your Finetta here at four as usual." She patted her shoulder again. "I shouldn't tell you."

Enid felt irritation rise through her veins. Carol was always making a nonsense of life, as if it was fun. "Tell me what?"

"Only Mandy thought you might like to know, seeing as it might be a shock." She bent towards her.

"Tell me what?" she said again, easing into the chair.

"She said last week not to say until she was here. But I can't see it matters, and we wouldn't want you to feel we hadn't thought. I never knew you had a son."

Enid looked up at her. "A what?"

"Ian." She raised her voice and leant close, a great, planet face in a universe of ignorance. "Is that right? I expect he's as handsome as Finetta." She straightened up. "I'll bring tea up with them, shall I? They'll be here at four sharp."

Enid tried to push herself out of her seat but got only as far as a slight lift before falling back. Her stick, hooked precariously over the armrest, fell to the floor. "Ian?"

Carol swapped the dress to her other arm and picked up the stick. "That's what she said."

"You mean Michael?" She must mean Finetta's son. Stupid woman must have got confused.

"No." She hooked it over the armrest. "Ian. She wanted it to be a surprise, but I thought, well we thought —"

Enid balled her hand into a fist, it jerked against the stick sending it flying once more. Her heart smashed against her ribs — seeing him in the Rolls, watching him not turn around, twenty-five years of silence. "You're certain?"

Carol picked it up again. "That's what she said."

This was what Joan used to do. "She's doing it on purpose." An uncommon sweat sprang over the dry parchment of her back, and her temples pressed in on her brain.

"Who's doing what on purpose?" Carol's fat face was too close again.

"Finetta." Enid turned her head the other way. "Hurting me."

Carol hooked her hand under Enid's elbow. "Why don't you lie down for a bit? I could get you a nice drink of milk."

"I don't want milk," she snapped, pulling her arm free. "My stick."

Carol put it in her hands. "Where do you want to go?"

"I need to telephone."

"She already said she'll bring the shortbread."

"Shortbread?" She tried to stand but she wasn't getting anywhere. She grabbed Carol's wrist.

"Has he been abroad?" Carol put her other hand on Enid's and helped her up. Enid shoved her stick out in front of her and took a step. "Why is he coming?"

"I expect he wants to see you," said Carol, gently.

"But I don't have any sons."

Carol let out a puff of breath. "Well I'm sure I don't know. Why don't you let me telephone?" She halted on the carpet, halfway across the room, the dress shoved into the crease of her elbow. "You don't have any sons?"

"You must tell her I'm not well." Enid marched another step across the room.

Carol took a sudden left turn and steered Enid towards the bed. "There's no need for you to come all the way to the office. I'll be done with my rounds in a tick and then I'll do it. Have a lie down till lunch. I'll come and get you."

"I don't want to lie down." They treated patients like imbeciles, as if upset could be cured by raised feet, but like a toy released, Enid found herself propelled towards the bed, unable to halt and turn, a victim of the rush of her brain, her very own Gallipoli, alive with a carnage she couldn't stop.

"Tell her I'm not feeling well today." She reached the bed. Her hands touched the counterpane.

"Of course you're not. I can see that. I'll come back and check on you in half an hour," said Carol. She whipped across the room and shut the door behind her.

3

.....

Enid, 1964

THE ROOM, LARGE but plain, had a cornice which disappeared into a modern partition that cut what was once
grand into a half-cocked idea of practical comfort. In the lottery
of room divisions, Enid's had won the fireplace. Around it were
two armchairs and a coffee table, and from her bed their emptiness felt like a warning. She lay on her back, as if she were dead,
and stared at the ceiling, her arms crossed over her chest. She
hadn't spent twenty-five years designing a perfect explanation for
her life only to have it shot down in one surprise attack. It wasn't
on. She wasn't prepared for it.

She eased off her shoes and flexed her toes. Three on each foot
responded. The others, fused in a united dispassionate nod, had
given up on independence years ago — they didn't care to join
in, they made no effort. She twisted each ankle. They were bony,
like misshapen sticks. It was unacceptable. Who'd stolen her life?

That's what she wanted to know. It was hers that needed answers. She'd given up her sons' lives long ago. She'd lost them both. If a man insisted on calling himself such, the correct course would be to write. Why hadn't he written? He'd had decades to compose a note that need only say, *Mother* —.

Her ankle joints creaked and popped. She wanted to break them. Snap, they'd go. Then she wouldn't be able to walk. They'd have to call for an ambulance, despite themselves and their stupid rules. For fifty years she'd lived by them. Fifty years of Mary Baker Eddy and Christian bloody Science. No medicine, ill health a result of a sin that can only be prayed away. Try praying this away, she thought, and then shut her mind. If she broke her ankles they'd have to send her to hospital because she'd be screaming.

She bent one knee and then the other. Agony. That was the word for them. They failed her with bitterness and revenge. What had she done to deserve this? She'd asked them only to perform the duty for which they were made. She hadn't tortured them or pushed them beyond reasonable endurance. Bend and straighten. Support her weight. Was that too much to ask? Yet they swelled and tore, they ground against the bone, they gave in sudden, jerking shatters that left her frightened of stairs.

Her eyes wept without emotion — they watered regardless of her mood. She reached for a tissue from the box on her bedside table.

If his brother had been perfect there'd have been no need for him. She'd said it then and she said it now. Forty-two years ago, she'd sat in the window seat of Cherry Trees, a clean dress on, her hair brushed for the first time in days. She'd stared at her new-born son while nanny held Finetta, and cried helplessly while her mother clapped her hands and looked the other way, while Douglas looked embarrassed.

Her heart spasmed, and she had to clutch her chest. He couldn't come. It was unacceptable. He couldn't just turn up as if he'd seen her yesterday and expect everything to have been kept on ice for him, as if she'd died when he'd left and could only be woken by his forgiveness. As if he had a right to stand in judgement. He didn't know. He'd been too young to understand.

She dug her hands into her hips — bony and collapsed, no hint of the widening softness that had made way for children. Giving birth had ruined them. There. She'd said it. Try me, she thought, as if staring a bull in the face. Just see if I can't think of those episodes of carnage. But her chest spasmed again and she had to open her mouth to breathe. She tried lying on her side but it didn't help. She might get it into her head to cry and she hadn't done that since he was born.

She sat up slowly and swung her feet to the floor, took her stick from where it hooked over the plastic rail of her bedstead and walked slowly across the room.

On the white walls of the corridor hung cheap prints of generic vistas: a seascape, a landscape; places no one had been. The floor was carpeted in green. To her left, the corridor ended in another room. To her right, it twisted out of sight down a small flight of stairs. She approached the first step, grabbed the wooden handrail and lowered her foot. Her knee gave quickly and she was thrown forward, but the other foot came spinning out to her rescue and caught her light weight. She stood for a minute on the second step, breathless. Her hand shook like her mother's used to; a bell that wouldn't stop ringing.

A draught whistled along, catching her at shin height. She lowered herself onto the next step until she was sitting down, one hand still holding the rail, her knees hunched together. It felt like the turn in the stairs down from the nursery at Strachur. She hadn't been back to her mother's house in Scotland since the whole terrible mess began. Crouched, knees bent, she could be twenty-eight again, halfway down the first flight, not daring to go further, not daring to go back. *I can't see.* Those had been his first words after the blood had stopped pouring and they'd bandaged him up. She'd wanted to smother him.

She wouldn't be accused. With one hand, she pulled herself onto her feet, her stick in the other, leant against the wall and looked around the corner. The door at the far end opened and one of the nurses came smiling out, throwing a comment behind her. She didn't notice Enid peeking around the bend. The nurse disappeared off down another flight of stairs. On the next step, the handrail swapped to the other wall. Enid made a grab for it.

Why had she chosen to be a Christian Scientist? Why not a Humanist or a Pantheist, or a Presbyterian like her mother? She could have lain down on that foul green carpet and refused to move; she could have said her heart was breaking. They would have had to call a doctor. They could have taken her away from here. But she hadn't chosen it. She remembered now. It had chosen her.

She walked slowly along the passage to the office.

"Enid." Mandy opened the door. Mandy had moles on her left cheek in the shape of two stars and a crescent moon. She caught Enid's arm. "Do you need something?" All the nurses wore blue uniforms and tan stockings and flat shoes. Enid looked for Carol, but her bulk wasn't filling any of the chairs. There was Mandy with her moons and stars, the girl with the poor complexion, and Dawn, who was almost as fat as Carol.

Enid said, "I need to make a telephone call." On the steps of the Basilica de San Lorenzo.

Dawn's uniform strained at her thighs, her calves squashed against each other under the chair. The room smelled of sweet perfume and cigarettes. Mandy walked Enid to an easy chair by the window. "Who do you need to call?"

It was his fault, Douglas's fault, and Joan's. "My daughter." She held on to the edge of the desk on which cups crowded amongst paper clips, a stapler, a box of pens. They'd made it happen. They'd both betrayed her.

Dawn pulled a drawer out from below the desk. It revealed files in manila folders.

Enid said, "Is Carol not here?"

"Carol's off till this afternoon," said Mandy.

"But I've just spoken to her." She'd only wanted God. She hadn't wanted marriage.

Dawn swung around in her chair, the squeak of it halted by

her firm foot on the floor, the other fat leg crossed over it. "Your dress is in the laundry. I'll bring it up after lunch."

"I don't want my dress." If they'd left her alone none of it would have happened.

"Carol said you were feeling unwell."

"I need to call my daughter." There'd be no Finetta, threatening her.

"Isn't she coming today?" said Dawn.

"Carol assured me she would call her." There'd be no Ian.

"This morning?" said Dawn.

There'd be no—

"Finetta," Dawn swung round to face the desk and ran her finger down a list. She picked the telephone from its cradle and dialled. "It's ringing." She looked at Enid.

Enid focused on the floor. There was a sweet wrapper wedged under one of the wheels of Dawn's chair. "I don't want to speak to her."

Dawn said, "It's still ringing."

"Stay on the phone until you reach her. Tell her not to come."

"Now, Enid," said Mandy, smiling at her, "I wouldn't normally say this, but I do think you might want to see her today."

"I see her every day," said Enid, thumping her stick on the floor.

"Every week," said Mandy, tilting her head as if Enid was a child.

"I don't want to see her today."

"No answer," said Dawn. She put the phone down and

squeaked round in her chair towards the nurse with the bad skin. "Put the kettle on, will you?"

Mandy said, "You'll be glad you did."

"I will *not* be glad. Ring her again." Once upon a time, she'd had servants who did as they were told.

"She did tell me not to say."

"I know all about it." Enid straightened her back as best she could. "I'm not in the mood to see anyone today."

"Are you sure?" Two stars and a moon tilted on their axis.

"I don't have any sons," said Enid. "Call her again."

"She's not there," replied Dawn. She got up and the chair groaned and rose.

On the steps of the Basilica de San Lorenzo.

While the girl with the poor complexion handed out tea, Enid leaned her head back and remembered. Nineteen years old, on a tour of Italian churches with her sister and aunt, and Douglas was, what? seventeen? Simple and handsome, sent away by his mother to meet people, presumably people a step up from a politician's son. She could see it now, how she'd dropped her guidebook and he'd picked it up, how he'd told her his name, and she'd thought: *never heard of you.* They'd made conversation while watching her aunt get her skirts tangled in the door of the gig, and laughed out loud and covered their mouths when the skirt had ripped and her aunt had been stranded with her leg out.

Somebody was holding her arm.

"There we are," said Mandy, "up you get."

"I don't want to get up."

"I'll try her again if you like," said Dawn, picking up the telephone and dialling the number.

"And I'll take you down to the lounge," said Mandy.

"I don't want to go to the lounge," said Enid. *Lounge* was a verb, not a noun, and on a normal day she would have pointed this out, but energy seeped from her like a plug pulled and she couldn't see. Her legs felt too weak to hold her up — she clung onto Mandy's arm. When they reached the top of the stairs, she said, "It wasn't my fault."

Mandy put Enid's hand on the bannister rail. "Have you spilled something?"

Enid took a step down. "I won't be accused." They took another step; Enid's stick, looped over her arm, swung between them.

Mandy patted her hand. "I'm sure it won't matter. I'll send Dawn along with a cloth. You can tell her what happened after lunch."

Enid's grip slipped but Mandy caught her. She let go and stood for a minute on the third step down, pulled her hankie from her pocket and wiped her mouth. "I had no choice."

She'd sworn it was better to concrete it over. On the new surface she'd constructed a story of her own and built into the walls a pact to hide his memory in death as she'd hidden his body in life. But after all these years, uncontrollably, the surface split, the buildings fell and the layers peeled back, through court and birth to the moment it began, before Ian was born, when his brother's sweet, round face looked right at her.

4

.....

Enid, 1921

FAGUS WAS LOOKING at her and she was looking at him and there was blood pouring from his head. It was seeping through her fingers and soaking her dress and there was screaming, his china-blue eyes almost white with glaze. Joan came running along the flagstone hall to where Enid held him on her knees. "What happened?" She crouched, her face inches from Enid's; two sisters holding the writhing child, who began to choke. "He's trying to be sick. Turn him over." They tipped him, and he threw up over the cracked floor.

She'd been walking in the garden. That's what happened.

She was walking in the garden of Strachur, Fagus in one hand, *Bleak House* in the other; a slow, agonising plod that was going nowhere, looking at how the sun glinted off the paving stones, and thinking about the castle across the loch. They used to live there. It was where she was born. If a child drew a picture of a fairy-tale castle, they would draw Inveraray — its spires and grey stone, its mullioned windows and bridges and moat, its flags that fluttered in the wind which blew, ever constant, across Loch Fyne. Inveraray Castle was where she was happy, where her brother had sat in the library with his pipe, ridiculous and young and honest; where her father admired the armoury with guests who pointed and asked questions of wars and tribes and clansmen. Where she and Joan could get away from each other and their mother could rule without grief.

It was chance that had given it to them, and chance that had taken it away. Her father was the youngest son of the eighth Duke of Argyll, but his eldest brother, who became the ninth, married Princess Louise and was whipped away to royal households — so Enid, her family, her father had got to stay instead. "Someone has to care for the place," her father used to say. "But is it ours?" Enid had asked, again and again, until she was old enough to realise that it wasn't — that nothing was owned, that everything could be taken away. Inveraray was taken away when her uncle died and her cousin, the tenth Duke, took over.

So they were here instead, for the summer, at the house her mother had bought across the loch — she and Douglas, Joan and Pat and Sybil. Her mother moved about it with authority; it was the family home, but though it lay in the same land it didn't feel like home at all. It felt like everything that was missing.

Fagus tugged on her hand and she smiled vaguely, not looking at him, letting her eyes travel from the paving stones to the house instead. It wasn't that it wasn't pretty; Strachur stood its ground in broad blocks of stone and ordered windows: eight on either side of the central body which rounded proud of the rest, as if the house stuck out its chest and belly for the height of all four floors. It was liveable, it was doable, but it was just a house — a second-rate version of the life they'd lived before. Douglas called it grand. Joan called it functional. To Enid it was simply A.M. — After Marriage.

Everything that had happened After Marriage had been bad. Or, to put it another way, after she'd got married, everything had gone bad. There was the small matter of the war which she couldn't blame on Douglas but wanted to. Then her uncle, and losing Inveraray. Then her father and his stomach and the awfulness, then a Turk had put a bullet in Ivar.

She hadn't meant to get married, that was the thing. She'd meant to have fun; she was only playing. But people love spilling secrets, don't they? She'd spilled and Joan had spilled and Douglas had spilled too. That last year at Inveraray, the year of the clock, she'd called it — when her father was still alive and her brother too, when Douglas was forced to a show-down in the library and her mother's gaze had settled into a stone frame from which it had not moved — Douglas had given her a clock *to watch time passing*. Their year apart was supposed to cool the waters, make them see sense — and it would have done too if his mother hadn't got it into her head to announce their secret engagement in *The Times*. Everyone knew why. Enid was a catch. Douglas wasn't.

And if war hadn't been declared? What then? If the date of their reunion at the Eton & Harrow hadn't fallen on the same day as the start of the war, and Douglas hadn't been one of the first to sign up? Could she have wriggled out of it then? Their love was already over. She'd spent a year away from him, and, if it hadn't been for the clock, well, she could have forgotten him entirely. He was a nobody, a nothing; she was meant for great things. She never wanted to marry. She'd already decided that she was destined to be a nun — a great sage of celibacy and wisdom, a constant communion with God, famous yet private. But war was declared, Douglas did sign up and her mother gave her the emerald engagement ring reluctantly, with a force that said *you don't deserve this but heritage dictates, and heritage always wins.*

Days before the wedding, their mothers had shouted at each other in the drawing room of Bryanston Square while London clattered outside and Enid sat on the stairs, listening. Her allowance was agreed, an income and a house that turned out to be a villa in Berkshire, but the row saw in a cold and empty church. She was shoved into her mother's wedding gown, the emerald ring on her finger, and Douglas, already in uniform, never lost the look of a man being carried hopelessly downstream. He'd gone off to war, France, not Gallipoli, and she'd wished it had been he — rather than Ivar — who'd never come home.

She wanted to lie down on the warm grass, but Fagus didn't like lying down anywhere. He wanted to run, anywhere, everywhere. They'd arrived three days ago, and she was already exhausted. At least at home the garden was small, and she had Everett to look after him. Parenting was consistently shocking. No one had told her. As usual, she'd simply been given orders.

"Ours is a substantial fortune." That's what her mother had said the day the telegram arrived with news of her brother's death. Even then she hadn't realised that it was all her mother's money, to do with as she liked, tied to no one, under no law but her own. She'd sat in the darkened quiet of the drawing room of Bryanston Square, shuttered and mute, Joan beside her on the settee, and wondered silently if the day of the telegram was the day to discuss it, but their mother had marched her words relentlessly over their grief, the brown paper wedged beneath her knuckles. "Ours is a substantial fortune. You," and she'd pointed at Enid, "must replace him." As if that were possible. She'd had no intention of replacing anybody.

She dropped *Bleak House* on the grass and swapped Fagus to her other side. He'd tired that arm from pulling. His sweet round face, his crystal-blue eyes — from the moment he'd torn his way out, she'd loved him, and she'd known too, as his squirming wet body was lain on hers and her heart cracked open, that the love was impossible — a handshake with the devil that would break her. Nothing good could come of such a force. It was too much. She could never un-love him — even if he died he would never cease to exist to her — and she felt now as she'd felt for the last four exhausting years of his life that she'd known all this before he was conceived.

Within a month of her marriage she'd started planning her escape. Her honeymoon at the barracks in Edinburgh over, she'd been delivered to Cherry Trees while Douglas went off to France, and she'd been glad that the awful motion carried out in an uncomfortable bunk at midnight hadn't borne fruit. Alone for the first time in her life, her childhood lost, the imprint of her mother's stony face firmly planted in her mind, her father already ill and her brother on a ship to Basra, she'd looked up *irreconcilable differences* in a law book she'd found amongst Douglas' things; it was to be a simple matter of pretending it had been *unconsummated*, like an unpalatable soup. It was how she was going to get out and right the ship that was listing badly; it was how she was going to get her life back. But then her father had died and her brother had died and her mother's hand had shaken, the brown paper wedged beneath it. In the shuttered drawing room of Bryanston Square she'd asked her mother, "What happens if I don't?"

"Joan is the eldest," Sybil had replied.

"But Joan's a girl, and she's not married."

Joan had laughed, "Well spotted."

It had taken the journey home to Berkshire for her to fully understand. It had struck her then, as the train rattled and she was thrown about, that if her mother could give it to Joan she could give it to anyone. Their fortune wasn't ruled by the laws of primogeniture at all but simply by the habit of tradition; Ivar was due to have it because tradition said boys came first. That boy was gone, that tradition stymied, her mother had nothing but the swaying of her heart. Joan was a girl. Enid was a girl. Joan had twenty-two reasons to hate her; one for every year that their father had loved Enid more.

So here she was now, walking in the garden of Strachur with Fagus; a slow, agonising plod that was going nowhere, looking at how the sun glinted off the paving stones and thinking about the castle across the loch.

Joan came trailing out of the glass doors, followed by Pat. They'd been Red Cross girls together during the war. Cross Red girls, Enid called them. They didn't find it funny. They found most things funny, but not if they came out of Enid's mouth. Smart, whip-thin and unafraid, Pat Dansey blew rules of breeding out of the water, and nobody cared. She was fun, she was a gas, and their mother loved her almost as much as she loved Joan. Pat was always there, always around, Joan's ever present confidante and ally, and this summer had joined them to escape the heat of a scandal of such epic proportions that even Joan, at dinner last night, had said it should probably be left alone.

It was all over the papers — Pat had been passing notes between Violet Trefusis and Vita Sackville-West. Both Violet and Vita were married to men, but, according to Pat, would rather be married to each other. It made Enid blush. Girls were often violently mad about each other, but this was different, and everyone knew it. This was a vice unsaid. Violet had been banished to Italy and Pat had been making the situation worse by going out there and delivering Vita's letters by hand. Joan was loving every minute, landing a balance between intimate and unsullied, in the thick of it yet clean. The gossip had careered around the table until pudding when their mother had said she just couldn't bear the thought of what poor Alice, Violet's mother and mistress of the King, or Denys, Violet's husband, were going through, and Enid, not a friend of any of them, had gone to bed. She'd woken this morning with the same heavy curl in her gut of being neither fashionable nor scandalous. She was tired, frustrated and alone and no amount of connection made it better.

It was hot. Fagus tugged heavy in her hand as Joan and Pat collapsed onto sun loungers, their arms to their brows. Snippets of their conversation and snorts of their laughter drifted across the garden. It made Enid mad. They smoked Turkish cigarettes, drank endlessly, and behaved as if the world would provide for them forever. Their lives glittered, they thought only of now, today, this minute. Not tomorrow or next year. Not who would care for them when mother died or their friendship rotted, not where they would live when they were old. She'd seen to that.

She'd thought she was saving herself but the sacrifice had been all hers. She'd provided He who would provide for all, as if all males could be relied upon to be fair, while Joan had stayed free to waft amongst her famous friends and help no one, sacrifice nothing; she'd lunch with Virginia Woolf, drink cocktails with Maynard Keynes, gossip with Katherine Mansfield. When Enid failed to catch her name in the society pages, their mother would fill the gap with, *Joan is marvellous. Do you know she* — and there would follow some long tirade about how terrific she was at running the house or having parties, how fascinating her friends were and so kind to include her in their evenings. If she wasn't sheltering from sandstorms in Egypt or playing blackjack in Monte Carlo, Joan was putting her feet up in Bryanston Square. She talked about getting a flat of her own, sharing with Pat, but why bother? Their mother's London house suited her too well. She had the life Enid could have had. Except Enid wouldn't have spent her liberty pouring cocktails down her throat. She'd have given up her worldly goods and devoted herself to God, or at least poetry, or at least something other than gin.

Fagus stood on her feet and leaned against her legs. "Why have we stopped, Mamma?"

She pushed his fringe out of his eyes. "I'm just resting." She did still believe in God, even after the war was over. She didn't have any other friends.

Fagus jumped off and ran towards the rose garden, with its steps and bricks and deep water, its every opportunity for damage. She called after him, "No, Fagus. Stay on the grass." Joan and Pat looked up briefly and she felt their judgement drifting like their smoke and laughter through the warm air, to see her launching after her little boy, who at four years old should have been steady, but they hadn't been there to hear the trip, smash, cry of another black eye. They didn't know it wasn't worth it.

His body was a battleground of scars. Douglas said she coddled him, but Douglas didn't know. He just whistled off to London every morning to play at the railway business in an office while she stared down the days and pretended she liked her son in hats. The worst had been at Epsom. Why had her mother been so insistent that she show him off? He wasn't a toy. He was hers, her boy, her precious boy, the only good thing to come out of bloody Berkshire. Her mother had insisted. "Slopping about as if you were at sea. Hiding him away," she'd scolded. "He won't know what the world looks like."

So she'd dressed him up, and dressed herself up, and out they'd gone to the Derby to pretend she didn't care when Douglas bet £10 on a horse that came last, or that her sister was off getting drunk with the worst kind of people and getting away with it. She'd join the living, that's what she'd sworn, as she'd pulled on her stockings and tried to imagine the day going well. But the noise and the crowds had popped his eyes; in his little white cloth cap he'd sat up and grabbed the blankets about him. Her mother had waved, the horses had thundered, she'd turned her back, there was a scream and there he was, splayed on the walkway, a volcanic red pouring from his nose and a split up the side of his head like someone had taken an axe to it. A course doctor had been found, and said lucky for them it was just a surface wound. "Heads bleed like billy-o," he'd exclaimed as if it was a joke, something funny. Everyone had laughed and patted Fagus' head in that vague way that won't get blood on a silk glove, and commented on how sweet he looked all bandaged up, but Enid had taken him home and he'd slept for a week, hardly moving, almost dead.

After that he was worse. The doctor said it was a matter of confidence, but Enid felt she was living in a madhouse where no one saw what she saw. *His head is too big.* She'd say it to herself in the mirror, practising, *Doctor, his head is too big. I want him taken to a specialist.* But then her mother would write and remind her that Fagus was the great white hope, and one day he'd take care of all of them as Ivar should have done if a bullet hadn't got him, and Enid would lose faith, panic, capitulate, close her eyes and pray. It was easier to belong in a lie than be outcast with the truth. She could push it down the road for another day, delude herself that some miracle would occur, that she'd wake up tomorrow and find it was just a phase, that he'd become a normal little boy, running wild with the others in the village, that the nightmare of his difference was over, and hers too — that she could join the other mothers with a normal shining product of her own.

She loved him, but he was different. She loved him, but he was different. She'd said it to herself again and again, until it felt as if others could hear her. He ran in circles, then set off towards the terrace. Enid followed. From the open nursery window on the top floor she heard the wail of the baby, Finetta, a year old, and this time actually perfect. Her birth had been a matter of hours, a surge, a split and slip; nothing like the hours of torment she'd had with Fagus. Finetta had been so tiny. She still was.

Murrell, the bird-like nanny from their childhood, had been dragged out of retirement for their summer visit and had the baby in her grip. Fagus, she couldn't cope with. The baby she adored. They all did. There was universal approval of Finetta's ideal looks and growth. Enid felt she'd churned out a better version, but that's where her feelings stopped. She had nothing for her, not even milk.

"Morning, you two." She'd reached Joan and Pat on the terrace.

Pat tried to sit up, failed and lay down again. Joan raised a hand. "Have some coffee." She was dressed in bloomers and a sweater, as if she'd forgotten to put on a skirt, which she probably had.

"We're making it palatable with brandy," added Pat. She looked vaguely for an ashtray, then used the saucer of her cup.

Fagus leant on Joan's arm. She touched his nose. "How are you this morning?"

"Come to the pond, Dodo?"

Joan groaned and put her arm around him. "I couldn't move if you paid me, darling."

He laid his head on her chest. What was it about Joan? Enid watched as she had before, the natural lean and tuck of her son and sister. Babies Joan kept away from, but as soon as Fagus had been able to talk, Joan had opened up and enveloped him like the most comfortable of blankets, the most unabashed of friends. Last summer it had begun, in nonsense conversations: Joan on her knees, hauling out the train set that used to belong to Ivar, or letting Fagus stand on her feet while she played croquet. She paid no mind to his childishness. She treated him exactly as an equal and he loved her for it. He was easy with her. He moved about her as if she were a part of him.

Pat shifted her legs to the side. "Do you want to sit down? You can share my coffee. It's making my head about ten times worse."

Enid squinted in the bright light of the sunshine bouncing off the stone. She perched carefully on the end of Pat's lounger and rested her weight on her arm. Pat passed her a cup. "Watch out for the brandy. I think I've overdone it."

Bitterness and alcohol hit the back of her tongue; she coughed into her hand and put the cup down. "I don't know how you two can stand it."

"You should have seen us last night," said Joan. She leaned over and stubbed out her cigarette.

"I heard you," said Enid, shielding her eyes. She'd sat up trying to read but Jarndyce and Jarndyce were just getting started, and the book, heavy on her chest, had felt too big to hold. She'd let it fall and listened to the distant laughter drifting up from the garden instead.

"We were all set for pontoon and then Douglas buggered off to the George and your mother wouldn't play, so we got out the backgammon instead," said Pat.

"I thought I heard you outside."

"Douglas wanted to play midnight croquet."

"After pontoon?"

Pat sighed as if to say: what does it matter? Joan let her hand drift from Fagus' head to rest on his shoulders, the other arm thrown over her face. "Whatever it was, it was lethal. Pat had me up till three, arguing over Persian rules."

Fagus ducked out from under her arm and sat on the warm stones, picking moss from between the cracks. Enid could see the top of his head, the halo of sunshine on blond hair, the tiny hunch of his shoulders. Far above them another wail escaped from the open windows.

From beneath her sleeve, Joan said, "Fetch some daisies, I'll make a chain." Fagus got to his feet and trotted off to the lawn.

Enid tried not to watch. She was beginning to get a headache. She could feel it creeping steadily around her temples. She took another sip of Pat's coffee.

Fagus returned with a handful of grass and three daisies. Joan sat up and put them on her lap. He leaned both hands on her thigh and skipped from foot to foot. Slowly, as Enid watched, a dark stain spread across the crotch of his navy trousers. "Oh God." She put the coffee down. "Fagus, quickly." She held out her hand. He grabbed the stain and hopped about, shaking his head. "You're peeing, Fagus. You've peed."

"Good Lord," said Pat.

"Go, go," said Joan. She held his hand and wheeled him around the end of her lounger towards Enid, then brushed the grass from her lap.

"My daisies," said Fagus.

Joan gathered the three flowers and put them by her feet. "Pee first."

"A little late, isn't it?" said Pat, looking away.

"He forgets." Enid hurried him into the house.

The air was suddenly cool and dark. In the hall she took off his wet trousers and pants, bundled them in her hand and wrapped him in her cotton shawl. "Stay here." She sat him on a chair beneath a marble bust of her grandfather. A little boy, swinging his legs, stared over by the blind white eyes of a Duke. In the laundry she dumped the soiled clothes in a basket and found a pair of clean pyjamas in a pile of ironing. The pile toppled as she pulled them out; somebody's shirt, a nightgown and a petticoat fell to the stone floor. She left them there. He was still sitting beneath the Duke when she hurried back through the green baize door. He shrugged the shawl off and untangled it from his legs. She lifted him to his feet and slipped the pyjamas on, one leg, then the other, and pulled them up to his waist. "Go up to the nursery." The stairs only narrowed for the top flight. "Nanny will find you clean trousers." The first three were wide and shallow. He was tall enough to hold the bannister. He'd gone up on his own before. "I'll watch from here." She needed a glass of water. Her lips were dry, her hands damp. "Nanny," she called up the stairs. "Go on."

She tried to mother, she really did, but it always felt like she was stabbing at something she couldn't fully see — time with him always ended in wet trousers or something broken, a pair of scissors he shouldn't have picked up, or a cup dropped. She had hopes for herself, always hope that she could do it — she watched him climb the first set of stairs, his little hand reaching up to the bannister rail — and then she'd run out of steam, get a headache, want to climb into her own bed and wish none of it had ever happened.

He reached the first turn. Her head throbbed. "Stay with nanny." It wasn't his fault. Even if — she watched his hand disappear — even if he— She couldn't even say it in her head anymore. Sometimes she thought he was just a normal little boy and she was imagining everything. She went back along the hall to the dining room. On the sideboard was a pitcher of water with a lemon slice floating at the top. She poured herself a glass and drank it in one. Her head was splitting. Nanny would have to cope.

That was when she heard the scream.

She dropped the glass. It hit the rug and rolled under the side-board. She ran down the hall. She could see him splayed across the bottom steps as though dropped from a great height, head first, the rest of his body stranded above him. She reached him and pulled him onto her lap. "Fagus. Oh Fagus — shh, quiet." She looked up the stairs and down at him again. "Oh God."

The screams must have reached outside because Joan came running in from the garden, flying along the flagstone hall towards her. She knelt too, her hands to his head, her fingers over Enid's. "What happened?" She tried to part his hair, but there was too much blood to see the gaping wound, from which the blood poured freely, warming their hands.

A maid leant over the bannister from the floor above. Enid shouted, "Get some cloths."

Douglas came pounding along the landing and down the stairs. He joined them, the sisters, their hands soaked, Fagus, between them screaming and scrabbling at his head and pushing at the arms that held him as if the blood and the pain were not his, as if they were something he could get away from.

Enid held him tight. "He was supposed to be going up."

"On his own?" said Douglas.

What did he know? He who was never there? Who skipped around as if they were the royal bloody family, and pretended, along with everyone else, that life was one long party?

With one hand, Douglas tried to pin Fagus' arm down. With the other he pushed the hair aside, but Fagus screamed louder and pulled his hand free of his father's, twisting in Enid's lap.

"He must have got confused." She tried to steady his body, but he slipped from her grasp.

Joan pulled Fagus towards her. "Where in God's name were you?"

"I just told him to go upstairs. He only had to go up, I was watching, I stayed watching, he wasn't alone, only the last bit, I only looked away for a minute, I needed a glass of water."

In Joan's embrace Fagus' efforts grew dim and his cries became low, constant moans. The maid, young, in uniform, brown curly hair under a cap, dropped towels beside them. They wrapped his head as best they could and lifted him into Douglas' arms.

Joan stood up. "I'll get Glendower."

"No." Enid put a hand on Joan's arm but didn't have anything except the hopeless wish that her sister would see the mountains of times it had happened before: what was coming, the long road ahead. A doctor would come, and another week of bandages and sleep would ensue, nothing would make it better but time, and she'd be looked at and not comforted. Rooms would grow quiet when she entered. All anyone would think to say would be, *how is he?* as if she'd vanished, as if her world contained nothing but a frightened, injured boy who should have been better looked after. Their care would be laced with admonishment and she would want to scream, *it's not my fault.*

Joan pulled her arm away. "What do you mean, no?"

The blood, his sobs, the very tableau of them in the hall was enough, wasn't it, for any normal mother to behave in a normal way? As he lay in Douglas' arms, Enid bent her face close, her nose to his, while Joan pulled on her boots at the door.

5

.....

Enid, 1921

THE DOCTOR CAME, a huge bear of a man taking up all the light in the attic bedroom. In the silence of crisis halted, he cradled Fagus' head in his hands and wrapped a bandage around the bleeding.

"Poor little chap. What a bang. We shall have to wait till morning to get a proper look. Best to let the body do its work. They're strong these little lads, you know. Bounce like balls. Attended a lad only last week who'd come rocketing down from a tree. We thought he'd broken his neck, but in twenty-four hours he was right as anything and asking to go up again. You'll see, he'll be fine."

Douglas breathed out and smiled as he shook Dr. Glendower's hand. "Thanks awfully."

"It's the mothers you want to watch," said Glendower, smiling idiotically at Enid. "Make sure she doesn't disturb him. It's sleep he needs. I shouldn't mind that it's sleep you need too, ma'am."

Enid ignored him.

"How do you know he'll be fine?" asked Joan.

"The swelling would be worse, and the pain," said Dr. Glendower. "I should imagine he's somewhat concussed. On the stairs, you say? Stone — he might have caught the edge of the balustrade to give himself a cut like that, but —"

Heads bleed like billy-o, thought Enid.

"Heads bleed like billy-o," continued the doctor. "Get cook to make up a dram of hot broth and drop a little whisky into it."

"Whisky?" said Enid.

"For the shock," said Dr. Glendower.

Fagus moaned into his pillow, patches of damp and streaks of blood stained the white linen. He reached for his head and pulled at the bandage. Gently, Dr. Glendower moved his hand away and tucked him under the covers. "If he starts to be sick, then call me immediately, otherwise I'd say get him to eat something — even a biscuit would do. You'd be surprised how many crashes are fixed up with a nice piece of cake. Young boys are very hardy, you know, as I've said."

"But he has been sick," said Enid.

Dr. Glendower gathered his belongings into his bag, the scissors and rolls of bandage, the violet antiseptic he'd smeared over Fagus' head. "I can't see that there's anything more to be done today. Fussing over him won't help. Mothers tend to worry more than necessary. Nurses need food and sleep too, ma'am. Make sure you get an early night."

Joan bundled the blood-stained towel under her arm and followed Douglas and the doctor out of the room. Enid was left alone. She listened to their fading footsteps, knowing they'd have some hearty conversation in the hall, when Joan would pretend she hadn't been as hysterical as Enid, and Douglas would clap the doctor on the back and exchange a look about women. She stared at the lump on the bed and she stared at her hands. A handshake with the devil.

When the door opened again it was Douglas on his own. He stood beside the bed and quickly touched the loose mound of his son's body that curled beneath the blankets.

"You see?" he said, as if Enid had spoken. "It was just a bloody awful crash."

But Enid knew better. Enid could only think of holding his writhing, bloodied form for the first time, when he'd been put on her chest and she'd cried with the love that had torn out of her; of cradling him as he grew, before he'd tried to walk, before she'd noticed for the first time that he couldn't stop falling over, before she'd cried in the bathroom and looked in the mirror practising, practising the words: *doctor, his head is too big.*

She didn't want to sleep. She sat up beside his bed, twisting her engagement ring in unconscious rhythm with his breathing, running it over her knuckle and back, her fingers playing over the precious stones. In the early hours she crept from her chair and lay beside him, her body curved into his, her back against the wall.

→► ◄←

She dreamt about Joan. They were children again in the grounds of Inveraray, playing on their bicycles, flicking gravel with their toes, and running for the steps where the sun warmed the stone and they could wait for their father to return. Joan pushed and Enid fell. As her face hit the ground she heard the voices of her family overlaying each other in greeting above her — her mother, her brother Ivar, her father, Joan — but Enid couldn't move to join them. Her body was stuck, pinned, glued, weighted to the ground, the cold gravel beneath her cheek. They were stepping over her and closing the doors.

She woke pinned against the wall, Fagus leaning heavily against her. She eased her body out, climbing over him like a spider, and slipped along the passage to the bathroom. By the time she came back Joan was there, sitting in the chair Enid had pulled up to the bed. "You go and have breakfast."

"I'm fine." Enid didn't know where to sit. She was going to sit there.

"You don't look fine."

"I'm not hungry."

"Glendower is on his way. Douglas sent a message. We thought he'd better check him first thing." Joan stayed put, so Enid gently moved Fagus' feet and sat on the end of his bed.

An hour later Glendower came tramping up to the nursery and unpacked his things. "How are we this morning?" he said jovially, but no one else was jovial except Douglas, who tried to smile a little. Glendower shut the curtains, dropping the room into darkness, and shone a torch in Fagus' eyes. Enid watched how the pupils stayed as dark planets despite the arrow-point of light. In that moment, as the torch shone and she held her breath, leant and looked, the mountains of times it had happened before became foothills. Dr. Glendower switched off the torch.

Douglas ran his fingers over his moustache and shifted in his flannel suit. Enid picked at the blood ingrained in the crevices of her fingernails. Fagus lay quietly, eyes open, not moving. Joan remained seated in the armchair, her hands folded in her lap.

Douglas leant his weight on the bedstead, as if to push it through the wall and said, "Well? How is he?"

Dr. Glendower went over to the window and opened the curtains. "He's not responding how I'd like him to."

Douglas persisted, he straightened up, he ran his hands along the dip and rise of the white metal, gripping and letting go. "Still in shock, is he?" He tried to laugh but it came out wrong, like a cough.

"His sight," said Dr Glendower, "isn't responding as I'd like it to."

His sight. That was the moment she'd got up and left the room. That was the moment Fagus stopped being the great white hope of anything.

Day after day she sat with him. She wouldn't eat, she wouldn't move. She asked one of the servants to get a cot — one of the ones they'd played with as children, when Ivar decided they should all spend the summer sleeping under the giant cedar in the grounds of Inveraray — and bring it to the nursery for her to sleep on. They hauled it out of some garage, she heard them struggling up the stairs, and then her mother's voice, "What on earth are you doing?" put a stop to it.

Douglas came and found her as another summer's evening crawled shadows across the lawn. "You must eat."

She shook her head. "I can't."

They hadn't changed the bandages yet, and his head looked wrapped in a tight turban, stained red on one side, as if he'd borrowed it from Joan as a prank and put it on, as though he'd been playing dress-ups with his aunt's hats.

"You can't do any good, staying here."

"Can I do good anywhere else?" she snapped, or tried to, but it came out tired.

"Glendower —"

"Glendower doesn't know anything."

"Glendower says sleep is the best thing for him."

"Glendower said he'd be fixed up with cake."

"He didn't know."

"No, he didn't, did he. He didn't know."

Douglas left and someone delivered a tray to the nursery landing. She pulled it across the threshold and sat on the floor eating cold mutton and bread. From the garden came the clack of a game of croquet gone on too long and the scream of Pat as more midges found their way into her shirt.

6

.....

Enid, 1964

WHAT IS IT to lose a child but keep them living? For everything about him to have gone except the body, the breathing lump on the bed, rucking the covers as he slept? Enid had watched and not breathed as if the focus of her attention could bring him back to normal life, but the lump of his body beneath the covers had stayed quiet and still. It had not moved.

If her family had listened when he was born, it might have been different. If they hadn't pretended that he was the perfect replacement for every slaughtered male, she might have trusted them enough to share the truth that had stared at her from his china-blue eyes since the day he was born; she might have gone to them for help instead of staring at his body, hour upon hour. But they'd lain an air of conspiracy across the nursery floor. They'd shut their ears and clapped their hands and turned their eyes to something else.

Enid looked at her hand and found it was Mandy's holding hers, not Fagus'. It was Mandy's young skin against her old spattered crepe, and she was guiding her towards the lounge.

"Last step," said Mandy, her other hand cupped under Enid's elbow.

If Joan had loved her. If it hadn't been a fight.

"There we are."

If she and Joan had been friends. If they'd been close. If they could have gone through it together.

"Now where would you like to sit?"

Why had her sister hated her? What had she done? Enid thought back through the years of their childhood; of funny, dumpy Joan in the castle, always dropping things, always getting in the way and saying the wrong thing at dinner. Clumsy, dumpy Joan who'd grown up, cut her hair and refused to marry, who'd said "men are dead," and been allowed to get away with it. What had Enid ever done to harm her? But while Enid had conformed, Joan had tripped up and landed on the pulse. Men were dead, millions of them, and she'd found freedom.

She'd had their mother's love. That was the root of it, wasn't it? She'd had Sybil's love as a panacea to not having the same from their father. Of course their father had loved her — he'd loved everyone, so had their brother — but he hadn't shown it like he'd shown it to Enid. Was it Enid's fault that he'd sought out her company more? When it mattered, Joan hadn't lost her defender like Enid had — their father was dead, but their mother was at Joan's side — Enid had had no one. She and her father were alike, it hadn't been her fault, it was no one's design but God's.

"Why don't you sit by the window?" said Mandy.

From slipping away with her father to talk about God on the shores of Loch Fyne, to a Christian Science nursing home in Hampstead. It was on another shore, the lake in Italy where she'd sneaked away with Douglas, that she'd first met the religion that would break them up and bring her here.

Christian Science wasn't new, even back in 1912 when she'd first come across it. Before the war it was a fad, one of the many she'd played with: New Thought, Humanism, Pantheism. It was just another she'd taken with her on her tour across Europe with her haphazard aunt. What else was she supposed to do? The Presbyterians had done her in. She hadn't wanted to be like her father, bursting to escape the confines of a God served in sermons, but too battered by rules to find voice or strength to defy the church and reduced, instead, to confiding in his daughter on the banks of Loch Fyne. She'd been young and optimistic. She'd seen no barriers. Who was a man in a black frock coat to tell her of the state of her soul, or stand as translator of holy words? She could translate them all by herself, thank you so much. She didn't need a pulpit and a wooden bench to keep her straight, or a numbing cleric to tell her who she was. She was Enid Campbell. She had thoughts of her own.

Before she'd stood beside Douglas in a cold and empty church and been married, she'd sat up till midnight reading her copy of *Science and Health*, the copy Douglas had bought her. There was no hierarchy in the movement. Every Christian Scientist was equal. Illness was a sign of sin that could only be cured through prayer. To treat the body and ignore the soul was tantamount to ignoring the words of Christ. Medicine was banned. Her copy had stayed with her through war and funeral service, hidden on the bookshelf and in her mind, put away between the Bible and *Gardens of England*, until one day she'd found it.

The lounge stank of rotten teeth and old sofas. The television was on. She'd missed the news, and, instead of Vietnam, a woman in a neat red cardigan was encouraging viewers to make soup from the ends of broccoli.

"I'll sit here." She waved her stick at a chair facing the television. Everett would have made soup out of the ends of everything, not just broccoli. If her family had given her one thing she was grateful for, it was the ability to find the right staff. Everett had come with the villa in Berkshire, and her comforting bulk had filled the kitchen with warmth and bubbling pots, ham hock and carrots in butter. What she wouldn't give to have Everett here now, taking care of everything, ordering the nurses, sending Enid to bed with a cup of sweet milk. Everett would have known what to do.

"There," said Mandy, her hand leaving Enid's. "You'll be happy here till lunch, I should imagine."

Should you indeed, thought Enid. "Wait." She caught Mandy's sleeve. "The telephone."

"Dawn's doing it. Didn't you hear her? She was dialling the number. She'll be trying now," said Mandy, her voice losing the patient lilt that marked her out as a nurse.

"You can't just *try*," said Enid. She'd always hated the word. "You have to do. You have to do it, do you hear?"

But Mandy wasn't a servant; she wasn't Everett or a lady's maid or a scullery girl. She was a nurse with two stars and a moon on her cheek, and she could do whatever she liked. "You sit tight," she said, patting Enid's hand quickly as she removed the claw nail hooked into her sleeve.

The woman on the television said, "Now don't be afraid to add plenty of salt —" Enid closed her eyes.

That summer, that awful summer, when the whole awful mess began — she saw it before her, she saw it swimming towards her in images pocked with fright and exclusion — the loneliness of the nursery, the doctors streaming in and streaming away, the fights with Douglas, her mother's face growing still, and conversations petering out every time she walked in the room.

She couldn't have spent a month up there. Enid opened her eyes; the woman on the television was recommending half-fat cream. She closed them again. It had felt like it but she couldn't have. She must have washed and peed and gone outside, but she couldn't remember doing any of those things. Once Nanny Murrel had brought Finetta up to see her, but she'd waived them away. Finetta's baby plumpness, her wriggling joy at life, were too much. Joan came up at the beginning, offering to sit with him. That hadn't lasted either. And Douglas had come up a few times, determined to get him up, as though by the sheer force of his desire he'd rouse his son from this fairy-tale slumber and see him run on the lawns again. A few times he'd hauled him to sitting, but Fagus had toppled like a teddy bear. All he did was sleep.

She remembered the bed pans, and trying to rouse him for a wash. She remembered spooning broth into his mouth and it dribbling down his chin, soaking the newly changed sheets. She remembered how quiet he was, and the day he opened his eyes and said, *I can't see*.

Halfway down the stairs, halfway up, stuck while her family waited in the drawing room. She remembered that. Glendower had been again; it must have been a few weeks after the accident, maybe three. They were due to leave, their trunks were packed, everything was ready, piled in the hall. Her mother had insisted Glendower come and see Fagus again — he'd arrived with callipers, but Fagus had screamed when they'd tried to put them on his legs. She and Douglas had stood on either side of him instead, encouraging him, hoping, pretending he was better than he was, but his legs had collapsed beneath him, and only Douglas' quick hand had caught him before he hit the floor.

7

.....

Enid, 1921

HALFWAY DOWN THE stairs from the nursery, not daring to go back, not daring to go down. Her mother, her husband and her sister waited in the drawing room two flights below.

Fagus couldn't stand up, he had hardly spoken since the day of the accident, and he couldn't see anything but the grey shapes of Enid's hand waving frantically before him. For a month he'd lain in his nursery bed and been fed soup. For a month she'd sat with him while the rest of the house grew quiet around her, and anger climbed the walls making dinner parties impossible. She'd held his hand in hers and cried. She'd shouted at him inside her head to wake up, stop it, to bloody well come back. She'd shouted at herself. There'd been moments of wild hope, surges of excitement when he'd tried harder than usual to push himself up on the pillow, or turned towards her when she'd spoken, but they'd died away as nothing followed; no great recovery that she could take running down the stairs and into the drawing room. He'd sunk down again and slept and slept as if he'd mostly left the world and was only passing through at meal times, to open his mouth and be fed.

Nothing the medics had done had made a difference. They'd carried him out to the garden to let him bathe in the light. They'd applied head compresses and massage. They'd talked of getting him to a hospital, but Glendower had said he shouldn't be moved beyond the grounds — any bump could make it worse. Enid had thought, *how much worse can it get?* but Douglas had agreed, and the family had descended into a new routine of Enid's absence, an absence shattered by talk of other things when she was there.

It was obvious that they wanted her and everything she recalled to go away. So she'd stayed away, from the drawing room and the quiet dining room and croquet on the lawn. She'd let them carry out their stoic summer efforts. Now, the day before they were due to go home, this last day of summer at Strachur, Enid sat on the stairs from the nursery, not daring to go down, not daring to go back.

But every minute more would make her mother's anger worse, and their voices grew louder as she reached the drawing room door. She heard Douglas say, "He's a child. He's not some —" Whatever he was going to say he stopped when he saw her. He leant his arm on the mantelpiece while Joan looked out of the window and Sybil, frills to her neck, her blue eyes locked on the fire, clenched her jaw, and kept her chin up.

Enid said, "Has Glendower gone?"

Sybil jolted to life as Enid sat down. They were in opposing chairs, one on either side of the hearth. The room, almost perfectly square, the windows shuttered, the fire lit, was hung with Japanese tapestry and lit with glittering lamps. A large black cherry-wood cabinet inlaid with mother-of-pearl stood against one wall. Enid had played with it as a child; she and Ivar pulling open the big doors then, up on chairs, opening each one of the thirty-seven drawers. They'd hidden special objects for each other to find: a clay pipe, a silver cross, a lock of hair. "How long has he been like this?" Her mother's voice grabbed her attention.

"How long?" said Enid. "Since he fell. You've been here. We all have."

"Enid," said Douglas. "She means, before."

"He was normal before." Enid looked from Douglas to her mother.

"No," said Douglas. "He wasn't."

"He's clumsy," said Enid. "He's always been clumsy." Like Joan, she wanted to say, but Joan had grown out of it.

"Anyone can see he hasn't been developing normally," said Douglas. He left the fireplace and sat heavily on the silk settee, his arm outstretched along the back, his legs crossed.

"You said I wrapped him in cotton wool," said Enid.

"A perfectly healthy child," interrupted Sybil, "does not fall and cut his head and instantly lose the power of sight and limb.

I've spent an hour with Glendower. He fully expected him to make some sort of recovery, or —" She failed to find the word, or the word was so insistent she refused to say it. Either way, Sybil gave a short, efficient sniff and tried again. "He has informed me that it is his view that a condition —"

"What condition?" Enid bit the corner of her thumbnail. Her teeth clenched on a piece of loose skin. She tore at it then looked down at the spot of blood, which rose with sharp, immediate pain.

"That is what I'm asking you." Sybil stared down at her, even though she was smaller than Enid and so encased in Victorian satin that her head emerged from the layers like a furious chick grown old in its shell. "You are his mother. What condition does he have? Glendower is adamant that a precursor of some sort must have been noticed. He noted a swelling of the frontal lobes —" She said the uncommon phrase carefully, its sound an effort in her mouth.

"He bashed his head," said Enid. She buried her hand in the other, pressing on the pain, but she kept her eyes on her mother.

"His head wasn't right before he bashed it," said Joan. "Anyone could have seen that."

For once, Pat was absent. At least there was that. Joan left the window and sat beside Douglas. She wore a long blue silk gown with a plunging neckline which made her look as if she were all breast and didn't suit her, and a sapphire necklace, which did.

"There's nothing wrong with his head," said Enid. She felt like Sisyphus, nearing the top of the escarpment. Loose stones slipped under her feet, the boulder was toppling. "He just needs more time."

"He's had a month, Enid," said Douglas.

"And no improvement at all," finished Sybil.

Joan said, "Well I've always thought his head was too big. We all have."

"His head's fine," said Enid.

"His head is not fine," snapped Douglas.

"What do you mean, not fine? You told me I should get up and get him out. You said I was shutting him away."

"We're not talking about Epsom."

"He's just —" She scrabbled for a way out, as Fagus had from the searing fire of his split skull. "He always gets better."

"Always is the point," said Douglas.

"I thought it even when he was a baby," said Joan. "It was obvious."

"Then why didn't anyone say anything?" cried Enid. The boulder fell, the drawing room fire let out a snap and an ember flew out and landed on the rug. Joan got up and poured herself a drink. Douglas stubbed out the ember.

Sybil raised her eyes an inch above Enid's head. "You're his mother," she said quietly. "You should have said something."

Enid hadn't changed for dinner. She was still in her walking clothes, put on after lunch when escape had seemed the best solution, when there was only one more night to go before they could get back home and hide and cry and wonder what to do. She'd been on her way out to sit by the loch and talk to the ghost of her father. She'd been going to pray again for help, but Douglas had caught her in the hall as she'd been putting on her coat and told her that Sybil had called Glendower back.

Douglas lit a cigarette. His hair flopped over his forehead. "Your mother has insisted —"

"I have suggested," corrected Sybil.

"Suggested," he kept his eyes on Enid, "that we think about his future."

"What future?" said Enid.

"Quite," replied Sybil.

"And our own," said Douglas.

"I mean," she changed tack, "he'll come home and —" for a month the obvious had crept and snarled at Enid from the shadows. She said, "There's always Finetta."

Sybil laughed, a short bark that had nothing to do with merriment. Enid cut into it: "Joan's a girl." Brown paper wedged beneath her mother's knuckles five years ago, her words marching relentlessly over grief, Joan's laugh.

Joan lit another cigarette. Smoke shrouded her face, and drifted above her.

"Joan," Sybil banged the flat of her palm on the armrest of her chair, "is not your concern." She looked at her quickly, a tight-lipped smile that Joan returned. Then she patted the armrest as if it were Joan's hand.

"But then what?" exclaimed Enid. Despair made her brave. "She hasn't got any useful children either, she hasn't got any children at all."

Colour rose through Sybil's pale, paper skin. Her soft hand became a claw, her blue eyes hardened and she seemed to rise in her chair toward Enid. "How dare you ask? You had one effort and one effort only: to provide this family with an heir. What I do now is not yours to discuss." She collapsed back, exhausted.

Enid left the room. She went out into the garden where the evening sun lengthened darkness into ghosts of fully formed trees. At the far end, before the fields began, a tangle of elder and willow grew beside a narrow river. She took off her coat and lay in the long grass.

The skin of her lips was torn and chewed, the crevice of her thumbnail stung. She sucked it, then rubbed her hands over her face and moaned quietly into the flesh of her palms. If she could have died today and taken him with her they could have buried them both in the tomb of her brother and father, and none of her family would anymore have the inconvenience of a daughter who couldn't and an heir who wasn't. Perhaps she could throw herself down the stairs, bash her head, end up the same way as him, and they could go together to whatever home for cripples her mother had in mind. Shut them both away. Forget them both in a cupboard, discard them both with the other of society's rejects, their name a taboo, never mentioned. Or leave him to his fate and throw herself in the river, put stones in her pockets and force her own head down.

But she was alive, and so was he. She arched her neck to view the river upside down, collapsed it straight again and stared at the drooping leaves of the willow above her. She couldn't do anything but live and go home. The cold ate into her back. She sat up. She brushed leaves from her hair and tried to reach between her shoulder blades with one hand, flicking at the burrs that clung to her jumper. Her blind and crippled son would return with his mismatched parents to a common villa in the home counties, there to sit in a chair and be wheeled about to sewing mornings where other women would look pityingly and say, *at least they have the funds to support him.* Except they wouldn't have the funds. Sybil had them and Sybil wanted him put out of sight.

She couldn't send him away. She wouldn't. Even if her mother decreed it, there was nothing she could do to force them. Fagus was discarded anyway — at home or somewhere else — he was out of the running and the prize was still there, out of reach today but not removed. If only she could contemplate the jump.

She screamed into her hands. She'd only stayed married to provide an heir. She was going to get out before it was too late, right the ship that was already listing badly, but Ivar had died and Sybil had pointed her bony finger and said, *you must replace him.* Everything she'd done from that moment had been designed for that: a concentrated, pointed effort to avoid the sentence of having to rely on Joan. Through the trees she could see the darkened upstairs room in the lighted house beyond the lawn. All of it, every hideous suffocating moment of it, had come to nothing.

The vileness of her thoughts made her want to tear her own eyes out. Who cared about the money? She had her allowance. They weren't going to take that away from her — Douglas' mother had fought for it and won. They had an income and a house.

Did she need any more than that? She and Douglas, Fagus and Finetta, they'd go back to Cherry Trees and live a quiet life. They could afford a cheap girl from the village, and Everett; they'd probably have to sack Gould and get rid of the motor, or Douglas could keep his driver and give up his London club. Either one. They'd all have to sacrifice something. Douglas and his bloody trains brought in a little. Sybil and Joan could drown in it.

But inescapably, in amongst the sorrow and despair, the practicalities of life rampaged through her brain, carried in torrents of jealousy, favouritism and distrust. She ran her nails through the grass, filling them with mud, and thorns, and pulled at the stalks, tearing them to pieces.

She shivered. Her skirt was damp. She got up.

Joan. Joan was the problem. Joan whom she'd spent her childhood laughing at. Whom she'd never taken care of when she'd seen her sat alone at a dance or lost for words at dinner. Whom she'd teased out riding, when Joan's horse was the only one who hadn't been able to fit through a gate, or at tennis when Joan's serve went backwards. She pushed a strand of hair from her face. But where had Joan been when their mother put her down? Where had she stood when Sybil had said for the hundredth time that Enid should be more like her sister and stop showing off? Next to Sybil, that's where, with a smug look of completion on her face, as if every guttural *oh* that escaped their mother's mouth, every lowering of the lids and rounding of the lips into that one, dismissive syllable had been designed to make Joan feel better. It wasn't Enid's fault she was younger and more beautiful. It wasn't her fault that their father had loved her more. She'd just come along at the end, the youngest born into a mould already set, yet Sybil took it as intentional, as if Enid governed all of them and deserved the consequences. She'd never said a single nice thing to her. Not once had she said, well done, or you look lovely. Just a turn of the head, a flick of the eyes, and a rush to love Joan.

She'd spent her whole childhood failing to catch her mother's attention. She'd tried and tried until one day, probably the day she'd met Douglas, she'd stopped. Why leap when her mother's gaze was always an inch above her head? She'd married Douglas. Doing something terrible had forced that indomitable gaze to seek her out. Now she couldn't escape it and they were going to punish her. This was it.

She peered through the darkening light and willow branches to the house. Someone was lying on a lounger, smoking. When she got closer, she saw it was Douglas.

His soft face was crowded with pain. He looked up for a moment, rested his head again and blew a long line of smoke into the dusk. When she reached him he said, "I should just get a train now. I should bundle him up, and get a train, and never come back."

Enid stopped at the edge of the stone, a few feet from him. "Keep your voice down."

"Don't you tell me to do anything. That's all I've had from the moment I met your family: orders from you, orders from your mother. Where are my minions? Who do I get to order about?"

"She's going to cut him off."

"She's suggesting we put him in a home, Enid." He got up as though he hadn't heard what she'd said, his eyes on the stone. "A home. For what? So that she doesn't have to look at him again? A home for useless, crippled little boys that no one wants, good-for-nothing little rejects, thrown from the tower for being hopeless. It's not up to her what we do with him."

"We'll have nothing, Douglas. Don't you understand? It doesn't matter what we do with him. She's going to cut him off."

He threw his cigarette down. "Why is everything money to you?"

Enid caught his arm. "Shut up, Douglas. They'll hear you."

He shoved her away. "What of it? Do you think we've any more to lose than we already have?"

"We'll have to rely on Joan."

"Who cares?" He pulled his arm free. "Joan's not going to abandon us."

"How do you know?" said Enid, her voice quiet. "She'll spend it all on brandy and say whoops, sorry, all gone. She'll have it siphoned out of her by Pat, or some other hanger-on."

Douglas sat down again. "Your mother will live for years."

"No, she won't, Douglas. One day she'll die and long before she does she'll give it up. It's us or Joan, don't you see? Joan hates me."

"No she doesn't."

"She does."

"You act as if she's done something to hurt you."

"You act as if she's your best friend." She sat beside him, not touching him, and picked at her thumbnail, making it worse. "And what if she suddenly does get married and have children? It's not too late."

He laughed. "That's not likely."

"How do you know?"

"Well it's not her thing, is it?"

"What do you mean, it's not her thing? It's everyone's thing. Just because no one wants her."

"Oh, someone wants her."

"What are you talking about, Douglas? She hasn't had a match in years."

"Little Enid, shut away," said Douglas, smiling. "London's moved on, you know, and so has your sister."

"Do you mean to say she's got someone?"

"It's right under your nose and you don't see it. You're as blind as —" he stopped.

She held her breath. "As what, Douglas? As who?"

"It doesn't matter."

She shook her head and chased away the image of their son, lying upstairs in his darkened room. "If my sister's got someone, you better tell me."

"Good God, Enid." He leaned a little toward her as if he had all the time in the world. "Have you really never thought?"

"Whatever you're saying, I can't see that it has anything to do with anything. Unless she's secretly engaged — is she secretly engaged?"

"I would have thought your family would have had enough of secret engagements by now, wouldn't you?"

"Then what is it?"

"They're lesbians." He sat back, as if satisfied.

"Lesbians? Who are? I don't understand what you're talking about." This wasn't what she was talking about at all.

"Sapphos. Pat and your sister. I think it's rather marvellous."

"Don't be ridiculous."

"I should say ridicule was the last thing on their minds."

"But Pat and Joan are just —"

"Companions? Jolly good companionship, if that's what it is. Up to their eyes in it, or should I say, breasts. And jolly good luck to them. I think it's thrilling."

"What rot." Typical Douglas, finding debasement in everything.

"I'll say it isn't."

"And I'll say it is. Mother would never allow it."

Douglas laughed again. "Your mother thinks sex is something a husband and wife do under the greatest duress."

"Douglas."

"What do you think Pat's doing all caught up in Violet and Vita's little tryst? You do know they're lesbians too, don't you?"

"Stop flinging that word at me."

"Too sordid for you? Your sister and our delightful Pat have been flinging themselves at each other, and quite probably a few other females too, for quite some time. So fashionable. It's been brightening my day for ages."

"We're talking about mother and Joan," Enid snapped. "Mother, and Joan and Fagus." She didn't want to know. She didn't want to know anything about any of it. She thought of Pat and Joan like shipwreck survivors, clinging to each other for want of a proper boat.

"Your mother and Joan and our son and all that money?" said Douglas.

"He's still her heir. There are laws."

"He *was* her heir and the only laws your mother abides by are her own. Joan's not going to breed. She doesn't have to, and for my money, she doesn't want to."

"You don't have any money."

"As you and your mother have made clear on any number of occasions."

"You married it."

"I married you."

"I came with it. At least I did. Fagus did."

"When I married you it was going to be Ivar's."

It was a trespass, always a trespass, to hear him say her brother's name. He'd hardly known him. He had no right. There'd been the awful scenes in the library at Inveraray, when Ivar had been sent to meet Douglas off the train and put him back on it again the next day. The wedding. A few months in France before he was sent off. She'd been stupid enough to think Douglas would keep him safe. "Joan's always wanted it. She's always had her eye on it."

"Are you saying she's pleased?"

"Of course I'm not. I'm just saying she could have stuck up for us. She could have said Fagus might get better."

"Fagus isn't going to get better."

"She'll promise mother she'll look after me, then she'll spend it all on blackjack."

"What are you suggesting, Enid?" He shifted away from her, and his foot knocked against her thigh. "That we have another son to spite your lesbian sister and hope to Christ this one turns out okay 'cos the first one was a dud?"

Yes. That's exactly what she thought.

8

.....

Joan, 1921

JOAN CROUCHED BENEATH the landing window, her hand over her mouth. It wasn't so much the words *dud* or *spite* as the other one. Pat leant against the bannisters. They'd heard everything, Joan on her way down, Pat on her way up. They'd stopped on the landing by the open window, caught by the voices, and listened to the row on the terrace below. At *lesbians* Joan had lost her balance, fallen forward and hit her head on the sill.

Pat peered forward to the window. Joan grabbed her skirt. "Get back. They'll see you."

"No they won't." She put her nose to the glass. "He's walked off one way and she's scampered in another. Poor Douglas. Too humiliating."

"How does he know anything about us?"

"I'm not talking about *us*. I'm talking about that foul wife of his."

"She's still my sister."

"She's a harridan."

"She's desperate."

"We all are in our own way," said Pat. "Where were you going? I was on my way to bathe."

Joan's legs ached, and her foot had gone to sleep. "I'll come with you."

"Let's slip a note under her door telling her we share bath toys."

"Stop it," said Joan, hitting Pat softly on the arm.

"Don't be such a schoolgirl." Pat took her hand and kissed it, right outside the drawing room, where anyone could have seen. "No one gives a farthing except perverts like Douglas. London is divided between those who know and don't care and those who don't care to know."

They reached Pat's room. She threw off the patchwork robe she'd been wearing all day and got into bed. "I do wish your mother would manage to warm more than one room at a time. My feet are glacial."

"You should get your fire lit."

"Servants never listen to me," said Pat, the covers up to her neck. Sometimes she looked as if she had too much chin for such small eyes — the distance between her features only just made it, as if she poised on the brink of physical catastrophe but never quite toppled over. She was designed for interiors, Joan had often thought it — anything with too much sky made her seem vapid, as if she might be swallowed by a cloud, or rise with the fog, but in this room of low ceilings and broad bed, heavy curtains and Persian rugs she looked beautiful. Tall, dark-haired, acute. Joan could remember the first time she saw her any time she wanted to — she'd seared it onto her mind and gone over it and over it, producing different versions like an artist who cannot let go, hugging it to her, never wanting to paint anything else. Pat's backside shaking and jiggling with the shake and jiggle of her arm as she scrubbed her way down a corridor at Charing Cross. Other nurses looked strapped into their uniforms, but Pat had made it look like a choice.

"I need a drink before my bath. Will you ring?"

Joan pressed the bell. "Bloody hell." She lay beside Pat, on top of the blanket, squashing her.

"Your family's scandals do bore me," said Pat.

"As opposed to other people's?"

"I go where I'm needed."

"I need you," said Joan.

"And as you well know, I need you," answered Pat, but she smiled as she said it and patted Joan's bottom.

"We'll get a flat together," said Joan.

"You always say that."

"I mean it this time. We need to get away from all this —"

"Money?" laughed Pat. "By the sounds of it you're going to have a windfall."

"You mustn't talk like that. I don't need it anyway. Mother said I'd always be all right."

"Even if she knew we're Sapphists to our core?"

"She wouldn't know the meaning of the word, and she wouldn't care. Look at Vita and Violet."

"Must I?"

"Mother thinks all they do is hold hands. She thinks Vita's seduced Violet with books."

"Hah!" Pat roared quickly and laid her head back on the pillows.

"She feels sorry for me. She thinks no one wanted to marry me, that I couldn't find a chap."

There was a knock on the door.

"Drinks!" said Pat, rising from the bed.

But it was Douglas. "May I come in?" He opened the door a fraction as if giving them time to dress or get untangled or whatever it was he thought they did. Joan didn't mind him but he was so simple, so *tan* — that was the word Pat used. Terribly nice, terribly easy to push around, you could wear him with anything. How he'd ended up in their family — well, it wasn't a mystery, was it, it was anything but mysterious. It was just another example of a bloody stupid accident. *Spilling* — that's what Enid had called it. *Why did you have to spill?* as if news of her secret engagement had bubbled up uncontrollably and breached Joan's mouth. *I was going to cancel him* — as if he'd been theatre tickets or supper at The Ritz. Enid had said a lot of things and Joan hadn't *spilled*. She'd thought she was saving her. Telling their mother was the only thing to do. As it turned out, she should have done it sooner, before he told his own mother and the whole thing exploded in *The Times*.

"Only if you're wielding two large gins," said Pat, getting back into bed.

"'Fraid not," said Douglas, closing the door behind him and standing in the middle of the rug as if he hadn't thought his entrance through.

"Come in, come in," said Joan. "We're huddling against mother's summer chill."

"Have you called down for drinks?"

"You can share mine if you give me a cigarette," said Joan.

"The sitting-room fire's not lit. I thought you two might be getting one in early." He took the armchair by their fire.

"You look like you've had a rocket," said Pat.

"I suppose Joan's told you the full blasting." He ran his hand through his hair.

"Poor Fagus," said Joan. "What are you going to do?"

"God knows," said Douglas.

"I don't know why you stick with her," said Pat.

"It wasn't her fault," said Douglas. "She hasn't been right since he was born."

"That makes two of them," said Joan.

"She's been completely off her head. I'm sure you've noticed, or perhaps you haven't."

"We never see her."

"She never comes to town," said Pat.

"It's as if she's on some sort of lockdown. Bunkered, we used to say in France. Ever since he was born."

"You hardly knew her before he was born," said Joan.

"That's not quite fair," said Douglas.

"Italy," said Joan. "That frightful house party, the even more frightful party in the library —"

"I wouldn't have called that a party."

"I was being sarcastic, Douglas. Banished till the war put a stop to everything and then you were off."

"They must have met at the altar," said Pat.

"We went on honeymoon," said Douglas, but his face didn't look like he'd enjoyed it.

"And by the time you came home proper, Fagus was born. I've known her all her life and I can tell you she's always been like this."

"Do you mean miserable?" asked Pat.

"I mean difficult," said Joan, rolling off the bed onto her feet. She thought she'd heard footsteps. She opened the door. "There you are." A maid entered with their drinks. She set them on a table at the foot of the bed. "Thank you," said Joan and closed the door after her. "Bloody difficult."

"Too beautiful to be anything else," said Pat.

"Thanks," said Joan.

"You know what I mean," said Pat. "She looks like a statue and acts like one. Fixed mouth, long stares, a waft of, *you'll never understand me.*"

"She's had the most bloody awful shock. We all have," said Douglas, giving Joan a cigarette.

"What will you do when you go back?" said Joan.

Douglas crossed his ankles. He took a sip of Joan's gin. "God knows. Get help, I suppose."

"If she goes any more mad, mother will cut her off too," said Joan, reaching for her drink.

"Would she?" He handed it to her.

"No, no, I'm exaggerating. She's not going to do that. I'm just saying her patience is almost worn out. She cares terribly for Fagus and Finetta, but the thought doesn't seem to cross Enid's mind for a moment. She hardly ever brings them up and since this —" she waved her hand vaguely — "it's as if Enid thinks she's the only one who cares. Mother cares, I care, you care, good Lord, even Pat cares."

"Don't tell anyone," said Pat.

"She pushes us all away and then complains that she's lonely," finished Joan. She sat on the end of the bed.

"If she cuts us off we really will have nothing."

"Never marry for money," said Pat.

"I didn't marry her for her money," said Douglas. "I married her because I thought I loved her and I thought she loved me back."

"And your mother announced it in *The Times*."

"We'd still have done it."

"Not according to my family you wouldn't."

"Well that's all past wounds, isn't it?" said Douglas, reaching for Joan's glass again. "The question is, what am I going to do now? I don't think her mind can take it."

"Another son?" said Pat.

"Another child, boy or girl."

"Is that what you're going to do?" said Joan.

"I didn't want any of this, you know." He looked at his watch. "I wanted a quiet life. Children, wife —"

"A house, a motor, a nice club in town," said Pat.

"I don't see you doing so badly out of it," said Douglas.

"Now, now," said Joan.

"She was a hell of a girl when I met her. You remember. You were there."

"She seduced you."

"I wouldn't put it like that."

"I would. Enid could get anyone she wanted. Men fainted when she came in the room. Father said the trouble with her was that she was too perfect."

"She was mad about God," said Douglas.

"God, wasn't she." Joan put her hand to her head. "*Mooning about*, that's what mother called it. *Enid, will you stop mooning about.*"

"I didn't know she wouldn't settle down," said Douglas. "I thought having babies would quieten her."

"How well you know the female sex," said Pat. "Mothers are the least quiet people of any I know."

"I didn't know she'd turn into — that she'd — I don't know, not cope in some way. Fagus —"

"She was not coping quite a long time before that, Douglas."
There'd been a fever pitch to Enid in those years, the men away, the
war on. She hadn't got a job. She'd sat in her villa and screamed.

"Your father —"

"We all missed my father," said Joan.

"I just wanted a quiet life," said Douglas.

"Then you shouldn't have married a Campbell," said Pat. "I
don't want quiet. I want life just as it is."

He looked quickly at Joan, and then flicked his eyes to Pat in
bed behind her. "I'd better bathe." He stood up.

"She won't come down, you know. It'll be just us for supper
as usual," said Joan.

"Just the girls." He patted his pockets.

"Isn't it always?" said Pat. "I say we need a few more men
around here."

"See you at dinner," said Joan.

"Right-oh," he replied.

After he'd gone, Joan lay down beside Pat again. "Poor Fagus."

"Are you going to carry on like this all evening?" Pat got out
of bed.

"When we get back I'm going to tell mother that we'd like to
get a flat. Get out of all of it. Don't you think?"

"You know perfectly well what I think," said Pat, kissing her.
"If you want to be free, the only thing to do is to be free."

She took a towel from the rail, stuffed Joan's bathing turban
on her head, and left the room.

9

.....

Enid, 1921

I T WAS NEVER her intention to remember, it just happened that on the train home from Scotland, as she sat watching Douglas turn the pages of the newspaper, she remembered the moment on the steps of the Basilica di San Lorenzo when he'd told her his name and she'd thought, *never heard of you*. If it hadn't been for the guidebook and dropping it, her aunt tearing her skirt on the gig, them laughing, she'd have never agreed to meet him again, they'd have never sneaked off with a picnic and sat on the shores of the lake and talked about God. His soft voice had trickled over subjects ancient and forbidden like her father's used to.

"Have you heard of Christian Science?" She'd shaken her head and he'd smiled. "It's a new religion, from America, Mary Baker Eddy." From his pocket, he'd brought out a pamphlet and read aloud: "Accidents are unknown to God, or immortal Mind, and we must leave the mortal basis of belief and unite with the one Mind, in order to change the notion of chance to the proper sense of God's unerring direction and thus bring out harmony. Under divine Providence there can be no accidents, since there is no room for imperfection in perfection."

"What does it mean?" The water had lapped at her toes, her face was near his.

"It means that there are no accidents. God decides everything."

He'd meant how she'd dropped her guidebook, and how her aunt's skirt had ripped on the gig — but watching him as the train rattled south, it hit her that he'd had no idea what he was talking about.

The journey was long and arduous. They kept stopping at vague stations like Newton le Willows and Rugeley where no one seemed to get on or off. Finetta held her toes in the bassinet, which was strapped onto the bed in the adjoining compartment; the connecting door was open. Sybil had lent them a girl to make the journey easier; Douglas' hands would be full now, grappling with Fagus' wheelchair, trying to get through narrow gaps, and up carriage steps that were too steep. The conductor had fashioned straps for it too, to stop it careering about. It was held fast against the sink now, knocking against the girl's knees — Enid could see bits of it all through the doorway: Fagus gripping the arms of his wheelchair, the girl's knees, the edge of the bassinet. She looked at Douglas seated opposite her, the newspaper open, a cigarette burning in the little metal ashtray by the window, and thought: *there are no accidents. You brought me to this.*

When they arrived home, grimy and tired, full of poor railway meals and hungry for sleep and stillness, Fagus was carried to bed while she sat by the fire and thought and thought, chasing the tail of some feeling that escaped her but left a trail of arrows vaguely scattered yet pointing at something, something she couldn't see. *There are no accidents, you brought me to this.* She thought it again and again until another memory surfaced as she put the guard up on the fire, that of watching Douglas' soft, embarrassed face as he said, *marry me*, and her thinking: *mother will be furious.* She crouched, stilled by it, her hands forgotten on the guard as realisation seeped from her centre into her veins until her body shook and the arrows swung into magnetic place across a map perfectly laid out in her brain. There it was, from flippant act to crippled son, via the deaths of the men she'd loved.

The house quiet, the children in bed, Douglas in the bath, she went to the bookshelves and ran the tips of her fingers along the spines until they stopped between the Bible and *Gardens of England. Science and Health*, by Mary Baker Eddy. She pulled it out and sat by the dying embers to read again of how there were no accidents, how the sins of the mother may be visited on the innocent child, how prayer was the maxim to pain. The pages were smudged where their hands had held them before.

It took a while to pluck up the courage. Perhaps even then she wouldn't have done it if Douglas hadn't knocked on her door one night, a week after they'd got back. He always knocked, even though it was their room. Since they'd arrived back from Scotland he'd slept in his dressing room, but tonight she'd made a special effort to be nice. She'd got Everett to make Coq au Vin, a dish she despised and took Everett all day, but Douglas loved it. It always prompted him to tell the story of eating it in Paris.

"How those chaps made it, I don't know."

He'd got to the bit about replacing mushrooms with corn flour faggots.

"They must have pulled out all the stops," she said, smiling.

"I should think we were the last ones to have it."

"I'll say." Did it never cross his mind that talking about the war was more painful to her than to him? He went on about such bloody camaraderie; he'd had every side — the slaughter, the brandy, the Coq au bloody Vin in Paris, the exquisite need to keep his chin up. She'd had silence and telegrams, no touch of it, a pure absence that hadn't ended. Paris was the last time Ivar was seen by any of them. Why had it had to have been Douglas who'd got the last look? Her mother had had all the letters, even the last, that arrived after the telegram. Enid had nothing of his to remember him by except Douglas' unbearable stories. Nothing. Not even Fagus could bring himself to look like him. "Will you have more?" She held the spoon.

Douglas patted his stomach. "Full to rafters. Marvellous. I say, it is good to see you looking brighter."

And there, he did it again, every reference, every word brought her back to where she was. Brighter from what? From watching her child curl into darkness? "Why don't we move through. Can I get you a brandy? I could rub your shoulders."

Douglas took to every touch and move and offering of crystal glass as if he accepted her new mood unquestioningly, as if this were a new beginning. In the sitting room she stood behind his chair. It was a comfortable, jolly room — a lovely big window with long window seat, a round table cluttered with photographs of his family, a rich warm rug from Persia on the floor, two easy armchairs by the fire, and an assortment of little put-me-up tables that held his things and hers. He kicked off his shoes. After he'd taken a few sips of brandy, she rubbed her thumbs in circles over his neck, digging down under his shirt to the skin of his back, softly moving her hands until he sighed.

She let go. "Do you know, I think I'll retire. Do you mind?" Her fingers trailed from his shoulders and rested for a moment on his arm.

"You must be jolly tired with all that cooking."

"I didn't cook it."

"No, but all the — you know. Lovely dinner."

"It was a pleasure. Goodnight, then." She paused for a second to see if he'd look. Perhaps she'd have to keep this up all week.

But no. She'd only just slipped into her best nightgown when the knock came on the door. She made sure she was looking as pretty as possible. Douglas came in to see her propped on the pillow with lace undone about her collar bone. "I say," he said.

She looked the other way as he undressed. She kept her eyes shut when he touched her. She could at least do that, but when she felt something other than his flesh against her leg, she had to look. "What's that?"

Beneath the covers, Douglas was naked but for a red spotted handkerchief tied around the base of his stiff private parts. They looked absurd, more absurd than usual, like he'd dressed them up to be a highway man. He was sweating and groping and trying to find position. He stopped and leant on one elbow. "Now come on darling, we don't want to take chances. Not yet. You've only just begun to feel better haven't you?"

He didn't look like he wanted to wait. "But what will that do?"

"A chap at the club told me." His chin was against her cheek. "It'll stop the swimmers."

"But I don't want to stop them." She pulled at it, but Douglas grabbed her hand away.

"Careful. Don't want to pull the old chap off." He was making light, and he was sweating. He was finding her, feeling his way.

"But Douglas —"

"We'll talk about it later." Too late, the piercing awfulness, the vileness of that entry when parts that should be somewhere else were forced up against each other, when some part of him was in some part of her and it was wrong, all wrong, all tight and pain and sweat, when it was all she could do to hold her breath until that moment, that last grunt and it was over.

He rolled away. Bastard, she thought as he got up and left the room. She heard the bathroom taps running as another kind of wet seeped between her legs.

But she didn't think bastard three weeks later. Three weeks later she threw up.

10

.....

Enid, 1921

S HE TIED HER dressing gown around her and went up to
kiss Fagus goodnight. There was an epidemic of Sleepy Sickness sweeping the country and her parochial medic had decided
that Fagus had caught it early on, causing him to fall in the first
place. His symptoms were exactly like the virus; all he wanted
to do was sleep. He'd found his voice again — he spoke when
she touched his head, he turned his face towards her, and his
hands reached for hers. He could sit up a little better too; not for
long, but enough to eat without spillage. When they changed his
sheets, he flopped in Everett's arms, but at least they could carry
him to the bathroom now, and he could use the WC.

The parochial medic said the general weakness came from
the virus, not the brain, and gave him medicine that was supposed to kill the virus and wake him up; he said both sight and
strength would come back once the virus was got rid of, but the

medicine only made Fagus weaker. She knew that now, now that she'd thrown it away. His wound was covered by new hair and he looked angelic, like he used to. She locked the door and pulled the armchair closer to the bed. From beneath it, she took out the book.

An hour later, in the sitting room, while she stared at the fire, Douglas drained his whisky and got up for another. "Can I get you anything?" His tie was loosened, his suit was creased.

She shook her head. He stank of trains. If only he'd have a bath the moment he came in.

"How is he?" He removed the cork stopper and laid it beside the bottle.

"Fine." He always asked that on a Friday night. "Perhaps a lemon soda."

He opened the cabinet and took out another glass. "Good week?"

She leaned back and resumed her gaze at the flames, which danced prettily in the hearth. He always asked that too. "Yes, fine."

He handed her her drink and sat down, his legs outstretched. He took another cigarette from the case on the table beside him. "I've had a hell of a time."

She picked up her embroidery. "Port Elizabeth?"

"They're chomping at the bit." He slugged his drink.

"Will you have to go out there?"

"I hope not."

He'd been going on about railways in South Africa for months.

ELEANOR ANSTRUTHER

His firm had the contract. Nothing bored her more. Her life was the nursery, her weeks a blessed, silent contract with God that broke only when her husband came home. All she had to do was give birth, heal her eldest son, and she could be gone. If it wasn't a boy there was nothing more she could do, but Christ was with her, and Christ had given her a chance.

"I'll just pop up and give him a kiss goodnight." Douglas drained his glass.

"Yes, do." He'd be asleep. "Finetta's in with Mary tonight." The new nanny was young but capable. When Enid had announced she was pregnant, her mother had insisted they get more help than Everett and vague girls from the village. She'd sent Mary from an agency in London. "She's teething," called Enid after him. She unpicked a stitch as he left the room. It wasn't as if what she was doing with Fagus would be completely foreign to Douglas. He'd introduced it to her, after all. He'd have no right to say anything. He knew perfectly well it was how they'd fallen in love.

She held her breath, listening for his steps returning, but the house was quiet. Maybe that would have been it, a brief conversation on the shores of a lake in Italy if they hadn't met again. If they hadn't met again he might not have handed her a copy of *Science and Health*, they might not have fallen in love over it, he might not have said, *marry me*, and she might not have thought *mother will be furious* and said yes. Was it worth it? Would she have found it anyway? She would have done, if she'd needed it — Christ was everywhere and she needed it now. But it was Douglas who'd

90

made it real, who'd said it was the real thing. If she hadn't met him and had Fagus, if Fagus hadn't fallen, if her mother didn't hate her — there, there was the soft shake of his footsteps coming down. He'd sworn it was the thing. They'd fallen in love over its pages, its doctrine, its words of ultimate comfort. She heard him reach the hall, the touch of his footsteps growing hollow. It wasn't the thing for him after he came back from the war. After the war he'd forgotten it entirely. She picked up her needle and thread.

He came in and collapsed into his chair. He'd removed his tie. He poured himself a second drink and took slow grateful sips as she held her embroidery and sewed another line.

On Monday, after Douglas left for London, she tied Fagus to a chair. It was an effort to lift him, his body heavy and resistant, but she was strong. She'd done it three times before.

"Put your arms around my neck." She heaved and manoeuvred until he was sitting upright in the little wooden chair she'd dragged from the kitchen. The ropes she'd found in the shed; they were heavy, a little dirty, and not at all suitable, but the alternative was string or the ties from the sitting-room curtains, and they were too short. He held his head well enough now, but his spine bent and swayed, and she had to support him with one hand while she wound the ropes around him. Next time she'd get a pillow.

"I know it's not comfortable." He was trussed like a prisoner, but he didn't complain. His eyes, unseeing, looked right through her. "Now, Fagus, we have to pray together." She knelt before him, her hand on his knee. "Dear God." She waited for his small words of repetition.

"God," said Fagus, his voice small and soft.

"Christ in Heaven," Enid continued, "send down your love and heal this child, the sin he carries within him. We are servants of Your almighty love, in Your sight, let his be healed, let his body grow strong, let the sin pass from him."

She rested her head on her outstretched arm. She'd accepted Douglas' proposal to spite her mother. She'd been forced into marriage for her sin; for her sin her brother and father had died, and for her sin again, Fagus had been crippled into half-life. But Douglas had brought with him a gift. With the devil had come the keys to salvation.

There was only one way out. The dreams she'd had. The horror. Fagus hanging by his feet from the giant cedar in the park of Inveraray, Ivar dancing beneath him, her father twisting in pain as his guts spilled out onto the grass, her mother raised on a plinth and turned to stone; Joan, mute and death-like, picking daisies on the lawn.

"Take this sin from him."

When her breathing had stilled she put him back to bed.

She went quietly down to the kitchen and filled the kettle. Everett was off getting a leg of lamb from the butcher. Mary had taken Finetta out in the pram. It was all going so well. Fagus wasn't making improvements but she felt better. He was calmer. The struggle of the first few months, her nervousness, and his fear of pain had made their sessions often end in tears. He hadn't wanted to move, and she'd often sat instead at his bedside, her hand on his head. But his lethargy, his uncomprehending muscles, the darkness of the room had got to her, and she'd felt she must do something more than just pray. She had to remind the shrunken body that it lived. She had to wake him up.

One time they'd both fallen on the floor, his body heavy on hers, and they'd both cried out. Everett had come huffing up the stairs wondering at the racket and found them piled on top of each other, Fagus crying. Enid had said he'd wanted to pee. She'd locked the door after that.

She sat at the kitchen table, her dressing gown wrapped around her, the room lit by one lamp in the corner, and sipped her tea.

11

.....

Joan, 1922

J OAN AND PAT were at the hovel, lent to Pat by a friend some years ago and never reclaimed. Joan didn't ask what kind of friend. It was enough they had somewhere private to go. She still hadn't broached the subject of her own flat with her mother. She was working up to it.

The hovel was old and twisted, with low beams and scalene windows, dusty floors, rugs overlaid, a huge fireplace, and sofas with the stuffing beaten out. Pat lay on the floor, covered in a blanket. She flicked ash vaguely toward the fire. "Another letter from the front?"

"Don't be brutal." Joan dropped the letter from Douglas on the table beside her.

"Has she had the baby?"

"Not yet. It's not due for another month or so."

"Whoopee," said Pat, rolling onto her stomach.

"Women like her shouldn't have children," said Joan.

"As opposed to women like us?"

"I'd be a good mother."

"You've sense, anyway."

"He says Fagus managed to walk a few steps last week. They got him out into the garden."

"Good old Spring."

"And Enid's ballooning. He says she's the size of a house. I can't imagine it."

"It must be dreadful."

"Unimaginable. Imagine having to go through it."

"I'd really rather not. It's only further proof that God doesn't love us after all. Is there any more gin?"

Joan shook the bottle beside her. "None. I'll make coffee." But she didn't move. She was too tired; not from the antics of the night before, or the day, but from the letter. Douglas' news always depressed her — there was so much he didn't say. She rubbed her hands over her face. "Can't we stay another night?"

"I was rather feeling like theatre."

"Tonight? I thought we had cards." Cards with the Forsythes, as usual. No one went to the theatre on a Wednesday.

"Blow cards. I feel like people."

Joan didn't feel like anything. "He goes on and on about the cherry blossom and how darling the sparrows look, and hardly says a thing about her. He's like Mr. Rochester without the frown — all jolly while this shadow lurks over his shoulder and empties every page. God, I wish she wasn't having another."

"Then it would have to be you."

"Why does it have to be either of us? There's nothing wrong with Finetta."

"Except she's a girl."

"I'm a girl."

"And you're delicious."

"Mother is obsessed with boys."

"Mothers tend to be."

"I wouldn't be. I'd give it all to the little moppet."

"Of course you would."

"Enid wouldn't."

"How do you know?"

"She hardly put up a fight, did she? She could have just stood firm. Mother wouldn't have had a choice. God knows what she'll do to this next one. She's not capable of looking after anything."

"Does it matter?" Pat propped herself up on her elbows. "It's like a fashionable craze, this having to be simply tremendous with one's offspring. My parents were distant mountains I had no inclination to climb. I cannot see the problem with it. Gushing one way inevitably means you'll have to gush another. I can't see the point."

Joan watched, through the dusty diamond window panes, a flock of starlings circle and alight amongst the birch trees. "You know what she's like. It's as if she's waited all her life for something to give her character reason."

"I can't imagine she's enjoying it."

"No, but I bet she feels justified. She can complain and feel sorry for herself. She can say everything is someone else's fault."

"She didn't push him down the stairs."

"No. The god we don't believe in did, though I don't expect she'd say the same. Douglas said something about her wanting to go to church all the time. Christ."

"Won't that please your mother?"

"Nothing will please my mother until she's holding a healthy grandson on her lap."

"And he reaches twenty-one."

"He doesn't have to reach twenty-one. She can give it away anytime she likes."

"And put Douglas and your sister in charge?"

"No." Joan looked on the floor for her hair clip. "No, I don't suppose she'll do that. Twenty-one then." She raised her empty glass. "Here's to my sister having a boy and him coming of age with all his faculties intact."

Pat put the guard up on the fire. It was getting dark outside. "Shall we go?"

"What's on?" Joan was dressed but only just, in a shirt buttoned badly, and long-johns that used to belong to her brother. "I shall have to change."

"I wasn't expecting you to turn up like that," said Pat. She found her slippers and put them on.

Even after six years, Joan couldn't help watching her: the way she dropped her glass on the table on her way out, left her cigarettes abandoned on the rug with the scent of her, the last of her brown hair disappearing through the doorway, a fingertip trailed across the frame. The stairs creaked as she made her way up to the sloping warm bedroom above.

The bar at The Adelphi was a mass of bright lights and bright people, amusing anecdotes and laughter. Joan glanced about at familiar faces, and faces so similar it was as if a pig had bred too big a litter; as though any of these people belonged anywhere but in their mother's womb or in their grave. Everything between was a trying, desperate attempt at being one with their surroundings when what, compared to womb or grave, could be anything but fake? It made their foreheads crease, their eyes strain, their mouths pinch. It made them drink too much.

What a bore. She wished she was at home. Pat handed her a cocktail. "Anyone interesting?" Joan shook her head. "You were staring at the door as if your life depended on it."

"I thought I saw Douglas."

"You did. He came in with that female in too much fur." Pat nodded toward a woman on the other side of the room who was standing alone, looking lost.

"With her?"

"Do you know her?"

Joan shook her head.

"Mabel Wormald. He's been seen with her rather a lot, apparently."

"How do you know?"

"Dotty told me." Dotty was a friend of theirs. Her name

suited her. She was laughing loudly with a group on Pat's other side. "You were staring so hard you didn't hear her."

"I suppose she's a friend of someone's."

"Some friend. According to Dot, he was seen compromising the living daylights out of her last Wednesday at a revue in Mayfair. Dotty went up to him while Miss Wormald was off powdering and asked him how he was. Apparently he blushed down to his toes and pretended he was on some sort of business excursion, entertaining the temporarily abandoned wife of a railway chap over from South Africa. Absolute rot, of course. Good old Dotty did some digging. She's as British as the next man and as unmarried as you or I. I say, he's coming towards us."

Douglas was pushing through the crowd towards the bar.

"Douglas," said Pat, loudly.

He looked up and saw them. His smile took a second to appear. "Hello, you two. Fancy seeing you here."

"Do we never come out?" said Pat.

"Oh, no, of course you do. I just meant — well, isn't this jolly?"

"Isn't it?" said Pat.

"How are you both?"

"Brilliant as usual," said Pat.

"I got your letter," said Joan.

"Ah. Oh — did you? Jolly good. Nothing much to report. She's getting terribly near."

"To what?" said Pat.

Joan pushed Pat with her elbow. "And I hear Fagus walked a little?"

"He did." He looked relieved to be talking about it. "Little chap took a few steps in the garden. Marvellous."

On the other side of the room, through the crowds of heads and jewels and feathers, Joan watched Mabel Wormald put a white gloved hand to her neat hair and tidy a curl into place.

"I think someone's waiting for you," said Pat.

"Is there?" said Douglas.

"Weren't you on your way to the bar?"

"So I was," said Douglas.

"You don't want to keep her waiting."

"Now, look here," said Douglas.

"Oh, don't get in a twist. We don't care, do we, Joan?"

"Can we change the subject?" said Joan.

"We all have our secrets, don't we?" Pat smiled at him.

"Well, good to see you," said Douglas.

"And you," said Pat, draining her glass.

He pushed away from them and Pat smirked.

"Stop it," said Joan.

"I told you," said Pat.

The bell rang and the lights in the bar flashed on and off, three times. The crowd surged, and Pat and Joan were taken with it. They mounted the stairs like slow salmon leaping upstream at their leisure, a trail of silk and chinoiserie, feathers bobbing.

In their box, Pat held glasses to her eyes. "Do you think your sister knows?"

"I'm sure she doesn't," replied Joan.

The lights dimmed, the curtain rose, and Douglas and Mabel were lost to the hushed dark.

12

......

Enid, 1922

IT WAS ALL going so well until Douglas came home midweek when he was supposed to be in London till Friday, rattled the nursery door and said, "Enid, let me in."

It had been a bad few days. She'd rowed with Everett over soup, failed to remember to kiss Finetta goodnight again, and lain awake every night, her belly huge, her ankles swelling; she'd had to take off her engagement ring, everything had got so fat, but even though her fingers still played over the place it used to be, she was unable to stop the thoughts that she thought she'd driven away. Was she too late, was it all too late, the path set irrevocably and nothing she could do? Yet it was all going so well — she remembered this in daytime when Fagus held his arms up, ready to be shifted to the chair; when he seemed to grow used to it as if he knew it was doing him good, like today, when it had only taken her minutes to tie him up.

"Let me in." This time Douglas shouted it. But Fagus was held fast, and the knot was stuck. The ropes weren't where she'd left them — she'd searched under the bed, then remembered she'd taken them out to the river to wash them; their dirt had got onto Fagus' legs and stained his skin. She must have forgotten to put them back. She'd decided to use her dressing-gown cord instead, but she'd pulled the knot too tight.

"I'm coming." Her fingertips stung.

Fagus said, "Daddy?"

"Coming," said Enid. Did it come out light? It was hard to tell.

"Enid." Douglas rattled the handle. Any minute now he'd break the lock.

The knot gave, she pulled the chord through, loosened the binds then put Fagus' arms around her neck and swung him into bed, her belly a mound that got in her way. She pulled the blankets over him, straightened her skirts, put a hand to her hair then twisted the key and opened the door. "Douglas." She smiled.

He pushed past her and stood at the end of the bed, a force with no clue where to go. "What were you doing?"

"It's his bedtime."

"With a locked door?"

"I must have turned it by mistake. The draught —" She stood hopelessly on the rug, her mind a blank. She could only concentrate on Douglas, his face, the way she hoped hers looked.

She saw him look at the cord, dropped around the chair that

in her hurry she'd forgotten to pick up. "What were you doing, Enid?"

She went over to the windows and closed the curtains. The room was a shelter of toys gone by; a basket of teddy bears and knitted rabbits, a merry-go-round of wooden zebras the size of little boys' hands, a hobbyhorse leaning in the corner. "I'll tidy up. Give him a kiss goodnight." The chair stood like an assault between them.

Douglas picked up the dressing-gown cord which stuck and twirled from around the chair legs as he pulled it loose. With it looped in his hand he leaned down to Fagus. He stroked the hair from his eyes, kissed him and walked out, the cord trailing after him.

Downstairs on the sitting-room table, the medicine bottles she'd been hiding were collected in a group. Douglas stood beside them, a whisky in one hand, a cigarette in the other. A fire danced prettily in the hearth. Enid sat neatly in her armchair and reached purposefully for her embroidery. So what if he knew? Who was he to judge? He went off every week to a life in London. He had her income and the freedom it bought him to go hunting and play with his car. What did he know of loneliness and a life lost, a son unable to look at her, a mother and sister who wouldn't? He had everything he wanted.

"Everett found these under the bed."

"That's where I keep them." She thought she'd pushed them into the corner.

"Empty."

"I've used them all up. I must have forgotten to throw them away."

He picked up one of the bottles. "The date on this one is from a week ago."

"Is it?"

"What have you done with his medicine, Enid?"

"Everett collects it. She has the prescription. She must have picked up an empty one from the chemist." She shoved the needle and it jerked suddenly through the embroidery pattern, piercing the pad of her finger. She sucked the spot of blood.

"But you haven't sent her out for a new one?" Douglas stayed by the table, the bottle in his hand.

"Apparently not."

"Even though he's supposed to have three of these pills a day?"

The parochial medic had swapped one prescription for another. He'd said *marked improvement*, and, in her head, Enid had laughed.

Douglas put the bottle down. "She called me at the office."

Enid unpicked a stitch that had got tangled at the back. "Everett?"

"She told me she thought I should come home at once. She said your behaviour, the way you've been behaving — she said she's been worried for quite some time, and then she found these, and ropes, under the bed. She said she'd noticed marks on Fagus' legs — and then she found the ropes."

She should have kept the door locked from the outside as well.

"She said you stay in there for hours and won't let her in."

Enid drew a long blue woollen thread through a hole, part of the eye of a pheasant in a pleasant country scene. "Can I not care for my boy?"

"She said you threw a bowl of soup down the stairs."

Everett had knocked on the nursery door and ignored Enid's shouts to leave the tray outside, she'd get it. Fagus hadn't wanted to get out of bed and Enid was sick of pregnancy. The soup had stained the walls.

She drew the blue thread through another hole. "Perhaps Everett would do better looking after the house than gossiping about me."

"Goddamn it, Enid." Douglas slammed his hand on the table, the medicine bottles jumped and fell over, cracked and smashed and little corks flew embedded in glass. They'd been so hard to remove. Every time she'd got one out and tipped the contents of the bottle down the WC she'd thrown the corks in the fire even though she knew cork didn't burn, but it didn't sink either. She'd tried reassembling the bottles instead. Better to shove the corks back in and hide them under the bed until she could dump them. She'd made three trips already to the woods and these before her, jumping and crashing, were due for disposal tomorrow. Out there, beyond the garden and the pipes of her house, she'd imagined little minnows getting frantic on Sleepy Sickness pills in the river. She'd gone to see if she could see any thrashing about, but it was impossible to count out the possibility of those discoveries too, now that she sat here, now that he shook his head and shouted.

He refilled his glass, the syphon cannoned soda into whisky. "What are you doing?"

She kept her gaze steady. "You should know."

"I need you to tell me what you think you're doing. What you've been doing, with his medicine — with *him*. Why haven't you been giving it to him?"

"It's against the law."

"What law?"

"As I said, Douglas. You should know."

"This isn't a game."

"Well, one of us was lying, and it certainly wasn't me. Filling him with pills for an illness he doesn't have, so that you can avoid the truth: he was born with sin, and I know what that sin was. This," she waved her hand in the direction of the nursery, the needle in her fingers, the blue thread, a line from hand to lap, "this thing that's happened to him, it was always going to happen. I took no notice. I pretended my actions had no consequence. He smashed his head and now he can't see and he has hardly strength to stand up. Pills aren't going to make any difference. He needs Christ."

Douglas came over to the fire, sat heavily and put his head in his hands. When he raised his head again it was as if he'd forgotten her. "You need help."

"I gave him my sin."

"It's the pregnancy. You're exhausted."

"Everything I did was wrong. I gave it to him."

"Have you seen the doctor?"

"I just wanted to hurt her." She leaned towards Douglas.

He put out his hand to touch her, but he was too far away. "You have to promise me you'll leave him alone."

"My sin killed my brother, it killed my father and now it's killing him."

"What are you talking about, Enid?"

"Us." She stared at him. Her eyes hurt. Her chest ached. She wanted to sink into the carpet, the floorboards, the stone and earth beneath. "We should never have been together."

"I'm going to call —" He was half out of his chair.

"Who?" she shouted. "Who will you call? My mother? Your mother?"

The syphon blasted another drink. Douglas took it to the window. He may as well know, she thought, staring at his back. He may as well know everything. Her belly churned as the child turned over. Her back ached, her legs were swollen, her hair fell ragged from the half bun she'd swept it into this morning when Fagus' secret was still her own. "It's my fault, Douglas, do you see? It's my fault, our fault, everything born of us, everything since us was damned."

"Finetta?" said Douglas — to the window, but she heard him.

"She's a girl," said Enid.

Douglas swung round. "You're just like your mother."

She wasn't. He was wrong. He didn't understand. "It's the men, don't you see? The men who suffer — father, Ivar, Fagus. You and I, we married in sin; we didn't love each other. I did it to spite her."

"Then what about this one?" He jabbed, loose handed, towards her belly.

Enid gasped and put her palm over the curve, shielding her insides. "That's why we have to heal Fagus. Do you see? That's why we have to do what we have to do. Christ is asking the question, Douglas." The baby kicked again and she felt the terror of the life inside her, the weirdness that was too much, the plain truth that her brain could not accept. A life that could hear every word, a human being that would emerge plunging from her, splitting and tearing, and making her mad. "We mustn't do it to him." She shouted back.

"Do what?" Douglas grappled for his cigarette case. "Do *what*? You haven't done anything. You didn't put a bullet in your brother, you didn't put a cancerous lump in your father's stomach and you didn't push Fagus down the stairs. None of this is anything to do with you. Fagus, our son, was born with something wrong with him. Our son. We all knew it, but you never let us say it. And now he's caught Sleepy Sickness or whatever it is — I'm not a doctor, I don't know. Maybe he's susceptible, maybe he's weak. It's just another brick on top of a ruined city."

"Stop it." She put her hands over her ears. "Stop it."

"Sin. The only sin that's being committed here is your inability to care for your children, or to be my wife. Fagus is desperately ill, and I get a call from the housekeeper telling me you're throwing away his medicine and tying him to a chair." He became still, suddenly, a cigarette halfway to his mouth. "You've got that book."

It had been getting dusty under the bed. She'd taken to leaving it in his toy basket, hidden under the largest soft rabbit. She stood up. "Don't."

"It was a long time ago, Enid. You can't think it had any seriousness."

"You seemed to think it was pretty serious when it gave you time alone with me. You said it was the future."

"It's nonsense. You know that. It's madness." He was already out in the hall, his hand on the bannister rail, his foot on the first stair.

She grabbed his jacket. "You don't know anything. You believed it too. We both did. There are no accidents. Illness is a sign of sin. Christ heals."

"No one's going to heal him, Enid. There's nothing anyone of us can do."

"But we can. I can. He's getting better."

He reached the first landing. "They don't let you use medicine, do they? They tell you to throw it away."

"I'm healing him, Douglas." She wasn't as fast, couldn't take the stairs two at a time. He reached the top floor before she did, and by the time she got to the nursery he had the light on and was turning picture books out of the shelf.

Fagus woke up. "Daddy?"

Douglas said, "Go back to sleep."

But how could he with Douglas crouched on the floor using the hobbyhorse like a minesweeper under the bed? Enid turned out the light. Douglas turned it on again, picked up the toy basket, and tipped it out. *Science and Health* fell to the floor amongst knitted rabbits and soft teddy bears. He held it up. "You've lost your mind."

That was all, just that. Almost the last time he looked her in the eye.

13

.....

Enid, 1922

T HERE WERE SO many people in her house these days. Douglas hanging about, midwives, neighbours all taking advantage of Everett's tea. A doctor because her mother had insisted. New techniques, she'd shouted down her newly-installed telephone, as if the study of midwifery was all she'd done since autumn. I'll really be fine, Enid had shouted back. You'll be fine, her mother had spat, when I say so.

All hanging about, getting in her way, preventing her from coming downstairs. What had happened to privacy? What had happened to getting out of the ship that was listing badly? She'd only added more cargo, more precious jewels that could not be lost, that had to be delivered. She moved like a cow from bed to floor to door to passageway, udders swinging, belly shouting at her to lie down, but nowhere was comfortable. The new doctor had cautioned against hot baths, but Enid didn't care. At least slopped into water she could feel weightless, a little.

She'd forgotten the impossibility of it, that this enormous mound would have to come out of the gap that resisted even the absurd protuberance of Douglas, that it would force her to stretch and gape and tear; that having carried it for nine months, fussed over by the stream of people in her house, she no longer mattered. It had reached the state of tyrant — any day now it would decide to come and wreak havoc on the warm body that had housed it.

In the bathroom, she turned the taps on full blast. Maybe she could boil them both alive. She leant her hands on the windowsill and stretched her back while the room filled with steam. She couldn't do it. She wasn't ready. It had all been a terrible mistake. For this past month she'd felt the alien kick of terrible life and had wanted to get a knife and cut the whole thing out, cut herself out, not be any more at all; and yet here she was, about to be, all over again, the bearer of God knew what.

Her waters broke as she stepped into the bath — warm, gushing liquid from between her legs met scalding bath water. She had one foot in, her hands on the edge of the tub, the other leg stranded on the bath mat.

"Everett," she shouted. It was confusing — the heat rising, the warm falling — she didn't know whether to get in or out. "Everett," she shouted again.

They filled her bedroom. They kept the curtains closed. They wouldn't let her off the bed to crawl on the floor and scream.

They made her put her feet up in a harness that dug into her back. When they laid his slithering body on her chest, all wrapped in cloths, his hair damp, she cried.

"I say, well done." Douglas sat gingerly on the edge of the bed. They'd cleaned her up — the bits that could be seen, anyway. The bits that couldn't bled and seeped and shot arrows of pain every time she moved. The baby was already pink; he'd lost the translucent blue-grey of birth when the universe still lay upon him, when he could be anything. He had a bonnet on, and slept. They'd timed it so he'd had a feed, she'd put her agonising nipples away, he'd burped and they could all look pretty, none of the blood and gore in sight.

He must think it's as easy as that, she thought, and said, "He's very sweet."

"What shall we call him? I was thinking Henry."

Henry was Douglas' father's name. She remembered how Douglas' face had fallen on first hearing Fagus' name; chosen while he was away. How he'd said, *oh, I was rather hoping*, and then tickled his cheek anyway.

"I'd like to call him Ian."

"Not Henry, then?"

"He's a Campbell."

"He's an Anstruther too."

"He's going to be a Campbell."

"He ought to have some Anstruther in there somewhere, you know."

"What about Fife?" She didn't mind the county Douglas'

family came from. "Anyway, his surname's Anstruther." How could she forget that? Every time she looked at her married name she still felt a wave of humiliation.

"Well, jolly well done in any case. He's absolutely dear."

A silence dropped between them. She shifted the weight of their son in her arms, hoping he might wake up, but he carried on sleeping, his little face upturned, his mouth slightly open, while Douglas carried on sitting on the edge of the bed as if the moment was precious, a shared intimacy that they may not have again. Yet his feelings weren't shared. That intimacy she saw written on Douglas' face, the way his hand lay on the cover almost touching her leg, the way his body leant an inch toward her, needing only a nudge to come closer, these were false patterns that described what he wanted: a passive wife made happy by childbirth, a raging woman made quiet, a female, lain on the pillows unable to fight, holding the hopes of all of them. Perhaps he thought everything would be better now. He made another stab at leaning closer, his chin up, his eyes down to see over the wraps, on his face an idiotic smile that Enid wanted to smash.

She moved away, further into the headboard, the pillows that propped her back. "Get Mary, will you?"

"Of course." Douglas got up quickly. "You must be tired."

"A little." She gave him a small smile.

Mary came in and took the bundle from her. Enid turned onto her side.

14

.....

Joan, 1922

JOAN SQUASHED BESIDE her mother in the rich, leather interior of the Rolls.

"I've torn a thread," she said, inspecting the hem of her skirt.

"No time to change." Sybil tapped the glass partition with the pewter end of her brolly.

"I wasn't going to. I'll snap it." Joan wound the thread around the tip of her finger and pulled sharply. "I'm terribly hot. May I open a window?"

The Rolls pulled out of Bryanston Square onto George Street, and immediately swerved to avoid a bus that had come to an abrupt stop to their right.

"Good Lord," said Sybil, gripping the leather handle beside her. "London is becoming absolutely hellish."

"You always say that," said Joan, letting in an inch of fresh air.

"I shall go up to Scotland for good, you know."

"You're always saying that, too. We could send Enid with you."

"At least she'd have proper staff."

"I thought you sent her a girl."

"I did. Will she keep her, is the question."

"Of course she'll keep her." Her mother hadn't stopped smiling — or worrying — since Douglas came to Bryanston Square last autumn to tell them the terrific news. That was the word he'd used, *terrific*; grinning with a look of pure fear in his eyes. *How apt*, Pat had said later, when she'd told her.

"Douglas tells me she sometimes doesn't get up at all," said Sybil. They wound through narrow streets, heading for the fast road west.

"The new girl, or Enid?" replied Joan. Cars always made her feel slightly sick. Or was it being encased with her mother, gunning towards Berkshire, unable to get out? She couldn't tell.

"Enid, of course. One can't go slopping about. It isn't good for the servants. One must set an example."

"She has been pregnant."

"I was recommended a good stroll every morning. The day after I had you, I was up Dun Na Caiuche."

"I'm sure you weren't, mother." The tower hill that reared above Loch Fyne was too high for any of them. But Ivar used to love it — he'd go up and come back with stories; he'd spun them so well her mother liked to think she'd been there too.

"Very nearly. I certainly got up every day. I wouldn't hear of staying in bed."

"Aren't you the legion." The way her mother told it, she and Ivar and Enid had simply popped out while she did her embroidery, hardly a blip in her daily life. But Joan had heard the screams when she worked at Charing Cross. The female ward was down the hall and not their domain, but all the Red Cross Girls knew it wasn't a matter of *there we are*, a slight spasm and a fresh new baby.

"Do you think she'll mope?" said Sybil, dabbing her nose with a lilac hankie.

"Of course she'll mope."

"If she's going to mope, I shall have to speak to her."

"She'll enjoy that," said Joan. The afternoon stretched before her: Douglas in a panic, Enid in a depressed fizz. She'd rather put her head in the oven than spend the afternoon with either of them. She hadn't seen him since the spring, not long after their unfortunate meeting in the bar of The Adelphi. He'd found her at home one afternoon and wondered if he might *have a quiet word*.

"You see, a man might have his jollies," he'd said, trying desperately hard to be casual. She hadn't felt like rescuing him from his awkwardness. She'd lit a cigarette and watched him squirm. "What with Enid laid up, and everything. Now you won't make a fuss of it, will you? Not that there's anything to make a fuss of, you understand. It's really just a bit of nonsense."

"I'm sure she'd be thrilled to hear that."

"Now, look here — you're not going to tell her are you?"

"I was referring to Miss Wormald."

"How do you know her name?"

"Everyone knows her name, Douglas."

"Everyone?"

"Oh, do be a man," said Joan. "It's hardly front-page news. Man takes mistress. I hate to tell you this, but you're not the first."

"Now, look here." He'd tried very hard to be a man then. "We all have our little secrets, don't we?"

She'd asked him to leave after that.

She hadn't seen Enid since last summer. How would she be now? No doubt the same. A depressed fizz, her pain strewn about like driftwood, a new baby to trumpet. Babies were nothing but a bore. Who cared until they were grown enough to stop puking and start holding a decent conversation? Fagus had been able to hold a decent conversation by the time he was three; better than his parents, anyway, and a lot more fun. In his last letter, Douglas had said he was *really quite up and about*, as if that made up for everything. She imagined he'd be propped somewhere — not the boy who'd picked daisies on the lawn, who'd chattered funny nonsense and pushed his head under her arm and called her Dodo, but the new, half-darkened boy who they would all have to get used to. Maybe he would call her Dodo again.

But what would she do to the next one, this next one whom they were, in an hour or so, going to see? And why did they have to keep shoving them at her, a woman so incapable that she'd lost one already? No, that was unfair. She knew it was unfair, but she couldn't help it. If it wasn't Enid's fault, then whose was it? If they'd got to him early, if the medics had been allowed to look, then none of it might have happened. Fagus might have had proper help and surgery or medicine, or whatever it was that he'd needed when he'd grown with a head too big. But now that was all washed over, wasn't it — a new baby to flatten the bumps, rake the earth, and make everything look rosy all over again.

Her mother appeared to have dropped off — her eyes were closed, her face rested in slow collapse; her mouth open, as if she had no teeth. That's what she'll look like when she's dead, thought Joan, when nothing is left but loose skin, the soul, whatever that is, flown. They will bury her next to their father, in the tomb that bears a plaque to their brother, and she, Joan, will come up and visit. Strachur will be Enid's. Joan will stay at The George; she won't stay at Strachur anymore. She'll come up and visit and remember the tower of old-fashioned loyalty that had got her through her childhood.

She knew she was watching her mother die — even though that final eclipse may not be for years — but everything had a beginning. She was pulling into another world, and as the veils dropped, closing her off, it made it difficult to see her face; it drained her skin of colour, while more and more her mind seemed to be wondering back to that godless unknown, as if she could concentrate less and less on what was before her. More and more often Joan would see her — in her armchair by the fire, or like this, in the Rolls, amassed in some interior vision or perhaps just switching off. What blessed relief, thought Joan, to give in to the insistent dragging. But she would rather not die in inches — how could she be sure there'd be anyone there to measure out her cup? Would Pat still be there? She didn't know. She didn't want to think about it. At least Enid would have her children, Douglas, conformity, normality, an acceptable order of things. However bloody their wretched marriage was, it was allowed. It could be spoken about, and guarded; things could be put in place, but what did she and Pat have? The thin excuse of companionship, having to put up with the term *spinster*, and deal with it because it allowed them to love unfettered. Just the two of them, neither wanting to go first or last.

She'd witnessed her father's gradual waltz, his painful deterioration made worse by the ruined love between them, and it had almost put her off loving anyone. He'd tried when she hadn't, she'd tried when he hadn't; their habit of misjudgement had continued right up until the end, when his last words to her had been *go away*, because she'd come to see him too early, before he'd been shaved. But Enid had known better than to knock on his door before ten — and Enid had been allowed in when no one else was, not even their mother. With Sybil, Joan will know better. She'll be the one to get it right, to stand as sentry when the time came, judging their dying mother's needs, telling Enid: *not now, you'll tire her.*

London was far behind them. They were on a lane of high-banked earth topped with trees in full May rush, a tunnel of green and sunlight.

"I do wish you'd get yourself a chap."

Her mother's voice made her jump. Christ. That woman. She behaved as though silence was only another waiting for her to speak. "I thought you'd dropped off."

"It would be such a relief if you could make an effort."

"Perhaps I can order one at Fortnum's." Joan looked out of the window.

"Thinking ahead is not funny, my girl, it's prudent. I've told you before. Enid is not to be trusted."

"She's not going to kill him." That was a stupid thing to say; she saw her mother's lips tighten. "I mean, I'm sure it will all be fine."

"Fine. Fine. Why must you girls use that phrase? I shall jolly well have to keep an eye on him, that much is certain. I've already told Douglas that I want regular reports, and that he's to bring him up as soon as convenient. I want to see him at least every month."

"There you are, then."

"You said yourself that it's like relying on a lifeboat to get one across the Atlantic."

"I did not."

"I heard you say it to Pat."

Goddamn it. She'd thought her mother was asleep that time, too. They'd been playing two-hand whist. Sybil hadn't moved from her chair for hours. Pat had replied: *let's give it up then shall we? Jump over board. Move to Casablanca or Khartoum, somewhere fabulous. We could have a life*, and they'd talked about it for hours.

"If I were feeling firm, I should say you have as much duty as your sister."

"I've no guts for procreation." She mustn't snap. She mustn't. Her mother was just flinging out ropes, hoping to be saved. She didn't mean to whip Joan. She knew nothing. If she knew — but no. If she knew, God knows what she'd say. She'd probably tell Joan that she'd got herself in a muddle, pat her hand, assume she didn't understand the world.

"Streatley," said Joan, reading the sign as they passed it. They drove through the village — a row of shops, a large, shapeless village green, the spire of a church through trees — and out again.

"Do you know where you're going?" shouted Sybil at the glass partition.

"I'm sure he does, mother. I gave him Douglas' directions."

They wound up a hill and pulled in at a gravel drive.

"At least there are gates," said Sybil, sniffing. Their driver got out to open them.

"There you are!" Douglas stood in the hall. "Let me take your things."

Joan shrugged off her coat and helped her mother from her fur wrap.

"And how was your journey? Not too long, I hope. Marvellous weather, isn't it?" he said, and rubbed his hands together as though he were cold.

"Are we to greet him standing up?" said Sybil.

"Good Lord, no! In here, in here." He opened a door to their right. "Come on in. Ma, why don't you take an armchair?"

There was a cot placed on the rug, all covered in white lace and frills, but with nothing in it. Sybil peered at it. "Where is he?"

"Enid's just changing. She thought she'd bring him in herself. He's absolutely bonny."

"And the others?" said Joan.

"Shall I ask Mary to bring in Finetta? She's simply dying to see you."

Joan couldn't imagine an infant simply dying to see anyone.

"I'm parched," said Sybil.

"Of course, of course." Douglas fairly ran from the room. They heard a door bang.

"Well, I must say," said Sybil.

"We need only stay an hour," said Joan. She wandered over to the window seat and sat down.

"An hour? It's taken us half a lifetime to get here."

"Not quite. Anyway, you looked more comfortable in the Rolls."

"They've had all morning," said Sybil.

She wants to make a show of it, thought Joan, staring at the garden. "Would you mind if I left you? You don't need me here, do you?"

"You might want to see him."

"I'm sure there'll be plenty of time for that. I need to stretch my legs. Do you mind awfully?"

"Oh, not at all," said Sybil, wafting her hand through the air. "I shall just sit here then, shall I?"

"I'll tell them to hurry up," said Joan. She went down the passage to the kitchen. She knew the way — she'd been here once before, when Fagus was born. "Hello, Everett."

Mrs. Everett said, "Oh, ma'am, I wasn't expecting —" and patted her hands on her apron. Her iron-grey hair was clamped to the sides of her head with clips.

"Mother's parched — and Enid's not down, with or without the baby."

"I'll see right to it."

"I think Douglas is seeing to it. How is he?"

"Mr. A? He's —"

"No. The baby."

"The baby. Such a poppet. You wouldn't know, I mean, he's such a poppet. Growing ever so nicely. Can't stop eating, and sleeps like a —"

"I heard babies didn't sleep very well at all."

"Oh, he wakes and shouts, I'll say. He had Mary up all night."

"And her?"

"Well, now." Mrs. Everett looked around as if searching for a prop. She found the biscuits that were cooling on a tray and started arranging them on a plate. "I should think it's quite taken it out of her."

"Does she get up?"

"She's up today all right." Biscuits arranged, she started on a sponge cake, cutting it into fine slices left standing so that by the time she'd finished it looked like an icing-sugar-dusted bicycle wheel.

"Where are the others?"

"Finetta's up with Mary. Will her ladyship wish to see the little girl too?"

"I think Douglas said he'd get them."

"Very good." She poured boiling water into the pot.

"And Fagus?"

"Well I should think he's out in the garden, ma'am, on such a lovely day. He likes to sit on the bench, listen to the wind, he says, and the birds and so on. He does go on."

"Out the back?" said Joan, pointing at the double glass doors that led to the vegetable plot and the orchard.

"The other bench, under the trees at the front, beyond the lawn. You'll find him there."

"Is anyone with him?"

"Oh no, ma'am, he's quite happy sitting alone. Since it's been warm he'll sit out there for hours. He always did like that spot, even when —" she looked from tray to countertop, but everything — the tea, the cups, the cake and biscuits, and sugar and milk jug — had been transferred. "I'd better get this in, hadn't I."

"Can I help you?" It looked too heavy, too loaded.

"Goodness me, no. What a thing. Her ladyship's daughter helping me with a tray, good Lord."

Joan held the kitchen door as Everett bore through it. There were voices coming from the sitting room. They must have gathered. There was no way she was going back in there. She opened the sitting-room door for Everett, but only to push it, and stand back. She heard her mother say, "Ah, splendid. And isn't he splendid, Mrs. E?"

She went out of the front door, crossed the gravel and walked quickly across the lawn. When she reached the trees at the far end, she looked back at the house. Enid was sitting in the window seat, side on to the glass, in a long white dress, her arms wrapped around her knees.

"Hello?"

Joan looked into the mild gloom of the trees. There on a bench, was Fagus. The trees took up a corner of the garden, a wall on one side, a hedge to the road on another; they grew in a spacious clump, like a miniature wood put in the wrong place. The bench was against the wall.

"It's me, Dodo."

"Dodo!" He held out a hand.

She took it and sat next to him. "Aren't you looking well."

"Am I?"

"Your papa's been telling me how well you've been doing."

"Has he?"

"Are you to stay here all day, Fagus?"

"Till Etty gets me."

She put her arm around him.

15

.....

Enid, 1923

IAN'S BIRTH TOOK up the isolated simplicity of snap-shots — the pain, the sweat, the humiliation of a doctor in the room — it all felt so long ago. He'd fed from her a little, and for a little while. She'd had something for him, and fresh goat's milk did the rest. He was growing splendidly. That was her mother's word. Isn't he splendid? when she'd come out to see him, daring a journey to Berkshire. Finetta had wriggled on Mary's knee, Everett had struggled in with an overladen tray, and Enid had sat in the window seat, a clean dress on, her hair brushed for the first time in days, stared at her newborn son and cried helplessly, despite him lying there so perfect in the frilly, white lace cot, despite her mother clapping her hands, despite Douglas looking embarrassed. If his brother had been perfect, there'd have been no need for him.

She must stop it. She must get up. He was splendid; everything a normal mother could want. She must stop these thoughts that were trying to kill her. She must at least try. That's what they all kept saying, anyway: the doctor and midwife, Everett, Douglas. Fresh air. That was their chorus: fresh air, a good walk, sunshine. *Come and hold him*, Everett had said again yesterday, after a week had gone by since the last time, but he felt as if he didn't belong to her; he was someone else's child opening his blue eyes, looking into hers, screwing up his face, and wailing. She'd gone back to bed.

Her bedside table was crowded with cups of half-drunk tea gone cold — a city of past calamities, from when she'd slunk away having failed again and Everett had come up with a tray. They kept bringing her tea, Everett did and sometimes Mary. Tea. As if it fixed everything. Come on, Enid, she thought, contemplating pushing off the covers and standing up. Come on.

She hardly saw Douglas these days. He came home at weekends, to tinker with his car. If she managed to get up and dress for dinner, he went on about trains, not meeting her eyes, looking anywhere but at her. Well, that was all right. It suited her perfectly not to see him. If only he'd leave her be completely, she'd probably perk up, but she'd learnt that messages got through, new messages about The State of Enid, as if she were a constitution in collapse. One day in bed usually passed unnoticed, two and she was pushing it; three in a row and a message would be sent, the troops called in, a doctor, sometimes two doctors, bearing tonics and opinions about blood. Was she eating enough? No. Was she getting enough exercise? No. Wasn't little Ian enough to make any mother proud? No, no, no. They kept shoving him at her too like the tea, as if all she had to do was have enough of him and she'd warm up.

She had no idea what time it was. She'd got rid of the clock, the one with Douglas' inscription on the back. She didn't want to *watch time passing* for a single second more, and she couldn't stand the insistent tick. She'd wrapped it in a shawl and stuffed it down the back of the wardrobe.

Come on. She swung her feet to the floor. Get up. Do something. She wandered downstairs in her dressing gown and stopped in the hall, the red tiles cold beneath her bare feet. Kitchen with Everett? Garden with Mary and the children? Sitting room alone? Perhaps she could eat something; tackle the stew Everett had made yesterday, especially for her. She could sit quietly in the dining room with a book and the stew. It would pass at least half an hour. Perhaps, after that, she'd have some new thought. *It all comes down to effort* — she'd heard one of the doctors say that outside her bedroom door, as if, just because she didn't want to sit up, she'd lost the power of hearing too. Effort. Yes. Perhaps by being upright the blood would do some magic trick of clearing her head and firing life into her bones. She'd remember who on earth she was, and what she was doing here in this neat and ordered house, where no one seemed to need her, but everyone seemed to need her to get up.

In the dining room she stood in front of the bookshelf. *Wuthering Heights* had been slotted in between the Bible and *Gardens of England*. She stared at it.

Those months and months she'd sat by his darkened bedside — the hours she'd prayed — it was strange now to see the vision of ropes and the bottles under the bed — who was the woman who'd done that? Was it her? Was there another Enid, living another life without another son, who still held her only boy in her arms and prayed? Who was passionate, and lively, and so full of strength that she'd dragged chairs and hauled limbs and thrown bottle after bottle of medicine far out into the river? Whoever she was, she was gone. This Enid, the Enid in front of the bookcase — she looked at her hands to be sure she existed — this Enid had two sons, and one had blotted out the other. This Enid had a husband who'd thrown her book on the fire and said that if she ever went near Fagus with that cultish, vicious nonsense again he'd take all the children away from her.

He'd improved though, hadn't he? She saw it sometimes when she caught sight of him, hobbling about on the lawn like a toy that needed oiling; a wobbly toy in a world of almost darkness. At least she didn't treat him like an abandoned pet, a stray they'd taken pity on, patting his head like Douglas did, as if she liked him but didn't know what to do with him. At least he wasn't slumped in a darkened room any more.

She'd missed the bit when he'd stopped lying down most of the time and become a child who was got up and dressed every day. Her body had got so heavy and unwieldy she'd stopped climbing to the nursery. She'd become the lumpen mound in a bed — they'd swapped places — and when her body began its deflation to normal size, her head became so heavy, or was it her heart, or her limbs or her eyes — she couldn't make it out — that bed remained the only safe place to be. She was too dense and fogged to be anywhere else; all she wanted to do was sleep. It was an effort just to stand here, looking at the books. She kept finding herself in places like this, staring at something, completely devolved of the reason. That's why being with anyone was so exhausting. She had to keep remembering to look as if she knew what she was doing.

Well, Fagus had improved, and stopped improving — like dough that had done all the rising it could — and so maybe it would be the same for her. That's what they said anyway. *You'll feel better soon*, until she'd stopped telling them that she felt unwell. It wasn't her body that was ill. The blood had been washed away, her belly had deflated, it no longer hurt to pee — she'd improved and stopped improving; his wobbly journey across the lawn was a triumph in the way getting out of bed was a success for her.

She took *Wuthering Heights* from the bookshelf, and *Gardens of England* tipped against the Bible leaving a little triangular gap. The Father, the Son and the Holy Ghost, she thought, looking at the three points. This is what keeps happening, staring at things, wondering whether to shuffle the books straight or leave that Holy Trinity hole. Either choice seemed worrisome. Stew. That's what she'd been going to do — ask Everett for a bowl of stew. She left the bookcase and the triangle, she put *Wuthering Heights* on the table and went out of the room, along the hall and into the kitchen. But when she came back in again, orders given, the indecision of the bookcase bore into her back, and she got up and shuffled the books straight.

She felt silly, sitting there, waiting for her meal like an imbecile in dressing gown and slippers, so she got up and went upstairs and got a shawl. She could say she thought she had the beginnings of a cold. When she came back to the dining room, her bowl of stew was waiting there, steaming on the table, cutlery and napkin beside it. *Wuthering Heights* was back on the shelf. Now she'd have to go through the whole thing again.

She decided against it and ate her stew instead. It was perfectly possible that it was delicious, but she couldn't tell — it was muted like everything else. Stew. Eat. Fork. Mouth. Later she'd perform some other function that showed she was alive, like washing her face or defecating, washing her bits in the bidet. Perhaps this was what life really was. Muted colours and bodily functions, an existence where nothing really mattered. Would anyone notice if she disappeared completely? Undoubtedly not. Stew. Eat. Fork. Mouth.

She managed half of it before she got tired of chewing, and gave up. It was only Monday — she had a whole week to rouse herself. She could turn on the taps in the bathroom and pretend to be having a bath, while lying on the floor and staring at the ceiling. Then she could go back to bed again, her thoughts covered with gauze, a bandage stuck with exhaustion and tiny hands, a white blaze of nothing through which she couldn't see and didn't want to.

16

.....

Enid, 1924

MARY TOOK IAN out of the pram and set him on his
little legs while she picked sweet peas with Finetta. Fagus
was propped on a bench in the sunshine; Enid sat at the kitchen
table, the back door to the garden was open; Everett cooked lunch:
ham hock, late summer salad and potatoes. From the garage came
the clang of Douglas and Gould tinkering with an engine.

Ian grabbed the bean canes and bent them towards himself.
"Watch him with those sharp points," called Enid to Mary.

With her great iron bulk — like a steamer, Enid thought,
watching her move across the kitchen; the vessel that kept them
afloat — Everett swept from cold store to stove and blocked Enid's
view. Enid moved to the other end of the table.

Everett dropped a pat of butter on a board, divided it and
dipped the knife in cold water. The kitchen was a happy clutter
of washed tiles and saucepans hanging, the broad wooden table

was crowded with bowls of suet, string and dishcloths. The air smelled salty and sweet.

Fagus kicked his legs and held his face up to the sky as if he was a dog, sniffing the air. "Is Fagus cold?" She thought she'd seen him shiver. His hands were stuffed together between his knees.

Ian pulled the canes again; they bent towards him, rucking the soil. Mary had her back to him, chattering with Finetta. Everett spilled flour on the work surface and clapped her hands causing a cloud that puffed then fell. Ian let go, the canes sprang back and he dropped onto his bottom.

"I'll get to him in a minute," said Everett, as she kneaded dough.

"I could get him a shawl." Perhaps she'd imagined it. Fagus was leaning back with his eyes closed, sunshine on his face. He was so big now. She'd forgotten somehow that he'd grow. She had tea with him most days.

Ian stood up, grabbed the canes again and yanked them clean out of the earth. His prize suddenly in his hands, the sharp tips waving in the air, he ran three steps away from Mary, holding his arms up as if he was a javelin thrower or a savage, spear aloft.

"Mary!" By the time her voice reached the nanny's ears, Ian had reached the edge of the plot. The cane stuck suddenly in the rabbit wire, ran through his hands and scraped along his cheek. He hit the fence head first and fell over.

Mary dropped her basket and was there, picking him up in a second, but it wasn't a second for Enid. Ian screamed, Enid's chair fell backwards, Everett, floured hands and red in the face, turned around, Fagus got off the bench, held the seat with one hand and said, "Etty?" Finetta carried on picking flowers while Mary scooped Ian off the ground and brushed his knees. There was nothing hurt, nothing wrong, but Enid held onto the table as Fagus held onto the bench.

If someone could have seen inside her head, the hairline cracks that at once began to spread, they might have known to say, *it's all right, Enid. He's fine. He's just a normal little boy.* But no one could and no one did. Everett brushed flour from her brow, adding more. Mary crouched in front of Ian, ran a finger down his nose, poked him gently in the belly and said, "Running so fast, clever little thing." To Enid she seemed to be saying it over and over, her finger running down his nose, a playful poke in the belly, a careful palm to the little boy's cheek, "Running so fast, clever little thing," while Fagus stood with one hand on the bench repeating, "Etty?" and Finetta filled her basket with purple flowers. Enid looked from one to the other, the fracture in her mind spreading like ruptured ground. There was too much life, it was too fragile, it hung on a finger-point of God. It was before her, in all its endless maybes — a thousand ways to travel, a trip on the stair, an heir ruined, another child she couldn't love for fear of loving.

She left the room, and not one of them looked up to see her go.

In her bedroom she felt for the suitcase kept on the high wardrobe shelf, and caught it as it fell. It was empty but for a bobby pin and a ticket stub in the elasticated pocket. She chose a few dresses, summer ones; her winters were in the attic. Light jumpers, three, in varying shades of green. Belts, stockings, shoes. Gloves: two pairs. Her jewellery — just her engagement ring. She put it on. The emerald and diamonds glistened and shone and felt heavy on her thin finger, a heaviness she'd missed — it had been years since she'd worn it, she'd forgotten somehow, after the balloon of pregnancy had deflated, that it was there in her bureau drawer; she'd forgotten to put it back on. She twisted it, remembering the feel, and ran it once to her knuckle and back. From the chest of drawers she pulled flannel nightgowns. They were light, they folded easily.

At the window she saw Douglas cross the gravel and stand back as Gould reversed the car into the driveway. Both men wiped their hands and looked it over. Douglas walked out of sight toward the house, but a few moments later he reappeared, pulling on his driving gloves. He got into his car without looking up. Enid could have caught his eye if he had. She moved a step back but he didn't check, didn't look up at the window at all and why would he? It was just another normal day in Berkshire. Gould walked ahead of him like an undertaker and opened the gates. Douglas revved the engine, turned left and was gone.

Carefully, quietly, she went over to the bed, flipped the lid of the suitcase shut and heaved it to the floor. One step at a time, down the stairs she went, to the tiled hall where, on the telephone pad, on a clean sheet of paper, she wrote, *Douglas, I'm leaving you. Enid.* For a moment the sounds trickling from the kitchen caught her — Everett banging pots and huffing, and a young voice calling amidst bird song — but she walked in the other direction and left the front door open behind her. The suitcase knocked against her shins as she crossed the gravel.

At the gates she turned in the opposite direction to Douglas, right, towards the station, a mile away. Up the hill, veer left and down the other side. It was a simple matter of putting one foot in front of the other. She heard a car approaching.

The only other house with a motor was owned by Douglas' friends, the McManners. Not her friends, not people she could talk to and laugh with, not humans with open minds and courage. They were his to invite over for backgammon and hers to tolerate, but Mrs. McManners, who considered everyone's business her business, had been waging a one-woman war to conquer Enid. She'd announced that all Enid needed was a hobby and something to commit to that would make her feel worthwhile: a seat on the Parish, a place in her knitting group. Enid had gone once and nearly died of boredom. What did these people know? Her band-aged mind had slipped for a moment but she'd shored it up with an excuse to leave and a brisk walk home in twilight. Her hobby had become Keeping Mrs. McManners Away.

She turned her face to the hedgerow and pressed her body into her suitcase, one hand down amidst the foxgloves. No one was going to stop her now. It was already set, suddenly, immediately, as if it had been waiting — the mile walk, the distant past of her children, the life she'd lived before. She thought of this morning, how she'd got up as usual, another normal day, and not known that this would be her last. How she'd looked in on the nursery, at Fagus being dressed and Finetta being fed, at Ian who had a sniffle and hadn't slept: her children, already separated from her by other, much better, hands who knew how to coddle and calm. With every step she took away from Cherry Trees, they became, more and more, an instant action that must un-happen, a play that was over, a fallacy that could not last. The car sped past and leaves flicked up at her shins. She crouched and steadied herself, stood up and faced the road again.

The light was beautiful, the air clean from yesterday's rain. Through the overhanging branches of an oak tree, sunlit blue mingled with white through intense green. A light breeze lifted the furthest leaves and cooled her face. Cow parsley leaned with foxgloves and daisies from the verge. A steady trickle of water, run off from the fields, dug deeper the groove at the road's edge. At the brow of the hill she put down her case and sat for a minute, perched on the flattened handle, the case precarious beneath her. The view spread out in waves of fields and woodland: a farmhouse and dairy indistinguishable from the land around them. There was no separation: man and nature met at rough edges, encroached and drew away, draped their limbs upon each other. No matter where one was, the other touched it. She got up, refreshed, and began her descent to the railway.

The boy behind the grill had blond wavy hair stuck under a cap that was too small for him, as if he was filling in for his little brother at a toy station in the countryside. He looked at her with eyes that said he didn't want to be there. "Which way?"

Which way. The tracks stretched long and straight in either direction. "London."

"Twelve-o-four. Further platform." He shoved a ticket through the dip and went back to his annual.

Enid dragged her case up and down the stairs, and sat on a bench at the furthest end of the platform. The wind blew a little colder. The sun shone through the trees and an address blinked repetitively in her mind. It had been printed in the flyleaf of *Science and Health*, the one Douglas had burned. Didlington Hall. Swaffham. She changed stations in London and boarded a sleeper to Norfolk.

17

.....

Enid, 1964

SOMEONE WAS SHAKING her shoulder. "Enid? Enid, love?"

She hated it when they called her *love*. So personal. She opened her eyes and saw Mandy.

"We should turn this thing off," said Mandy, switching off the television. "Lunch is ready."

Lunch. Another meal. She looked at her watch. Eleven-thirty — always too early. She moved her stiff limbs, willing them to take her weight, respond, get her up. Herded in at eleven-thirty to be sure to be seated by twelve. Who ate at midday? Servants, that's who. Servants who had no choice, and old people too used to being fed.

She'd been dreaming, or perhaps it had been the television. Something about trains. Mandy helped her up and they joined the slow surge toward the dining room: men humped in cardigans, women shuffling in collapsed slippers. Was she really like that too, locked in pretence of something, oblivious to the carnage, still smiling and talking about beef? The dining room was a collection of tables seating four and a floor covered in blue linoleum.

"Will you sit with Bridget?" said Mandy. Bridget never spoke. Enid liked her enormously. All the Franks and Georges and Mollys and Janes had given up on saving her a seat at their tables. Mandy held her chair for her as she sat down. "You'll be glad to know we got through, though I've a mind to say I'm not pleased. Your Finetta wasn't best pleased either. What a shame."

"To whom?"

"Your son. Him coming all this way —"

"How do you know how far he's come?"

"And your Finetta —"

"My Finetta should learn to watch her tongue." She was sure she heard the word *ungrateful* as Mandy walked away.

Ungrateful my hat, thought Enid. She hadn't changed her mind in the least. That's right, she'd been dreaming; dreaming of the train that had taken her away from Cherry Trees, away from Douglas, from Fagus, from Finetta and Ian. He had no right to come marching back in now. So they'd got through. Good.

Bridget lifted orange squash to her lips and spilled it down her front. Disgusting, thought Enid — but if they will give us plastic cups that crumple at the slightest touch it was hardly Bridget's fault. The nurses were handing round plates and tucking paper napkins into soiled collars. Teeth were being put in. Enid waited.

She'd written to Didlington Hall twice before the ban and the burning of the book. They'd been letters of practice enquiry — how to apply the rules of marital duty without betraying the soul, and the methods of prayer for a child in the stages of recovery. The replies, helpful if poorly written, were signed, *Yours In Christ, Ruby Smith*. She'd taken a buggy from Swaffham station. It had turned in at gates fit for Inveraray and wound slowly along a drive which opened, a mile or so later, onto a red brick Palladian mansion set in parkland. Its chimneys were reflected in the lake that lay before it.

A small girl with ringlets had opened the door. "Yes?"

"I'm Enid." It was all she'd been able to say.

The girl had taken her suitcase. "I'm Ruby."

She'd followed her in like a puppy, grateful for the short reply. Ruby had shown her to a library festooned with animal heads, where Enid had lain down on a large, collapsing sofa. Ruby had put a tray of tea and biscuits down on the table beside her. She'd sat with her while she ate, not speaking, only smiling.

When she'd finished Ruby had led her to an attic bedroom. "This is yours," she'd said, showing her the wardrobe, the window, the chest of drawers. "You can stay as long as you like."

The saw of a chair across lino brought her back. Bridget was being removed for a dry shirt. "I'll be with you in a minute," said Mandy.

Enid stared at her empty place.

It wasn't easy to remember it, none of it. But that bit, that moment in her life when she'd — what? — gone off? Like bad milk or soured cream, she thought, watching Mandy approach her with a plate. Is that what had happened? Had she soured and turned bad, become unpalatable? She remembered walking out, she remembered arriving, she remembered thinking that her family were better off without her. She'd lain on the bed in the room she'd been given, in the vast red brick Palladian mansion in Norfolk and thought, *I'm falling.*

18

.....

Enid, 1924

S HE SLEPT LIKE the dead that night, a sleep free of dreams, and when she woke she was confused and didn't know where she was; didn't recognise the bed, the curtains, the room. She thought this isn't my bedroom and then remembered. She got up and wandered down the corridor of many doors that Ruby had led her along last night — the long, long rug perfect for children to run madly on, past the paintings hung on red flock walls, the half-moon tables holding trinkets and vases of flowers — until she reached the grand staircase that led down to the hall. Leaning over the bannisters, she heard the droning tone of words united coming from behind vast double doors below.

Inside, a prayer meeting was in full swing. Ruby got up from the circle and came towards her. "Enid." She led her to a chair and sat beside her. Someone threw a shawl over her shoulders. The group held hands again, a stranger and Ruby taking hers on either side, and the words began: *For Mrs. Smith's ankle, we bring healing, for John and his three children, we bring healing, for Miss Elizabeth's gout, we bring healing.* On and on it went, in and out of Enid's head as she rocked and swayed between them.

Ruby sat with her in the library afterwards. They each had a bowl of soup. "It belongs to friends of mother's. We moved in two years ago. Then everyone did." Ruby bit off a piece of bread. "Endless bedrooms, we've had eighty here at least. Not now, now we're down to about thirty-three — thirty-four counting you. There's a heronry, a racecourse and a dairy. The lakes are stacked with trout."

"I've left my children," said Enid.

"Have you?" Ruby tilted her head to one side.

"I'm a terrible mother," said Enid.

"Mothers have the greatest task," said Ruby, as if she could possibly know.

"I am better away from them."

"We'll take care of you."

"My family will try to get me back."

"You're safe here."

"They're bound to follow me."

"In Christ we trust."

"You have to help me if they try to come and get me."

"We are all one in God's love."

"They won't understand."

"Christ heals."

"They'll try to make me go back."

"You can stay as long as you like," said Ruby for the second time.

It was so new, so completely foreign to anything she'd known. There were crowds of them, crowds and crowds of believers, all swamping the mansion in Norfolk, gripping their books and standing in a circle holding hands. A minister from America came and stayed for three weeks. He told them they needed money for the upkeep of a grand church in London. He asked for donations. Enid thought of the money in her purse, all five pounds of it, and went and fetched it.

She joined the routine of Didlington, her name on the rota of jobs. Prepare breakfast on Mondays, wash up on Tuesdays, help with luncheon on Wednesdays. There was the prayer room to keep tidy, and charitable works pinned up on a board, where you could tick your name off if you'd made more than three visits in a week. Dairy duty and butter-making, laundry and ironing — she never knew sheets were so large. There were servants, but only a few of them — boys covered in coal dust and girls who swept the floors, an ancient nanny who lived in the attic bereft of charges, and a footman who'd found new cause in operating betting at race meets. Ruby's mother commanded the running of things: the butcher's list and the vegetable plot, the fruit cages and hens. Ruby skipped about gathering volunteers for fund raising, and encouraged anyone lagging to join her on energising walks.

Some sort of rhythm began, of washing and dressing and going downstairs to prayer meetings, and meals, and charitable works. Chores done, Enid spent hours in the library, a book dropped on her chest when the effort to read became too much. The animal heads, as she lay on the sofa, seemed to stare at her as if they would eat her, or eat her brain. They seemed to say *come here, we will rid you of this terrible thing called life, we will release you, if you give in,* and she did give in, to some sort of rhythm, the new normality of washing and chores, of prayer meetings and visiting the sick, of Ruby's insistent smile — and she would have given in more, if only she could feel her body.

She knew she had one — she could see it as she moved about; she saw her hands and feet, her chest with a book dropped on it, but these were the only signs, and she wondered, often, if she existed at all. Of course she did — there were her hands and feet doing chores and visiting the poor, there was Ruby smiling, and a visiting minister booming in her ears, there was the wide open sky of Norfolk, and the Palladian mansion of brick and prayer, but where was she? She was with the drip-drip memory inside, of everything brought with her.

Like reading a book backwards, her actions explained themselves after the event. It had been her presence keeping Fagus from full recovery, from the health he deserved, that was his, that was coming to him. She hadn't given up on him, she'd just forgotten, and leaving made everyone safe. Ian would be safe. The meaning of the moment in the kitchen when he'd run into the rabbit fence and Fagus had held onto the bench became clear.

The devil had whipped about in that late summer air, but she had taken the evil with her; she, stronger than them, who knew where to go, who could commit the act of sacrifice to save her family and in turn be saved by the great presence of Christ, shored up in a red brick mansion in Norfolk. The devil couldn't pass through the gates and they were all free.

That word kept coming back to her. They were free of the curse of her and she was free of duty, of blood, of all the ties that bound. That explained the strange lightness in her limbs, the sense of something missing. All of this — the unravelling of the bandage in her head, the piercing of her brain with light, the enormity of knowledge — everything made sense. A vast expanse of nothing stretched from morning till night and this, she tried to live with.

But without the bandage her brain was seeping, and as the weeks then months passed, the picture became confused. She'd walked out on her family. That's what she'd done, hadn't she? Was she remembering right? They were all there, had all been there — the kitchen and Everett, the sunlight and garden, and Mary with Finetta, and Fagus on the bench, and Ian, running. Was that her who had left? She saw the suitcase on the bed, and Douglas pulling on his driving gloves. She saw Gould walking like an undertaker, and the car turning left. What had they done? Were they still all there, going round in circles, repeating that scene over and over? Was she there too, or had she stopped all those lives, the existence of them; had they vanished with her? And what of the night — if they did still exist, if they were all there — what of the night when she hadn't come back, when Douglas returned, or supper was made, or the phone rang and she wasn't there? What had they done? How long had they waited before they did something? She couldn't imagine them beyond that moment of her leaving, she couldn't picture it at all, and as the weeks, then months, passed, the freedom in her limbs became the lack of something; a weight she was used to gone. Ruby encouraged her on energising walks with increasing regularity, but everything in her resisted. This wasn't what was supposed to happen.

Little, happy Ruby never seemed to tire or lag. She never complained or got ill — she had enough for everyone, and especially for Enid; rapping on her bedroom door when she stayed in there too long, or seeking her out in the library, greeting her with a smile that was enough for both of them. Enid found herself honed in on, as if preferring one's own company was strange. Did it really make her look so hopeless? Was she not allowed to die quietly? She tried to appreciate the little kindnesses, she really did. She tried very hard to settle her mind when Ruby came up with another bright idea to cheer her; she tried not to think, *leave me alone.* They made breakfast together, they flapped sheets together and on Tuesdays they shared a sink. Ruby asked her one day, as they stood side by side, "What is it that you want, Enid?"

Enid stared at the suds, her knuckles appearing like mountains above bubble clouds, and thought: *why haven't they tried to find me?*

19

.....

Enid, 1925

ONE MORE MONTH. One more month, and if they didn't come, she'd write. She was in her attic bedroom, avoiding people as usual. She took off her dressing gown, pushed her slippers from her feet, took the towel from her shoulder, threw it over a chair, went back to her bed and lay down. She'd had vague thoughts of dressing, and had got as far as washing her face.

Her room was tiny, the bed too large, an overhanging bedstead in a place of narrow angles where there wasn't enough carpet to lie down. She pulled the eiderdown over her and turned onto her side. She'd begun lots of letters. Her mother, she'd settled on first. She'd sat in the library, paper at the ready: *Dear Mother, You must be wondering where I am.* She'd torn it up — *wondering* had sounded like the sentiment for a lost hat. *Dear Mother, please don't be angry.* But her mother had been angry with her, well, forever. *Dear Mother, I'm sorry.* But she wasn't, and she'd thrown that one on the fire too and gone for a walk across the wide, open parkland.

The next month it had been Douglas. *Dear Douglas, I think I will have made my point by now. How are the children?* Hopeless. He'd laugh at her and she didn't know what her point was. To say she couldn't cope? They'd have her locked up.

Light flickered through the thin patterned curtains and for the millionth time she swore to remember to get something heavier, something that would give her dark when she needed it — like today, when constant doubt in a compound of believers had almost done her in. When she would have left, if she'd been sure of where to go.

Last Christmas they'd opened the hall to the poor, and scraped together food to feed five hundred, even though only fifty had turned up. With snow on the ground and the lake frozen, she'd written *Dear Mother, I know I've made a terrible mistake, it all got on top of me, Fagus, Ian, I simply lost my nerve, I got confused but I've had time to calm down.* Written and crumpled up.

Dear Douglas, I'm very surprised you haven't tried to find me. The children must be anxious. What have you told them? You needed only to sit down and listen to me and all of this could have been avoided. I was unhappy for the longest time. You left me alone to go mad in that house and everyone blamed me for everything. I couldn't stand it. How is Fagus? How are they all? Please send them my love. That was after the snowdrops but before the crocuses. She hadn't sent that one off either, and now bluebells coloured the woodland floor. She pushed the covers off and got up. It was time for chores anyway. She padded along the hallway in socks, an old woollen jumper thrown over her dress. She could do the potatoes before anyone else turned up, and be back in bed in an hour.

Down in the kitchen, cream tiled arches dominated a series of connecting rooms, rooms of sinks and chopping tables. A wall dividing the narrow hall stretched the length of the house and was lined with glass cabinets that stored bowls, platters, tureens and plates — enough to feed the five hundred who never turned up; a hangover from when the house was a social whirl and not the least bit dedicated to God. Ruby could plan her next big adventure into healing, and Enid could play the game of finding matching crockery when she was bored.

Sunshine pushed through windows at the far end, and the stove gave out black-metal heat. At a sink, Enid took off her ring, picked up a scrubbing brush and set to on a potato. She brushed a stray hair from her temple with her arm. Today she'd failed to join the picnic walk to the estuary and snapped at John, a gentle-man in his eighties, whose widower son of the same name lived in eternal struggle to care for his constantly sick offspring. She'd gone round there once, with Ruby on one arm and old John on the other, to see young John in his cottage by the park walls, but the sight of three limp children had made her ill too, and what good was that? Did she need to be reminded? She'd gone back to bed and cried for a week. No one had suggested it again. She'd said his name only once, at her third meeting, when Ruby had asked if she had anyone for healing. "Fagus." Her voice had come out rusty. But he could never have enough; the further away she got, the closer he seemed to come. She dreamt of him, he clouded her days. She couldn't get away from him. Ruby had written it down.

She picked up another potato. On her right hung a calendar, hand-drawn by a resident intent on celebrating time. Each month had an emblem — April was symbolised by cherry blossom. Her gaze drifted down the dates. She lost track of the days here — every day was the same; only the seasons stood out. She knew it was Wednesday because she was doing potatoes, and she knew that in two weeks they'd have a celebration of the beginning of summer, so that made today — she ran her eyes along the second week, Wednesday the seventeenth of April.

Fagus' birthday. He'd be seven. She looked at her sleeve, and noticed it was soaked in dirty water.

Someone else could do the potatoes. She patted her hands on an old towel left hanging over the back of a kitchen chair, put her ring back on and ran up to her room. In bed, a book for a table on her raised knees, her hands still damp she wrote,

Dear Douglas, I want a divorce. We've been separated long enough and I'm sure you'll agree it's the right thing to do. She crossed that out and wrote, *course of action. You see I've made a decision. You're tremendous at organising things, you always have been and I'll say you've had a pretty*

fair crack of the whip this past while, while I've been away. I feel quite sure you're doing a splendid job but it's time I came back, don't you agree? I'm quite sure the children need me. Mothers are so important, without us, well, there'd be nothing, would there? I am sorry I left you all in such a shock. It had got on top of me and little Ian, he'd begun to grow up — how is he? I did feel he needed a chance to grow without my worry all over him. Perhaps old Dr G was right after all — mothers do worry more than others or whatever it was he said, and I did need to rest. I'm quite aware it's been a simply dreadful long time but now that I'm rested I'm ready to mother again — and I want to! I do so want to. I think I can do it now. I just needed a little time. But I'm also quite sure I can no longer be your wife. Don't you agree with that too? You and I, we really were not made for each other. But now the children are produced (I sound like a cow that's been bred from, don't I? I don't mean it like that, but we've done our job), now that all that's over, you and I can have the rest of our lives free of each other. It doesn't matter what anyone thinks. I know mother will kick up the most almighty fuss but it's really not up to her. She has her little heir after all. I, we, we've done as we were told, haven't we? I'm quite sure the family will see its way to furnishing you with a little place of your choosing. Do be sweet and agree, Douglas. I'm happy for you to choose any terms you like.

Yours etc,

Enid

✦ ✦

Her children. Fagus. What had she been doing? What had she been thinking? Where were they? Why weren't they with her? She must have gone mad, she'd forgotten; she'd let this place get to her, she'd let everything get to her. Her children — they beat their way through her blood into her heart, her heart that had almost stopped beating, that had slowed to such silence that she'd almost forgotten everything. It ran now, it ran as she had from the scullery and the potatoes when her hands were damp and her sleeve soaked in dirty water.

She would be everything her own mother had failed to be. She'd chatter with Ian and choose dresses with Finetta, go for little walks with Fagus. She'd just needed rest.

She sealed the letter in an envelope, put it aside and closed her eyes. Her fingers played over the emerald and diamonds, the gold band as she twisted it, turning it this way and that until she fell asleep, her hands falling still, one over the other, and dreamt she held Fagus in her arms.

20

.....

Enid, 1964

S HE CAME TO over a plate of beef and gravy, boiled carrots and cabbage. There was no one in her arms. Her arms were empty. Her hand shot up like a schoolgirl. "I say." She waved at the nurses, anyone of them could see her. They were milling about with cloths and plastic jugs of squash. "I say." She got out of her chair.

The girl with the poor complexion came trotting over. "More squash, Enid? You haven't touched your plate."

"I've made a mistake."

The girl glanced under Enid's chair, as if she'd peed herself. Stupid child. Enid said it again. "I've made a mistake. I need to telephone."

"Telephone? Who is it this time?"

"My daughter."

The girl with the poor complexion held Enid's arm and looked helplessly at Mandy, who was down on her knees wiping carrots off the floor. "Mandy?"

Mandy came over, the cloth and carrots bunched in her fist. "What is it, Enid? Do you need the lav?"

"I've changed my mind," said Enid.

"You don't the need the lav?" Mandy was about to walk away.

Enid grabbed her stick. "I have to see him."

Mandy and the girl with spots exchanged a look. Mandy said, "Perhaps we should take her back to her room."

Enid pulled her arm free, wobbled, held the table and sat down with a thump into her chair. "If I don't see him, I won't know."

"Oh, Enid," Mandy sighed. "You are having a day of it."

"I am not having a day of it." Her hand hit the table, and her fork went flying. "You have to call my daughter and tell her I've changed my mind."

"We did say," said Mandy.

"No," said Enid. "No, you don't understand."

"We could try," said the girl with spots.

"She was just on her way out," said Mandy.

"Out where?" said Enid.

"How should I know?" She tucked a paper napkin into Enid's collar.

Enid pulled it off. "You have to get hold of her, you must tell her Ian must come. I have to see him. Tell her I've changed my mind."

"Of course you have," said Mandy.

"We can try if you like," said the girl with spots.

"Try," said Enid. "Try." That word again. She didn't care anymore.

"All right, all right." Mandy raised her hands, her palms towards Enid.

"I can cope for a minute," said the girl.

They had to do it — Enid was sure to keep an eye on Mandy, sure to watch her scuttle from the dining room and not get caught on someone else. They had to do it, because Ian was the only one who knew.

21

.....

Finetta, 1964

A S SHE SHUT the front door, the phone in her hall rang
again. She paused for a moment, one hand still on the
handle, her keys in the other. It would be her bloody mother
again. She wasn't going back inside for that. Whatever it was
could wait. Under a warm coat the colour of oatmeal, and che-
quered with thin red lines, she wore a lemon-yellow winter dress
that narrowed at her slim waist. Her hair was coiffed in waves,
suspended above her shoulders. She looked at her watch. Perfect.
Just under an hour to get there. He'd be early and she wouldn't
have to wait.

She shivered as she climbed into her car — a little white Sprite,
convertible and natty, but uncomfortable and terrible in winter;
her brother had bought it for her. The windscreen was completely
fogged up, and she had nothing to scrape it with. Ian would have
had a little tool kit in the boot of his car for just such an occasion.

He had a tool kit for everything. She put the quilt, wrapped in tissue paper, on the passenger seat, turned on the engine and waited, with her hands huddled in her lap.

Her bloody, bloody mother. Now she'd have to tell him that she'd told them and they'd told her. She'd only wanted to make her suffer a bit. She hadn't wanted to scare her so much that she'd cancel him completely. It was absurd. Twenty-five years and now she'd cancelled him, damn it. Finetta blew into her hands and rubbed them together. A tiny patch of clear glass began to grow at the bottom of the windscreen.

Should she lie? Say nothing? She got out again and lifted the windscreen wipers out of the grasp of the frost. The Sprite chugged plumes of vapours into the air. The street was quiet, most of the cars and people had gone off to work. A front door slammed further up the road and a woman with a dog crossed to the other pavement, shopping bags in hand. She wondered if she should get a dog. Get some company. Stop being so bloody alone. In her seat again she switched on the wipers. Damned car never warmed up. She'd have to go. She didn't want to be late.

She set off towards the pub where she and Ian always met. It was halfway between them, and an hour from Hampstead. They'd have time for lunch, and perhaps a walk, before she'd have to go. If she went. Maybe she should cancel too.

The traffic was clear; she chugged along. On the main road to Windsor, she tightened her grip on the steering wheel. It had been his idea, not hers. She slowed behind a truck. They'd never spoken of her mother. He'd gone off to Eton, she'd gone to

Vienna, the war had broken out. After it was over, he'd gone to Washington, and come back again a few years later. The truck turned off and she pressed the accelerator. He'd got married, had a daughter, got divorced, married again and had a son. He'd written that there was another child on the way, and six months later that she'd died.

Was that why he'd chosen now to see her? Some sort of misjudged effort at forgiveness? Didn't he know their mother was rotten to the core? That she didn't feel anything? That she passed over sorrow and death as if she was made of the same brick as her frightful nursing home? If he thought he understood her, he was wrong. Maybe he knew she was dying, nearly dead. Not dead enough, but almost.

God, she was an awful daughter. She indicated left and checked her mirrors. She'd had just the same thoughts when she'd had her children, a moment of wild compassion when she'd thought *now I see* but it hadn't lasted. As soon as the real Enid had been put up against the mother in her head, she'd realised her mistake. Real Enid didn't change. Real Enid was the same as old Enid, the one who'd dragged her through it all like so much discarded Christmas wrapping — useless, but too pretty to throw away.

She could not tell him. She could just take him there, and see what happened. It would be too late by the time he walked in the door, and all sorts of things would take over — there might be flying crockery or shouting. Her little lie would be forgotten completely. And was it a lie if she said nothing? She slowed and turned right.

He'd asked her not to tell. He hadn't said why — he'd said *best not tell her, don't you think?* and she hadn't promised either way. She hadn't written back. He'd assumed she'd do as she was told. She could just say, *I decided against it* — but that would ruin their lunch and she didn't want that. She wanted her few hours of happiness. He had something to him that comforted her, his presence, as if something greater was watching. Without him she wondered if she existed at all.

There was the pub. She'd been a million miles away. Of course she existed. She was thinking of before, those other times, when they were little and he went off and she was left alone. She drew up in the car park of the Herod Arms. It was convenient and anonymous, it had adequate food and no music in the dining room. The sort of place a businessman might bring his mistress, or a mother take her son for lunch. Or a brother his sister, who met once a year for lamb chops and roast potatoes.

She parked, turned off the engine and checked her face in her compact. She looked almost the same as she had last year — Ian never seemed to age either. *Campbell blood*, Joan used to say. Nothing about Anstruther blood. Campbell blood dominated everything. She walked up the steps and pushed open the half-glazed doors.

Ian was already there, seated at a table near the windows. He got up and kissed her. "Got here all right?" He held her chair.

"Fine. No traffic." A waitress brought them menus. "Thank you." Finetta put hers on the table without looking at it.

He did look exactly the same, not an inch older. Terribly

smart, well-cut, clean-shaven and dapper, a nervousness covered up. He brushed the fingers of his right hand over the knuckles of his left and didn't look at the menu either. He looked at his watch. "We've plenty of time."

"I'll have a sherry," she said to the waitress.

Ian ran the ice around his glass of Cinzano. "You look well."

"So do you."

"Bloody cold."

"Bloody."

"Car started alright?"

"Just about. Thank you." Her sherry arrived.

"What'll you have?" He picked up his menu. "Shall we have a starter?"

She picked up hers. "Yes, let's." They always did.

"I'll have the paté and the lamb," said Ian to the waitress.

"The soup, please," said Finetta, "and the fish."

"Cod or plaice?" said the waitress.

"Oh," Finetta looked at the menu again, "I hadn't realised there were two."

"Have the plaice," said Ian.

"The plaice," said Finetta, handing her menu to the waitress.

"And what have you been up to?" said Ian. He flapped his napkin onto his lap. "Did you get a new boiler?"

Her letters were all about boilers and gas leaks, his about estates. "I had to get a completely new one. Such a bore."

"I wonder if you shouldn't move."

"Do you?"

"I saw the most darling house in Newbury. Perfect for you. I thought of you in an instant."

"That's sweet of you."

"It's got a little bridge over a stream to the front door."

Turn up and risk him being furious. Tell him and ruin lunch. "How darling."

"We can go and see it if you like."

"Won't my house be a bore to sell?"

"We needn't worry about that."

Hurt him. Hurt her mother. She finished her sherry, he drained his Cinzano. Their first course arrived. He dug into his paté, she sipped a spoon of mushroom soup.

"Do you know, I'm not so sure it's such a good idea you coming today after all."

"Why's that?" He buttered a triangle of bread.

"She's terribly confused."

"Do you think the shock might kill her?"

"There is that." They both smiled. He poured her a glass of water. "Thank you." She sipped it.

"You don't have anything against it, do you?"

She picked up her spoon. "No, not in the least. I don't expect you'll find her changed." She'll make you mad. She'll break your heart. "Old, of course, terribly old and wobbling." She breaks everyone's heart.

"I won't stay long."

"She likes tea sharp at four."

"I shan't stay for tea."

"Oh." Finetta dabbed her mouth with her napkin. "Not for tea? Then perhaps another day really would be better. Wouldn't it be simpler if you just popped in on your way up to town?"

"I am on my way up to town."

"On another day."

"Are you trying to put me off?"

"On your way up to town today? So you just thought —"

"I just thought I'd like to pop in and get the portrait."

"What portrait?"

"The Augustus John, you remember the one. It used to hang in that dreadful corridor upstairs."

"The one of her?"

"He's become rather valuable."

"Augustus John?"

"Yes. I thought I might have it."

"You're going to ask her for it?"

"I'm going to take it. I think she owes me that, don't you? It's about the only thing of value."

"And the ring."

"Does she still have it?"

"Never takes it off."

"Dodo was always convinced she'd sold it."

"She'd rather have cut off her own hand."

"Then she'll give it you, I expect."

How many times had she watched her mother run it back and forth to her knuckle, turning it absently, her fingers playing across the precious stones as if they held some sort of charm that only Enid was aware of? Years and years of sitting in hard silence, watching her mother grip the burnished gold. Finetta had asked to look at it once, when she was little, thinking it might amuse her mother to see her taking an interest, but Enid had snapped that Finetta meant only to squirrel it away. She'd said she wasn't old enough to touch it.

She should have given it to her when she'd got married; that would have been the correct order of things, that's what their grandmother had done for Enid. It was an engagement ring. It was supposed to go to your daughter when she got engaged. *Whether you like the chap or not,* Joan had added, when Finetta had asked about it. Still, even though that ship had sailed, there was no shirking the female line. Joan had told her it had been passed down from mother to daughter for generations.

"Well, she hasn't anyone else to give it to." Finetta put her knife and fork together. The waitress came and cleared their plates.

Ian said, "I had a lovely letter from Michael."

"Did you?" There, the thrill, the lightening of her heart whenever her son was mentioned. She smiled.

"He's doing rather well, north, isn't he. I was fascinated to hear about Shrewsbury."

"He's terribly happy," said Finetta, seeing her son in her mind, imagining him walking across the room, the sensation of his company; precious, delicate, there as long as she didn't reach out and touch. She watched their second courses approach.

"I shall be out with Barbie next week," said Ian.

It was always a shock to be reminded she had a daughter too.

Her son vanished as she pushed her daughter aside. "The thing is," plates of steaming fish and meat were put in front of them, "I'm afraid she knows."

"Knows what?"

"That you're coming."

"Of course she knows. She wrote back a month ago."

"You wrote to her?"

"Of course I wrote to her. I can't just turn up at her school unannounced. I'm taking her to Gstaad for Christmas."

"Oh." Finetta lost control of her fork, the prongs clattered on her plate, and a speck of sauce flicked onto the tablecloth. "Barbie, of course. You wrote to her."

A dish of boiled potatoes, cauliflower and carrots was set between them.

"You didn't think I'd written to our mother?"

"I—"

"Why would I write to her? The last thing I want is a fuss."

"No, I quite understand."

"I've never written her a single letter."

"But you see it was all rather a shock, as you say."

"My wanting to see her? Did you think I never would?"

"I mean, for mother." Ian looked uncomprehending, and so she ploughed on. "As I say, I had to tell the nurses; they're frightfully particular about visitors."

"Why did you have to tell the nurses?"

"Because they're frightfully particular about visitors. They all thought it was frightfully exciting." She'd chosen the wrong word. "Thrilling. I don't know."

"Did they?"

"And they told her. I am sorry."

"Well, I don't suppose it matters." He cut into a lamb chop. "I won't stay."

"Yes, but you see they telephoned —"

"Has she had a collapse?"

"I was in the bath."

"What a bore."

"Wasn't it?"

"I'm only after the picture."

"I can get it for you."

"I'd like to get it myself."

"But you really don't have to."

"Shall we talk about something else?" It was an order, not a question. He finished one chop and cut into the next. Finetta ate a slither of plaice. It dripped with a white, insipid sauce. The vegetables between them went untouched.

But then he said, as if he hadn't heard himself, "Do you remember how she put her head round the door?"

She remembered.

"We carried on playing with my boat."

"She won't talk about him, you know."

"I don't expect her to."

"That's not why you're seeing her?"

"I've told you why I'm seeing her."

"She won't say his name."

"I expect she's forgotten it," he replied. "I thought we might walk after lunch, to pass the time. Would you like that? Is it near the Heath? We could have a stroll to settle ourselves."

"Quite near." She hadn't been hungry in the first place and she couldn't eat. Another scene of hatred and regret, a decrepit blast of shots long fallen wide that would spatter Finetta and leave her bleeding. She'd be the one that was left — not their mother, not Ian, but her, Finetta, left to stand in another ruined city, forgotten again, picking up the pieces of a family that didn't care to be whole.

"All that God," said Ian.

"Frightful, I know."

"Does she still shout out Christ's name?"

"I think they have prayer meetings, I'm not sure. Most of them can't get out of bed and the ones that can just shuffle about. It should be illegal, not calling a doctor when they fall or their hearts give way."

"Sounds perfect to me."

"You'd think they'd die off quicker, but there's plenty of them."

"I'm sure God will get to each of them in the end," said Ian.

"Extraordinary to pray for life to a deity that specifically designed the body to die." Finetta sipped her water.

"None of it ever made any sense."

Finetta tried a carrot. "The thing is, they said not to come."

"Who said?"

"The nurses. They said she won't see you."

She'd made sure she was ready. She'd swallowed the carrot and rested her cutlery on her plate, she'd said it as clearly and as honestly as she could, but instead of raising his eyebrows or storming out or giving any other outward sign that their mother had broken his heart again, he just cut another small piece of lamb and popped it in his mouth.

"I am sorry." She leaned forward quickly. "Does it matter terribly? She hasn't changed and I can get the picture. I am really, frightfully sorry. I shouldn't have . . ." she trailed off.

He put his knife and fork together.

Finetta did the same. "I mean, to turn up unannounced is one thing, but — you see I — I just can't see what good could come of it now, now that you've been announced and — and, well, you've said there's nothing you want from her, apart from the picture, and I can get that for you. You needn't go through it at all, honestly you needn't. I just don't think you should. She's old, do you see, and the nurses said she was really quite —" what was the word? Mad? Spiteful? They'd said *shaky*. "— adamant. Need you come? She'll never forgive me if —"

"You go against her wishes?"

"You said you didn't want fuss."

The waitress removed their plates. Ian looked at his watch. "Shall we have pudding?"

"You do agree, don't you?" She wanted pudding. She wanted sweetness to chase it all away. "I am sorry," she said again.

"There's no need to be," he said to her, and to the waitress, "I'll have the jam roly-poly."

The waitress wrote it down and turned to Finetta. "And what'll you have, madam?"

Madam. She didn't feel like a madam. She felt six. "Have you the fudge?"

"We've assorted ice cream."

"Vanilla," said Finetta.

"And two coffees," said Ian. He ran the fingers of his left hand over the knuckles of his right.

The dining room had filled up while they'd been talking. At another table, a woman was picking daintily at a prawn cocktail, while her large companion dug into a scotch egg. On the further side a child swung his legs, while his mother told him to eat up.

Ian's roly-poly arrived making the table smell of the nursery. Her ice cream was the colour of daffodils.

After coffee he walked with her to the car park. They touched cheeks lightly as they said goodbye.

22

.....

Enid, 1926

ENID WALKED BACK from the dairy, a churn of milk
in each hand. Across the lawns, jogging up the drive of
Didlington Hall, she saw the post boy, the mailbag slung over
his narrow shoulders. It was months since she'd written and not a
word. Nothing. Her mother had probably put the screws on, but
if he wouldn't divorce her, she could file for an annulment. She
knew about these things. She'd made enquiries with a solicitor in
Swaffham.

She stopped for a minute to rub her nose. She hadn't expected it to be instant, but she had thought she'd hear by now.
Where was he? Africa? Last June she'd conceded that perhaps he
was. He'd gone on about Port Elizabeth enough. She'd thought
about writing to his firm to enquire of his whereabouts, but had
discarded the idea along with the letter. Too personal, too imper-
sonal. Not the thing at all. She'd concluded he must be in Africa.

She'd addressed her letter to Cherry Trees, someone would have forwarded it; there was nothing to do but wait. She picked up the churns and carried on.

Thank goodness she'd left. She still felt that, although now she had to push a little harder to feel pleased. She'd done the best thing imaginable. It was impossible to comprehend any life with him again, and nothing could have made her point clearer than walking out. She'd gone over it and over it — despondency had been trampled in the rush of determination that day; the day of Fagus' seventh birthday, and whenever it tried to stand up she hit it again with the same conclusion. What happy woman would have left her children? None — only one desperate, as she'd been, who'd had no other choice. But he'd understand now, especially as she'd made it clear that she was ready to take up the only mantle that mattered. She was ready, at least she felt ready; at least that's what she'd said in her letter so she'd better be.

Her children tugged on her, they sang at her, they came in flashes as she was going about her day. Ian's chubby legs, Finetta's curls, Fagus' sweet round face. Where were they? She searched for them as if they'd run off over the lawn playing hide and seek; she felt them about her and could not see them, and wondered at the tug that had awakened and shouted and hadn't stopped shouting since April. Had it been shouting all along, this blood pull that made her think of them constantly? Had it only been muted by exhaustion?

She'd thought such terrible things — she'd thought that her heart had gone bad, but it hadn't; it had only frozen over. It had only covered itself in ice so as to sleep. She was a creature thawing out — the first sign of life back in April, the drip-drip awakening over the summer months as she waited for Douglas to reply, and now her heart was in full bloom again, perhaps for the first time since forever; pumping blood through a body alive, every nerve in her body awake, every piece of her singing. She was ready, wasn't she? She didn't want this rush to pass with no word; a silent revolution was no revolution at all. Didn't they know she was awake again? Didn't they know she was alive?

Ruby said it was only a matter of time. They'd gone together to post the letter, and though her life was not a drama existing solely for Ruby's excitement, Enid hadn't been able to help feeling a little thrilled. It was nice to have a friend, even a silly one. It was nice, just occasionally, just this once, to have someone to talk to, to feel jolly with, or nervous, or sad. Ruby had tucked her arm into Enid's and said *I'm so jolly proud of you* and they'd walked home as if they were girls locked in conspiracy; a secret that they threw in looks and smiles as the days passed. As the weeks passed Enid's smile became a little less willing and after months she'd stopped catching Ruby's looks at all. That was when Ruby started making a habit of taking her hand unexpectedly, of leaning a little too close and saying, *it's only a matter of time, Enid. I'm sure you'll hear something soon.*

Of course, there was a mountain to sort out, lots to think about, all sorts of plans to get straight while she waited: where she would go, who she would employ, what she would say to her mother. Cherry Trees was out of the question. Nothing on earth would make her take up there again as if nothing had happened. She'd need to go back initially, of course — she'd have to gird her loins for that, it made her feel sick to even think of it, but these things must be done. It would only be for a week or so, to organise what needed organising: gather the children, pack, but she'd certainly sell, take Everett and Mary with her, perhaps get a second girl as housemaid as well as a maid for herself. Surely her mother would be pleased to see her equipping herself with proper staff — it might even make up for having a divorce in the family and her mother could hardly weep over Douglas. Wasn't it what they'd all wanted all along? The heir produced, and the commonality of Anstruther, gone? Ian would be cooked in Campbell fires as if his father's blood was just a blip, a spark to light him, consumed with the match and the kindling. He wouldn't remember him at all. She was sure she'd allow Douglas to visit and teach Ian to tinker with engines.

She rested the churns on the grass again. A buzzard wheeled above her, crying into the wide Norfolk sky. She'd suggest to her mother that she move to Strachur. That's what she'd do. Why not? It was closed up most of the year; they only opened it for summer. It would all be Ian's one day, so why not now? Yes. She had it all mapped out. That's what she'd do. She and the children and plenty of staff, Strachur all hers, her mother up for summer, Joan too if she absolutely had to, but for no longer than a week, a fortnight at most, and Douglas could visit occasionally. It was going to be perfect.

Scotland would be good for Fagus too. Apart from the

stairs — would he remember? Would he feel his way and say *mumma, was this where I fell?* But she was assuming he'd be just the same. For all she knew he was up and running, he could be skipping about like Ruby by now and she'd missed it; the great rise, the seeing, the bloom to full health — and even if he wasn't, even if he was, what? A little ragged round the edges? He'd be a young man one day. He'd need her.

She'd watched mothers at summer fairs all summer long, and thought *I can do that*. She'd watched them chase their children across the grass, seen the happiness in their faces, the ease with which they held each other, and thought *it can't be that hard*.

But at night she'd lain awake, unable to sleep, a light flickering on and off in the darkest recesses of her mind, keeping her awake; a signal of something feared, a tail she half chased but it escaped her. There was a letter, drifting like a magic carpet, to Douglas, somewhere, wherever he was, and whenever she thought of it she heard a voice, saw the imprint of that half-chased tail, that thought that began *you?* and left her hanging. Yet it was too late. She'd made her decision. The letter was on its way.

She picked up the churns. They knocked against her shins, and a splash of milk slopped onto the grass. Of course she could do it. She was a mother. She'd given birth three times, for goodness' sake. All that fuss. She'd been tired, that was all. She'd been fractious. She was recovered now.

The post boy, mailbag jumping on his back, ran the last steps. He reached the house as she did — he to the front door, she to the rear, and in the darkest recesses of her mind the light flickered on and off.

In the scullery, she put the churns down. Making butter was something she'd become rather good at. She set to with spoons and lids, pouring and sieving. It took her an hour at least, and by the time she'd placed two earthenware pots in the cold store, she stank of milk, her arms were tired, and her hands sore.

In the adjoining room, the long wooden table was stacked with breakfast bowls of leftover porridge and dirty spoons. It wasn't her turn to wash up, she knew that. She filled the kettle and heaved it with two hands onto the stove. It was only after she'd refilled the burner with logs that she noticed a fat brown envelope, lying on the table, addressed to her. With concentrated slowness, she washed her hands.

> Enid,
> You can have your divorce. My terms are custody of the children. Please find all necessary paperwork enclosed.
> Yours etc,
> Douglas.

She put her feet up on the rungs of the chair beside her.

When she pulled out the rest of the papers she found receipts from a hotel in St. James', and an affidavit from the doorman, reporting on Mr. Anstruther's comings and goings with a woman called Miss Wormald. They'd been seen on many occasions, entering the building in the evening and emerging together the next day. Beneath the receipts were a stack of forms from his lawyers, asking her to sign here and here.

Three girls, all wearing long white cotton dresses, came gossiping in at the far end. They wore their hair in straight plaits down their backs. The girl with the darkest hair put a platter down on a chopping board. Enid read the letter again. The light in her head flickered on.

"Has it come?" Ruby was standing beside her. Her face was full of awe and expectation, drenched in the height of excitement as if watching a kitchen drama by the Swaffham Players, but this was Enid's life. It was her life.

Enid stuffed the papers back in the envelope. "It's nothing."

"Enid." Ruby pulled out the chair, knocking Enid's feet from the rungs, and sat beside her. She put her hand on Enid's arm.

Enid shoved the envelope towards her.

Half an hour later, Ruby had made tea and Enid was covered in a blanket on the sofa in the library.

Ruby sat across from her, crossed-legged in an armchair, her ringlets held back in a scarf. "What are you going to do?"

What was she going to do? If only she could stop feeling so damned pleased. "I don't know."

"The law is on your side."

Ridiculous, coming from such a child. "Is it?"

"Of course. Mother told me about this frightful case — it happened to friends of hers, the Pratts. Perhaps you know them?"

"I don't know them."

"Mr. Pratt wanted to take the children away but the judge wouldn't have it."

"I walked out." She felt — what was it? Relief. She felt relief.

"Yes, but aren't there — circumstances?"

Enid adjusted the blanket. She could get a little cottage nearby, near Cherry Trees but not too close. Out of the village, somewhere with trees, a garden, a stream. She'd always fancied a stream. No staff; perhaps a girl and a housekeeper, but no army of staff watching and gossiping and judging her every move. She could pop in to Cherry Trees — she saw it in happy clutter: Everett at the stove, ham hock bubbling — she could pop in and walk away at her leisure. She could stay in bed all day, and no one would call a doctor or say she was off her rocker.

Ruby carried on. "You said he was —"

What had she said about Douglas?

"When you got here — I remember, even if you don't — you were in a pretty bad state."

It was the strongest language Enid had ever heard Ruby use. Enid tried to concentrate.

"You said he was —"

"Neglectful," said Enid. That's right. That's what she'd said.

"Neglectful," repeated Ruby, giving the word the full array of meanings that Enid had never bothered to pick apart.

"He was," said Enid.

"Well, there you are then," said Ruby. "You said you were a terrible mother. Do you remember? We sat here, right here, and you said they were better off without you. I knew at the time that no woman could possibly say that without reason, and I knew you weren't — I could see it in your eyes, the effort, the distress, I mean, that must have made you leave them. He did that to you. You didn't begin that way, did you? No one begins broken. He broke you. Of course you walked out. If it comes to it I'm happy to say how terribly ill you were, what a simply frightful state you were in."

I'd rather you didn't, thought Enid.

"He trampled you to pieces and now he's robbing you of your children."

"I walked out, Ruby," Enid said again.

"And he's been with this woman, this —"

"Wormald. Her name's Miss Wormald."

"Does he mean to marry her?"

"I've no idea."

"But then she'll have your children."

She hadn't thought of that. Another woman being mother in her place. "They'll always be mine." Let's see how she liked it.

"Don't you care?"

"Of course I care. I don't see what choice I have. It wasn't him who left them."

"Any woman would have done the same."

"Would they? Then why aren't there thousands, hundreds of thousands of women running for the doors of their houses? Why do I know of no other woman who hasn't been able to stand it?"

"Mrs. Pratt," said Ruby.

"I don't know Mrs. Pratt," snapped Enid. "Look, I'm just

being realistic. It's a pretty black mark, whichever way you look at it." She could have the best of both worlds.

"But you're their mother." Ruby leant on the word as if she knew what it meant.

There was the light, swinging like a beam from a lighthouse, her fear the jagged rocks in an ocean she'd drowned in once before. If she lived in a sweet little cottage nearby, with trees and a stream, she'd be free of the daily chance of pain — no guilt that she hadn't kissed Finetta goodnight, no heart-stopping trips on the stairs or bandaged heads. But no normal mother could want that. "I don't see what I can do."

"You have a right to them," said Ruby.

"I'm sure the law would see it differently." So would her family; they'd never condemn her again. They'd always accused her; they'd always doubted her. Now they'd have nothing. No one could blame a victim. He could make all the decisions — she could waft by with presents and flowers and kisses. *He took the children from me, but I'm still their mother.* She could hear herself say it to some friendly passer-by as she held their hands on the village green, straightened their hats, knelt before them to do up their coats. *How dreadful,* the stranger would say — some respectable middle-aged woman in a felt hat — and Enid would reply, *yes, dreadful* and walk them home to Cherry Trees, kiss them goodbye at the door, walk away on a daily basis, go to her own sweet little house and do what she wanted. She could wave at them from the gates as they watched her leave, hear them shout: *bring us more sweets on Saturday, Mamma,* or some such chirrupy, happy fare-well. She couldn't harm them. They could love her.

"Don't you miss them, Enid?"

She'd forgotten where she was. "Of course I miss them." Her body had grown so used to the ache she didn't feel it anymore.

"I'm sure they miss you terribly," said Ruby, putting down her cup.

"I'm sure they don't," said Enid. The light shone spots on Fagus in his darkened room, on Finetta so unknown, on Ian running with the bean cane.

"Do you mean to accept him?"

"He has Everett and Mary. There's no difference to them, is there?"

"To be without their mother?"

"They won't be without me. He doesn't say I can't see them."

"But Enid —"

Ruby had such a rosy view of everything. Perfect families, perfect friends, everyone good and whole. "He isn't there most days, or wasn't. I can't see that that could have changed. And, for the time it's taken him to answer, I shouldn't wonder if he hasn't been away too."

"Then who has been looking after them?"

"The staff, I just told you. It's a matter of logistics, Ruby. I never knew he'd want them. You're right, I was in a state, I was —"

Who would understand this? Must she keep pretending

again — this time that she was sorry to give them away? Whatever normal mothers were, she wasn't one of them. She loved her children, she must do, she'd felt the tug of them, she'd written and had moments of absolute confidence, but this — this solution — it hadn't crossed her mind that it was possible. She'd given them up completely because to have them completely had killed her. She wasn't a normal mother, but did she have to be? As long as they were safe, cared for, loved, as long as they knew she loved them, that she existed. They'd thank her in the end. She was certain of it.

"You're giving him everything."

"He's giving me everything. He can run the house, the staff and I can live somewhere near. It will be exactly the same, except I can be —"

"Divorced," said Ruby.

"You make it sound so dreadful."

"It is dreadful."

"Only to someone who's never been married," replied Enid. She wrote back that evening.

23

.....

Enid, 1926

THE JOURNEY FROM Didlington Hall to Cherry Trees took her all day. Her decree nisi had arrived in time for her to get out of the Didlington Hall harvest festival, and all that was left to end her marriage as coldly as it had begun was for them to sign custody papers together. He had the files, and she had a pen in her purse, along with some boiled sweets for the children. By the time she walked up the hill to the wrought-iron gates, the sun had dipped below the trees.

The first thing she noticed was the chain. Its heavy iron links were slung through the bars of the gate and pulled down by a thick padlock. She rattled it, but it stayed put, locked. She could see a corner of the villa, the sitting room and her bedroom above, but there were no lights on. The air was still, and the evening filled with birdsong. Dandelions grew amongst the gravel of the drive. The lawns hadn't been cut; the grass, long and straight, was thick with summer flowers gone to seed, cowslips collapsed, and hog weed that waved in the evening breeze.

This time the walk back to the station wasn't sunlit and bold. It started to rain. The man behind the grill, in smart cap, looked at her with kindness. She sat in the waiting room for an hour, waiting for the train back to London. When it arrived, she had to run the stairs. She slept again as it rocked. It drew into Liverpool Street at ten forty-nine that evening. At the taxi rank she leant into the window and said, "Bryanston Square."

The butler carried her case into the hall. She breathed in the familiarity of that place — the chandelier that shone high above her, the black and white tiles that glistened beneath her feet. Her shoes made a shooshing sound as she mounted the stairs, her hand slipped quietly on the bannister rail. As they reached the first landing she said, "Is no one here?"

The butler walked two steps ahead of her. "Miss Campbell and Miss Dansey are out for the evening. I understand your mother is in Scotland." He began the second flight and she followed, echoes of her childhood in the walls around her: running down, in a game of hide and seek, going up in fear of the portraits at night, descending in her wedding gown to her father and brother, who'd waited in the hall.

The butler stopped outside a bedroom on the third floor. "May I arrange some supper for you?" He put her case down, opened the door and stood back to let her pass.

She walked into the bedroom that used to be hers. "Tell cook to send something up."

She heard Joan crashing about in the middle of the night. There was laughter, then a shut door.

At breakfast the next morning Joan didn't look up as Enid came in. She wore a pale silk kimono dressing gown over red velvet pyjamas, a dragon reared over her shoulder. "Have you had a nice trip?"

Enid stared straight ahead. It was bad enough coming down to Joan in a house of memories, let alone dealing with her sister's face, set as if she owned the place. She wasn't about to go explaining anything to her. She'd slept badly; she'd lain awake for hours, wondering what on earth was going on. "Where is Douglas?"

Pat came in. Her dressing-gown cord trailed across the floor, and the bells on her slippers tinkled with each step as she moved between the hot plates, taking an egg and three slices of bacon. The silver lids of the jam pots glinted in the sun; the sideboard was a palace of fine china and starched, monogrammed napkins.

Pat, plate in hand, made her way slowly to a seat at the shining oval table. "Morning, all." She sat down with a sigh.

Enid hadn't realised how different she'd become until that moment, in the breakfast room, watching Pat's steady descent to the table. The opulence, the shine, the grandeur of people with nothing to do — sat amongst it in her plain brown skirt, hand-dyed cotton shirt and hair in a simple twist, she was a twig blown in through the window. She pulled the cuff of her sleeve straight. "Why is mother in Scotland already?"

Joan said, "She lives there."

"Since when?"

"Since years ago, I don't know. When was it, Pat? Last summer?"

Pat poured herself some coffee. "Last summer." She made a stab at her egg, put her fork down and reached over the table for Joan's newspaper. She only got half way — her arm wouldn't reach further than the salt and pepper pots.

Joan handed it over. "Are you going up to see her?"

Pat laughed, and coughed, and dug into her egg again. Joan poured herself a glass of lemon water. Her hair was dishevelled, her limbs elegant and long.

Why did she think of Joan as fat when she wasn't with her? There was nothing fat about her; the largesse of her childish body had gone long ago and been replaced with something full but neat, a majesty that Enid remembered now. "I went to Cherry Trees."

Pat struggled with some bacon. Joan said, "If you're not going to read the racing, can you pass it back?"

"It was shut up."

"Did you expect everything to be kept on ice for you?" said Joan, folding the pages into a manageable size.

"Do you know where Douglas is?" Her egg looked over-cooked, and the black pudding was collapsing.

"Don't you mean the children?" said Joan.

"I expected the children to be at home."

"Looked after by whom?" Joan tipped the coffee pot but only a few black dregs dripped into her cup.

"Everett and Mary."

Joan pushed her cup away. "It's been two years, Enid."

"I'm well aware of that."

"You can't just walk out with no explanation and expect nothing to have changed. No one knew if you were coming back."

"No one asked."

"We didn't know where you were." Joan scrunched her napkin as if to discard it, then stretched it out again and laid it back on her lap. "You just walk in here as if it were yesterday, happy as you like, sitting down to breakfast. You arrived last night, did you? Was a telegram too much?"

"I don't plan these things."

"No." Joan picked up her napkin again and threw it on the table. "You don't. You just disappear at lunch and reappear for breakfast, two years later." She flipped open her cigarette case.

Pat looked up from the paper. Her savage finesse had narrowed into a single, fine point of elegance. "Where were you?"

"Norfolk." Enid stared back.

"Very flat, Norfolk," said Pat and returned to the paper.

Enid looked at Joan. "I shall need to stay here until I've made arrangements."

"You can't."

"Why not?"

"You just can't." She got up and went to the window.

"But I've nowhere else to go. And I don't have any money — I had to borrow the train fare. I need time."

"Two years not enough?"

Enid snapped back, "I'd forgotten you know everything."

Joan leant against the glass. Her cigarette sent strands of smoke about her head. "What have you been living on?"

"I told you, I've been in Norfolk, with friends."

"How very kind of them," said Joan. "I expect they were frightfully understanding."

"We were a family," replied Enid. "We worked together. We took care of each other. Some people do, you know."

"Did you wear sackcloth?" asked Pat.

Enid picked up her knife and buttered her toast with quick, precise movements. "Quite the experts, aren't you, on being a mother. What it's like to be shut up all day, day in day out, in a villa. If you refuse to get dressed they call it a lark. When I did it they called a doctor."

Joan came back to the table, sat down and rubbed her eyes. "Can't you get hold of your allowance?"

"I haven't been to the bank yet."

"Then get a room on tick."

"You could at least tell me where he is."

"How should I know?" said Joan.

"You can't tell me you haven't seen him? You must have seen him. He has the children. He must be somewhere. Hasn't he been in touch? Mother must be going spare."

"Mother is perfectly well."

"Then where is he?"

Pat said, without looking up, "Can't you reach him at his club?"

So casual at the family table, so very at ease at someone else's expense. Enid snapped, "I thought he might be here."

"Whatever gave you that idea?"

"If Cherry Trees is shut up then he must be somewhere."

Pat got up and fetched a silver pewter from the sideboard. She poured more hot water into her cup. "We thought you'd dropped off the edge of the world."

"I don't understand what business it is of yours," said Enid.

"You dropped off the edge of the world," said Joan, "and now you turn up as if you've a right to ask questions."

"Someone could have tried to look for me." Enid spoke to the table, her plate, the congealed skin on her egg.

"Douglas did try. He couldn't trace you. How was he to know you were in Norfolk? Mother nearly had a coronary. None of us knew what to do."

"And since when was it up to you?"

Joan shook her head and laid her hands flat on the table. "I was there."

Pat turned a page of the paper. "We had to cancel our trip to Khartoum. I, for one, shall never forgive you."

"He's been back a month," said Joan, getting up. "You can find him at his club."

"Back from where?"

"Port Elizabeth. He looks rather well on it. I'm going to bathe."

Enid said, "He's not living here, is he?"

"He's taken a house in Hertfordshire somewhere." She was at the door.

"And the children?"

"They're with him," replied Joan, not looking round.

But it took Enid three days to realise that Joan had neglected to finish her sentence.

24

.....

Enid, 1926

D OUGLAS' CLUB INFORMED her that he'd be there on Monday evening and suggested she send a note to his office, so Enid took a room in a hotel in Mayfair for the weekend. She didn't want to stay at Bryanston Square, anyway; it stank of smoke and judgement. On Monday she went to the bank with her decree nisi and explained it would soon be absolute; she needed to change the names on the account. She would be Miss Enid Campbell again. It was, after all, her money. The bank manager told her his hands were tied until the complete paperwork could be shown and offered her a loan instead. She spent the day shopping at Selfridges, and by the time she descended the stairs to the Ladies Side of Boodles, her sackcloth and ashes were crumpled in her hotel bin, along with her long brown skirt and hand-dyed shirt.

How odd to see him, she thought, as she was led in, as she

saw him, waiting in an armchair in the hushed quiet of the gentleman's club that kept visiting ladies safely in the basement, that
kept the lighting bright and the carpets thick — this man who
was once her husband, who'd found someone else long before
she'd let him go. It was funny that it didn't touch her, that she
didn't mind. All those evenings alone when he must have been
with this other woman; all those stilted suppers when he'd talked
about trains, his face betraying nothing. His Miss Wormald had
been filling in since Fagus was five — she'd worked that out while
packing her suitcase at Didlington. Romping with him, in some
vile hotel.

The image revolted her. How could anyone want that? Her
sexual episodes with Douglas had been a duty she'd performed
with eyes shut. Her body was a disconnected vehicle, a means
of travel and manipulation, a thing, once of beauty, once used
to seduce — it had given an aura of plenty and class, but it had
never defined her, had only disguised the unconfined soul of her.
Lined in the silk of her untouched childhood, it had torn in small
places to let him in and her children out; in the spaces between
birth and conception, she'd pushed him off. It had never occurred
to her that anyone would do it for fun. He'd snapped, more than
once, that she should have told him that before they were married,
but then he'd stopped complaining or knocking on her door and
now she knew why.

He looked different. He was tanned, and he'd filled out a bit.
He stood up, didn't know what to do with his hands, and sat

down again. From an attaché case he brought out a file, and from his breast pocket, a pen. He held it out to her.

"How are the children?" She ignored the pen.

"Very well." He put it on the table, beside the file, and beckoned to a waiter.

"I understand you're no longer at Cherry Trees."

"Tea, for the lady, and a whisky."

The waiter nodded.

"When did you move?" said Enid.

"I assumed you'd wish to sell."

"I bought it."

"And you shall have the proceeds." The change suited him. He had a steady handsomeness which only came with age.

She said, "How long will it take?" A floral tea pot and plate of sandwiches arrived.

Douglas poured. "A month at most. I'll have the furniture put in storage, if you like."

"And the children?" She put two sandwiches on her plate.

"Do you wish for them to be put in storage too?"

She took a bite — thin ham, butter, fine slices of white bread. She chewed quickly and chased it down with a sip of tea. "I assume you've proper help for Fagus?"

Douglas lit a cigarette. "He's at school."

"School?"

"I just thought —"

"Which?"

"Which school? Castlemere. It's in Shoreham, run by a Miss Barnes. Your sister found it." He stopped and started again. "His mind's as sharp as anything, you know, within reason. I didn't see why he should be chained in some sanatorium when his brain's perfectly good. He's learning French. They keep him there, all year round, as it were. Miss Barnes runs it as a boarding house during the holidays. Quite a few of the boys stay on. It really was the best I could do."

She sat back and took in the confines of the room, the scattered groups of ladies leaning forward over dainties, the uncomfortable men in suits; the everyday comfort of a life lived normally.

Douglas ran his hand through his hair. He was greying at the temples. "You must know you left me little choice."

She got up and went to the powder room where she stared in the mirror at her ageing skin. When she returned to the table, Douglas' glass was full again. The ice clinked as he raised it. "And what are your plans?"

"I'd like to settle somewhere near you, so as to be near Ian and Finetta, you understand —" There. She'd said their names out loud. They were real. "I hear you're in Hertfordshire."

"You've seen Joan?"

"I had the pleasure of breakfasting with her on Saturday. She told me as little as possible."

"Where were you?"

"Where was I?"

"I mean, where did you breakfast?"

"At Bryanston Square, of course. I was forced there when I

discovered the chain on the gates at Cherry Trees. I arrived on Friday night."

"And you had breakfast with Joan?"

"And Pat, if you must know the details. They were both in nightgowns. Of course they could have separate bedrooms, but —" The thought of what they might do flattened her brain and made words fail. He'd been right. She'd known it as Pat walked in, as they shared the paper, as Pat coughed into her breakfast and Joan failed to pour coffee. Something in the ease of them — it had frightened her. Sexual intercourse with a man was one thing, but with a woman — she was glad words failed her. She only wished the images failed her too.

But who cared? It was their sordid business. She wasn't interested. She tore off a corner of sandwich, as if giving it to a child, but left it on her plate. "I should like to come out to Hertfordshire, to see the children as soon as possible."

"Damn it, Enid." He turned his cigarette lighter over and over in his hand. "You walked out. We were all at a loss. Joan was marvellous. God knows what we'd have done without her."

"So I keep hearing. Do you expect me to buy her a present?"

"I didn't know what else to do."

"Then you buy her a present. I don't see what she has to do with any of it."

"She's become very attached."

"We shall have to discuss whether she can come and see them."

"You don't understand." He shook his head. His hair fell over his forehead like it used to do, and through the better glow of his skin she saw lines beneath his eyes. "You're not having them, Enid."

"I don't want them." She stopped, halted by her own admission. "I'm happy for you to carry on; if they're cared for, then I really see no need to step in. I only think it would be good for them to have their mother nearby — for me to be near, you understand — and I'd like to say hello, see them — well, really as soon as I can —" She trailed off.

Douglas, divided from her by a thousand-mile drop that was shunting and pushing and cracking them further apart, shook his head again. "We didn't think you were coming back."

"We?"

"Joan and I." He put down his whisky.

"And? What? Did you tell them I was dead? I'm only asking for a visit, Douglas, really." She dropped her hands to her lap as if this were a simple row, a confusion over luncheon dates or plans for the summer, but she didn't feel relaxed. Her lips were dry. Her jaw hurt. "We can arrange the details, how to do it, I could take them for tea every week, perhaps see them at school — Ian and Finetta are at school also, are they? Or have you employed a governess?"

"Ian is four," said Douglas.

"Of course, and Finetta, I expect a good governess is all she'll need in good time. I'm happy to arrange any system you like; and for now, if I could come for tea, I'll only stay an hour or so. We've got to start somewhere, Douglas. I don't see what Joan has to do with it. It has nothing to do with her whether I see my children or not." She picked up her cup.

"They're not in Hertfordshire."

"But she told me they were with you."

"Did she?" He stubbed his cigarette. "They were," and held his glass up to a passing waiter, "for the weekend. This one just gone. More soda."

"For the weekend?"

"I've been abroad. I imagine Joan told you that."

"But they must have been with Everett?" Her tea was cold.

"How could they be?" He ran his hand over his mouth.

"They were for all the years you weren't there either," said Enid. "Everett, Mary. What difference did your presence ever make?"

"I had a wife who assured me she was there too."

Enid put her cup down as carefully as she could, but it still rattled in the saucer and wouldn't sit straight. She pushed it away. "Did you send them to Scotland?"

"That summer, I did." The waiter returned with Douglas' glass. He took a sip. "You must know he's become her heir, Enid."

"He's always been her heir. I don't see what difference that makes."

"Not your mother's." He looked as if he'd give anything to leave that sentence unfinished. He took another cigarette.

She stared at him, daring him.

"He's Joan's," he said, and when she didn't speak he cannoned his sentence at her again, as if she was stupid or deaf or blind. "He's Joan's heir."

She opened her mouth and closed it again. He must have got the wrong end of the stick. He'd been away. The family had never trusted him anyway. She smoothed imaginary creases from her lap. "Don't be ridiculous, Douglas. Joan has no more money than I do. Ian is mother's —" but all of a sudden, as Douglas dropped his gaze, as his hands shook and he couldn't make the lighter work, all of her worlds imploded at once. Just like that. In a flash of pure clean understanding.

She stood up. Douglas stood up too. "Surely you must have realised that would happen? What did you think she was going to do with it all? Put it in a savings account for your eventual return?"

"She promised it to Ian."

"And he shall have it."

"From Joan."

Douglas nodded. "From Joan."

"And Joan has mother's estate."

"Yes."

"And mother is still alive."

"Yes."

"In Scotland."

"Really Enid, it can't be complicated to understand. You walked out. Your mother is old. She wanted to be sure everyone was safe."

"Everything, you mean."

"Everyone, everything, what difference does it make? Ian is heir. It doesn't matter to whom, does it? He needs guidance."

"He's four."

"We didn't think you were coming back, Enid."

"Where is he living, Douglas?"

"She stepped in, Enid. I told you. She's been really marvellous. I just didn't know what else to do."

"I'd like to go now."

He picked up the file and shoved it into his attaché case. The pen rolled onto the floor. "Someone was always going to have to manage it, Enid, and he's happy with her. They both are. They've really settled in quite well. He doesn't know any different. He won't remember Cherry Trees at all."

"You mean me."

He shoved his cigarette case back in his pocket, the unlit cigarette discarded on the table. "Your mother's old. She couldn't carry on. She needed help. What else was Joan going to do? She's been marvellous. Fagus is settled, and Finetta's as happy as —"

"I want to see him."

"You can see him any time you like." He hurried after her. "There are no visiting times. Miss Barnes is very accommodating, and it will be no problem to arrange —"

"Not Fagus." They were out on the street. "Get me a cab." The doorman went into the road and raised his hand.

Douglas grabbed her arm. "You can't expect everything to have been kept on ice for you, Enid. We were frantic."

She pulled away from him. "That's just what Joan said."

A cab pulled up. She dropped into the back, leaned forward and slammed the door.

Was it then, in the cab from St. James', that she chose revenge over life? Or was it packing up Cherry Trees? Or standing at the railings watching Ian play happily in the gardens of Bryanston Square? She went, when Cherry Trees was sold, when the money had allowed her to buy a tall narrow house in Fulham and the sitting room was crammed with packing cases, straw spilling out onto the floor, her belongings strewn everywhere. She gave up putting things away and walked across the park.

She might not have recognised him if she hadn't arrived on the corner of George Street at the very moment he came out of the house, his hand held by a nanny. She might have stood at the corner, watching the windows, and not registered a little boy playing in the gardens opposite, not gone to lean against the railings to see him, a toy train in his hand, his teddy on the grass. But she did. She saw his nanny lead him across the road and enter the gardens. She followed at a distance and when they'd shut the gate behind them she leaned against it, her hands gripping the bars. He looked so happy.

25

.....

Enid, 1926

A T THE KITCHEN table of her new house in Fulham, she wrote a note, another simple jot of words.

> *Dear Joan,*
> *I wish to see Ian for tea. Please send him at four pm this*
> *Friday, 27th.*
> *Yours etc,*
> *Enid*

After she posted it, she came home, got out a fresh sheet and wrote another note, which she folded and left on the hall table beside the front door. Joan's reply arrived a few days later.

She waited by the window. Her sister's Rolls Royce slid to a stop outside number thirty-nine Evelyn Gardens at precisely four o'clock. From the rich interior came the same uniformed nanny, followed by Ian. He was dressed in another smart little suit with the same teddy bear squashed under his arm. She ran downstairs, picked up the note, opened the door, smiled and said, "Hello."

The nanny didn't smile, but Ian raised his eyes to meet hers. She grabbed his arm, shoved the note into his nanny's hands, pulled him across the threshold and slammed the door. It could only have taken her seconds to read it.

The woman started hammering and shouting. Enid opened the cupboard under the stairs, scuttled him into it and flattened herself against the wall. He screamed and went quiet. After the nanny left she got him upstairs and looked at him in the light of the sitting-room window. There was a dark stain spread across his trousers. No matter. She'd already organised a box of Fagus' old clothes to fit him.

"It's all right, Ian. I'm — you're here for tea. Nanny will be back in a minute. Shall we get you out of those wet things? Here, wait here." She'd already made Ian's room, look just, almost, nearly, like Fagus' used to. When she'd gone to pack up Cherry Trees, she'd found their things barely touched, as if Douglas had taken nothing — a ghost house, the occupants disappeared, their things left perfectly in place. She'd taken everything, like an automaton set on a future some other part of her could see; as if she'd known she'd need the basket of knitted rabbits, the merry-go-round of wooden zebras, the hobbyhorse leant in the corner, the blanket spread on the single bed.

She came back with a pair of trousers and held them up to

him. "Will these fit you?" They looked too big. "Perhaps I can find a cord to tie them." She fetched some string from her sewing box and looped it through the belt holes. "There. Shall we have tea? You're hungry, aren't you?"

She picked him up and plonked him on a chair at the tea table. It was set and laden and completely ready. Cake, sandwiches, tea for her and milk for him; she'd bought the cake especially, but he didn't eat and neither did she.

"What about your room? Perhaps you'd like to see that instead?" She lifted him from his seat again. He said nothing. He didn't resist, but when she pushed him into the corridor he ran down it.

"In there Ian, that's right," she said, running after him. He disappeared into his room, but when she got there she saw he'd hidden under his bed.

She tried for ages to get him out.

"Please, Ian. There's nothing to be afraid of."

He crept further in.

"Aren't you hungry? I can make boiled eggs and soldiers."

He pulled his teddy closer.

"You can't stay under there for ever."

He didn't move.

"I shall have to pull you."

She tried, but he kicked so hard her knuckle bled.

26

.....

Joan, 1926

THE BELL OF Bryanston Square rang at twenty-seven minutes past four. When she'd buttoned his coat and put her cheek to his, not more than an hour ago, she'd said to Nanny Duncan: "He need not stay long, do you understand?" Nanny Duncan had nodded. She was an excellent woman, firm and correct; she'd come within a week of the children. Joan kept her hand on Ian's shoulder. "You are to leave sharply at four-thirty. No dallying. Do not be persuaded to linger. You must hold onto him tightly, and not be drawn into questioning."

"Yes, ma'am." Duncan's hat was squarely on her head, and her gloved hand was ready to take his.

"And under no circumstances are you to be persuaded to leave the room. He must not be out of your sight for an instant."

"I understand, ma'am," Duncan had replied.

She'd gone up to the drawing room and waited. She'd made her driver do the trip the day before just to be sure of distance and time. She knew exactly how long it would take. Finetta had been somewhere — upstairs, or in the library. She was a resourceful little girl. She didn't seem to mind being left alone.

So when the bell rang at four twenty-seven, Joan was not expecting it, and she spilled her liquorice tisane down her front. Nanny Duncan's hat was not square on her head anymore; it was cocked sideways, as if she'd been running. But her face wasn't red. It was ashen. She held out a note.

I have decided that Ian should live with me. Enid

"She was so quick. She just took him. She grabbed him from me, I couldn't have expected it, she grabbed him and —" Words were pouring out of Nanny Duncan, but Joan wasn't listening. Pat came clattering down the stairs. "What is it?"

She must have been screaming. The note was crushed in her fingers.

"Go back to your book," said Pat to Finetta who'd appeared in the hall too.

"She's taken him," said Joan.

"Come upstairs," Pat held her.

"I can't move."

"Come," said Pat again.

The drawing room swayed in firelight, a standing lamp was switched on, the curtains were drawn, and a brandy decanter was open on the table.

"I told you she would do this," Joan shouted into her hands. "You said I shouldn't worry. You said it was the right thing to do."

Pat stood by the fire. "I said you had to."

"You said she wouldn't dare."

"I want it finished."

"You knew."

"I knew she wouldn't let be."

"Why? She's let be before. Two years, remember?"

"And then she came back."

"And if we hadn't, she'd have gone again."

"She'd always have come back. She's his mother."

"I'm —" but she wasn't. She wasn't. For two years she'd thought she was, that's all. Two years ago, Douglas had arrived with three children in tow, and she hadn't known what to do. Where should she begin? This wasn't her life. This was someone else's life. This was her sister's wretched mess, not hers.

Fagus she'd dealt with first. He couldn't manage all the stairs at Bryanston Square — it was impossible. He was becoming a young man, grown up from a child, and his limbs were everywhere, crashing into vases and knocking against tables. Every time he broke something, he sat still for an hour after saying sorry, clinging onto his chair or wherever she'd sat him to keep him safe. The girl Mary, the nanny Douglas had brought along too, didn't help one iota. She treated him like an imbecile — she may as well have put a lead around his neck. He wasn't deaf. He wasn't stupid. He just couldn't see.

He needed normal. He needed school, like every other young man. She'd sacked Mary, employed Nanny Duncan and taken Fagus to Castlemere. Eton was out of the question; he'd needed somewhere he could get used to and manage, somewhere that could manage him. Something realistic. They didn't all have to go off their heads, and she'd felt like the only one thinking clearly. She'd kissed him goodbye, she went to see him as often as she could, once a term at least, and she'd made the right choice; he was happy, he was safe. Finetta had slotted in prettily, there was nothing to do with her — a doll of a child, all ringlets and smiles — and then there was Ian. Little Ian, with his teddy squashed under his arm. Before he arrived she'd thought she'd known what love was.

"She's taken him." She couldn't stop saying it.

"Yes," replied Pat.

"I'm calling the police."

"Call your lawyer."

"We'll have her arrested."

"On what charge?"

"Kidnap, of course."

"A mother has her son?"

"You know it isn't like that."

"But they don't. Call your lawyer. Wire Douglas."

"I'm going to stop her allowance."

"Let the courts deal with her. The power rests with you. Any judge will see that."

Joan's elbow hit the table beside her and an ashtray spilled onto the floor. "Why should I have to fight for him? He's mine already. He loves me. He belongs here." Her body shook. Across the park, somewhere, in some dishevelled room with her dishevelled, mad sister was her boy, and she wanted to tear out of the house, she wanted to run, she wanted to rip her sister's eyes out.

"And he will be, legally. It's the only way," said Pat.

"I shall never let her see him again." She cried great heaving sobs, her face wet, her hair bedraggled, her sleeves a mess.

"Darling," Pat came and sat beside her, "you won't have to stop her doing anything." She put her arms around her. "After this, he shall never want to see her again."

She missed supper. She couldn't eat. She went to bed and couldn't sleep. Every piece of her shouted to get him back, and visions of him tortured her through the dull slow hours till dawn. She got up, tired of waiting for light to seep in around the curtains. While Pat slept, she splashed cold water on her face and dressed quickly. As the sounds of breakfast began to filter through the house, she wrote to her mother.

Two hours later she waited in the hall for Pat to change into something warmer. A bitter wind knocked pigeons from the branches of the trees.

Pat came downstairs, wrapped in fur. "Have you ordered the car?"

"It's outside," said Joan, her own fur clipped to the neck.

They drove to the offices of Bircham & Co; from Bryanston Square past Marble Arch, whizzing along Park Lane to Victoria, and into the narrow streets of Westminster. A woman in tight, wiry glasses. They were offered refreshments while they waited in an anteroom of comfortable chairs and low tables. The last time she was here had been two years ago, with her mother.

Pat dropped a copy of *The Lady* on the table. "Do they always keep you waiting so?"

"Mother used to make him come to Bryanston Square."

"That's what we should have done."

"But not when Ian came. She brought me here. She said we must modernise."

Pat laughed. "What did your mother ever know about modern?"

"I suppose she feared I'd entertain him in my undergarments."

"She was handing you over."

"She wanted me to know where the office was, I suppose."

"Miss Campbell." Mr. McKinley launched into the room and held out his hand. "Do forgive me. Come right this way." He was tall, kind and gracious. Her mother always said he was exactly what one wanted in a legal man. Masses of manners, and masses of brain. He led them to a meeting room: a polished table, a stack of papers, a sideboard set with glasses and a jug of something. Of the hurried wires she'd sent the day before, three had been to him.

"Can we stop her money?"

McKinley opened one of the files. "Do you wish to make her destitute?"

"She has as little right to him as she does to an income."

"It was your mother who set her allowance."

"It was my mother who asked me to control it."

"If she has him, she will have to live off something. It will put the courts in a most unhappy position: to have to choose between wealth and a mother."

"I'm not suggesting we cut him off."

"I should think not," said Pat.

"Her income is one thing," said McKinley. "His, quite another. I have here the details of his Trust."

"Can she get hold of it?"

"No. If you recall, it will pass to him on your death, and thereafter to his son and so on."

"We tied it very tight?"

"We did," said McKinley. "Your sister is not entitled to any of it. However —"

"If I make her destitute, he'll suffer."

"While he's with her, yes. Thereafter is another matter. I suggest a sensible line is to leave her allowance in place while demonstrating absolutely that she is an unfit mother. It will make you appear most reasonable."

"I am most reasonable," said Joan.

"Of course, Miss Campbell. What I meant was —"

"When will I get him back?"

"We shall have to apply to the courts in the first instance."

"But that could take months."

"I'm afraid the wheels of justice —"

"Jarndyce and Jarndyce?" said Pat.

"Don't say that," said Joan.

Jarndyce and Jarndyce. She'd read *Bleak House* the summer

that Fagus had fallen. She'd found it splayed on the lawn, bleaching in the sun.

"We shall apply in the first instance —" repeated McKinley.

"He can't stay there all that time, however long it takes — months."

"I quite understand your discomfort —"

"Discomfort?"

"But until we have an order from the courts —"

"She stole him."

"She's his mother," said Pat.

"He's lived with me since he could walk."

"I understand it's the most terrible shock," said McKinley.

"She's only his mother by biological coincidence. She means nothing to him. He won't know where he is. He doesn't know her at all."

"Yet she is his mother."

"I don't need that pointed out again," shouted Joan.

"It's only in the short term," said Pat, her hand on Joan's. "Try to be sensible."

"You try and be sensible." Joan pulled her hand away. She was going to lose control, here, in front of McKinley, in these sensible offices with these sensible people. She pointed at the pitcher on the sideboard, and McKinley got up and poured her a glass. Lemon water, with too much lemon. Too sharp. She put the glass down.

"Would you consider offering a settlement?" said McKinley.

"It's what she's after," said Pat.

"What kind of settlement could compare to Ian?" said Joan.

"She's only after money," said Pat.

"And to make me suffer."

"We could turn over an increased allowance, or a lump sum if you prefer, in return for settling out of court."

"She gets enough as it is," said Joan. "She doesn't deserve a penny more."

"You'd get him back," said Pat.

"How do you know?" snapped Joan. "She'd laugh in my face. She'd keep putting the price up. She'd ruin all our lives. If it was money she wanted, she'd have sent him back this morning with another one of her notes. She doesn't love him, she doesn't care for him, but without him she has nothing. No lump sum is going to make up for having the heir to my fortune."

"She can't win," said Pat.

"But she can try, can't she? If Fagus had been heir it would have been him."

A car roared past the window. Joan tried more lemon water, but the acid stung her tongue.

McKinley closed one file and opened another. "Do you propose to continue to care for your niece, whether or not her brother is there?"

It hadn't crossed her mind. She'd simply assumed Ian would be back.

"If you want to drive a mother mad, send her all her children," said Pat.

"Her argument will be that she is his mother. Her man, whichever chambers take her case, will veer away from money having anything to do with it. I would suggest you send the little girl to join her brother."

"See how she likes that," said Pat.

"After all, from what I understand, she asked only for Ian to come to tea, is that correct?"

Joan nodded.

"And this was following the disclosure from her husband that Ian had become your heir?"

She nodded again.

"Very well, then. The case, put like that, is relatively simple. All roads point to an act of revenge, the vicious heart of a woman intent on hurt. Not care, not a mother's love, but outright vengeance on you and your mother, and no doubt the boy's father too."

"Send Finetta to Fulham?"

"I fear you must," said McKinley.

"And Fagus?"

"Who pays his school fees?"

"I do, of course."

"Then perhaps you might have a word with the bursars. Surely it is a mother's duty to take care of all her children?"

"No favouritism," said Pat.

"And apply for custody of all three?" said Joan.

"No." McKinley shook his head. "Yours is a special case. Ian is your heir; he is set to inherit not just a fortune, but a life. For him, a steady hand is required. He will have position in society. Society needs men of his position to hold a steady course, and only you can give it. The rules of inheritance dictate, Miss Campbell, and they will dictate to court."

"The papers will have a field day," said Pat.

"You will face some very unpleasant questioning," said McKinley.

"I have nothing to hide," said Joan.

Pat crossed her legs the other way. McKinley wrote a note in the margin of his file. Joan took another slug of lemon water.

"And what of the boy's father?" said McKinley, smiling bleakly.

"You may well ask," said Pat.

"We have his full support," said Joan. Douglas had sent a wire back last night. It said: *do everything you can.*

"Has he agreed that you should have custody?"

"He agreed to that two years ago."

"He applied for custody of all three of them," said Pat.

"It was a condition of divorce," said Joan.

"But they are not divorced."

"She didn't sign," said Joan.

"Douglas is a simpleton," said Pat.

"If he'd carried it out in an office, none of this would have happened," said Joan.

"He had some ridiculous notion of fairness." Pat peered into Joan's glass, sniffed, and put it down again.

"Then he must continue his line," said McKinley.

"No," said Joan. "I will not let this become another chapter in their wretched marriage. Let him divorce her."

"He means to marry his mistress," said Pat.

"Then I take it he will speak on our behalf?" said McKinley.

"Oh, Douglas." Joan stared angrily across the table. "He'll do anything we want."

Out on the street, Joan took Pat's arm. "Let's walk. I need the air." She leaned into the car, and spoke to her driver. "Meet us at The National." The car eased away and Joan tucked her other hand into the deep fur pockets of her coat. They turned left along King Charles Street to Horse Guards Parade and St. James' Park. A pair of swans floated quietly on the lake; the cold fluffed their feathers. Joan and Pat increased their speed, as the warmth of the offices of Bircham & Co receded and winter took hold about their ears. Across the Mall they marched arm in arm, through Admiralty Arch, past Nelson's Column, and up the steps of the National Gallery.

They sat before a Stubbs, a horse rearing, a look in its eye of power and fear. "I can't think straight," said Joan.

"You don't have to," said Pat. "They can't possibly leave him with her. He'll be home in no time."

She'd wanted to holler out an animal pain all the way there, but had kept her head down instead. In the stillness of the gallery it was harder to be quiet. She wanted to cry out and shout, she wanted to scream, but that would get her called mad too, and she'd never see him again. She was expected to behave reasonably and decently when her child had been ripped from her, as if any person who could stay calm should parent at all. To love and be still. Impossible.

Pat stared at the painting. "I love its eye. So wild. I've always thought Stubbs must have had a rather Catherine the Great sort of fancy."

"How vulgar," said Joan.

"I'm designed to think badly of everyone. You know that. It has the added benefits of leading one to a place of few disappointments."

"You don't think badly of me."

Between them, hidden under their furs, Pat touched her hand to the small of Joan's back. The gallery was quiet, there were few others there. A gentleman with two ladies following him, guidebooks in hand, stood before a Millais; a guard was seated by the wall; a couple, arm in arm, walked swiftly past into the next room.

"We could just go and get him," said Joan.

"Of course we could," said Pat.

"You know I'm not given to hysteria, but when this is over I'm going to tear her head off. When he's home again."

"He'll come home again."

"I can't bear the thought of where he is."

"Don't think about it. Imagine it's a game of Patience. You're good at that. We hold the whole deck. She has nothing."

"What about us?" She could feel Pat's thumb tracing circles over her spine.

"She has no evidence."

"Half of London knows."

"The half that will be with us. No one will speak for her."

Two men walked past, their hands clasped behind their backs.

"Let's stay home tonight."

"I promised Otty I'd partner her at bridge. We won such a lot last time."

"I think I'll stay home," said Joan.

They left without taking tea. In the car, Pat said, "Drop me on Piccadilly, would you? I've shopping." Outside Fortnum & Mason, Pat got out. As the Rolls pulled away, leaving Pat on the pavement, Joan was tempted to tell her driver to go to Evelyn Gardens anyway. Why hadn't she gone straight there last night and grabbed him? Pat had talked her out of it; they couldn't all appear unhinged. But Joan felt unhinged. The gate to her composure swung wildly from hatred to revenge. The former made her want to burn her sister's house down; the latter, to see this through to its end, to punish her slowly, in inches, like death.

Sleet began to batter the pavements as the Rolls drew to a stop in Bryanston Square. Pat would be caught in it.

27

.....

Enid, 1926

WHAT HAD SHE done? He wouldn't look at her. She knelt before him, as she had yesterday. "Ian?" She held his arms. They were clamped to his sides. "Ian?" He kept his eyes on the floor. He was wrapped in a towel, he was shivering, standing in the middle of her bathroom while the bath tub ran.

Everything of yesterday had felt like running. Running for the door, running for trousers that weren't stained, running after him down the corridor. But today, everything was still.

This morning she'd woken on the floor beside him, beside his bed, him still under it. She'd meant to pull him out when he was asleep, but she'd fallen asleep before he did, his pillow under her head, his blanket pulled over her. There was a stench — it was the stench that had woken her. He'd crawled to the further end, and lay on his teddy. She'd tugged his legs, and this time he hadn't resisted.

Now he was in the bathroom, she'd got him as far as that. "Ian? Please say you're happy. It shan't take long. I can take you back in a jiff, if you like. You do need to wash, though — have a nice bath, and then I can make you breakfast, and everything will be all right. Won't it?" She shook him gently. She was sat on her heels so that she was lower than him, so that she could see into his face, but he kept moving it away. "You remember me, don't you?" He said nothing. She let go of him, got up, turned off the taps and tested the water. "Come along then, let's get you in." He let her unwrap the towel and lift him, her hands hooked under his arms. He looked so little once he was in, so small in the shallow hot water. She gathered up his soiled clothes, dumped them in a basket and carried it to the area steps at the back of the house. Peel could deal with it. She'd employed the housekeeper last week.

She sat on the loo while he sat in the bath, neither of them moving. She'd never washed a child before. She wasn't sure about any of it. She offered him a sponge. "Will you wash your face?" It wasn't his face that needed washing. The water was slightly brown, and bits floated in it. "You'd better stand up." He did as he was told. She rubbed a clean flannel over his body and squeezed the sponge over the crevices she didn't know how to touch. "You'd better get out again." No point in sitting down in that water. He let her lift him onto the floor and wrap the towel around him again.

She used to hear the children squeal at bath time. From behind the bathroom door at Cherry Trees came peals of laughter and squawking and splashing. Ian sat quietly on the floor as she dressed him, standing when he was asked, lifting this leg and that arm, popping his head through a jumper, saying nothing at all.

She tucked him up in bed. As far as she was concerned he could stay there until Joan came. He looked exhausted, and it was obvious neither of them were going to eat until this was over. Anyway, she needed to be near the sitting-room window — its view of the street was too good. They'd be here any minute. It was a wonder they hadn't come last night. She pulled her chair up and got out her embroidery.

An hour later the streets were as noisy and silent as ever. No screeching tyres had come tearing into Evelyn Gardens, no siren wail of the police to make everyone stare, no hammering on the door. She looked at the clock on the mantelpiece. Almost midday, almost luncheon, an entire night followed by an entire morning — and nothing. Not a peep. It came to her in inches, the feeling she remembered from the early months at Didlington: the realising, too late, that she was waiting, and then having nothing to do but wait. Where were they? Why hadn't they come? Didn't they care after all? Was it all going to be much simpler, a matter of forgiveness and getting on? Had she misunderstood completely?

But this hadn't been the plan, you see. She was speaking to someone in her head. She said aloud, "You were just supposed to see that I existed, that I mattered, that I have a right to my children whether I want them or not." She said it to the window, the street below, but the window and the street below took no notice. "I just wanted to make a point." She banged on the glass. "Make you listen." She imagined Joan on the pavement below, pleading. "I just wanted to make you see you can't have everything, that you can't just take what you want and expect everyone to make way. But you —" She stopped. It wasn't true that Joan had always hated her. Joan hadn't always hated anyone. Joan just got on being everyone's friend; she'd never done a damned mean thing in her life. Joan was supposed to have come rushing over London and pleaded for him back. They were supposed to make an arrangement. She bit her lip.

Mother. Enid took a sharp breath in. Why hadn't she called either? No matter how high she jumped, her mother's gaze was always an inch higher, and now she'd sunk so low that her mother would never see her again. Perhaps she should write. She got half out of her chair and sat down again. What was the point? Hadn't she made her views clear? She'd given Joan everything, even things that were not hers to give. Her perfect Joan, and her errant, awful Enid, who'd done nothing more alarming than be born and be loved by her father, perhaps more than he'd loved his wife. It hadn't been her fault.

Perhaps she should send him back. It would be simple. A mistake, another note, a promise that it would never happen again. She pushed her fingers against her forehead. How absurd, to think this would be forgiven. They'd destroy her. They'd leave her with nothing.

She looked in on him, but he appeared to be sleeping. He was perfectly still, like Fagus; Fagus after the light had been shone in his eyes and he'd stopped being the great white hope of anything. No. She closed the door softly. Not like Fagus. Ian was a healthy, lively, full of hope young boy and he was here.

She returned to the window and the hours ticked by. *Now what?* she thought. It was like the day after childbirth, when excitement drifted away and she was left with what she'd been planning. Where were they? Why hadn't they come running?

Peel arrived, all bustle and shopping baskets. Enid met her in the hall. "Go and sit with Ian. He's in his bedroom." She put on her coat. "My son, he's come to stay. See that he has everything." She fixed her hat. "I have to go out." She didn't, but she couldn't stand the silence.

She walked for an hour around the streets of Fulham. When she turned into her street again, she half expected to see the Rolls, but instead she saw a post boy, handing Peel a letter.

28

.....

Enid, 1926

T HE LAWYER SHE found, from an advertisement in the back of *The Times*, had fat wobbling lips and a cheap-cut suit. Her chair was lower than his; she had to look up at him. "Can you help me, Mr. Crowther?"

"A most complicated case." He smiled, showing uneven teeth. His desk was loaded with files slipping across the ink blotter, hemming in a glass tankard packed with pencils. Weak sunshine forced its way through an overcast day; it hit the windowpanes behind him and highlighted the dust-laden glass. "Might you give the child back?"

She gripped her purse on her lap and flicked the metal clasp with her thumbnail. "I can't."

"It would save a great deal of bother."

"She'll stop my money."

"Wouldn't she have done that already?"

"She can't, while I've got him." It sounded cold. She meant it to be brave.

"Can you not return him on condition of an assurance that your allowance is safe?"

"She hates me. She'll say one thing and do another. She's never going to give me anything without him."

"But you don't want him?"

It was a simple question. Too simple. "I can't think straight if I'm destitute, can I? She's taken my son and she's taken my money —"

"Your mother's money."

"It was supposed to be my son's."

"Has that changed?"

"Of course it hasn't changed. But the rider has: she who holds the reins. Don't you understand? My sister hates me. It was only a matter of time before my funds dried up; it was lucky I came back when I did, and if I hadn't divorced I'd never even know. Douglas, my husband, he had all the bank accounts in hand, I had nothing of my own that he couldn't touch. I'd have come back, divorced, given him custody, and hey presto my bank account dries up."

"Did it?"

"It didn't have time."

It was all lies and she knew it. That wasn't what she'd been thinking about at all. She'd been thinking about Joan — clumsy, dumpy, mother's girl Joan, tripping up and landing on the pulse, getting everything. "She's stolen what's mine."

"Your son?"

"My inheritance."

"We are defending custody."

"Of course." Enid flicked her thumbnail against the catch.

Crowther licked his lips. "Her man will drag you through the mud."

"You think I'll lose."

"I think you'll have a fight." He picked out a pencil from the tankard. "It's never too late for measured judgement."

"It's too late to let her win," replied Enid.

She took a bus from Gray's Inn to Chelsea. Outside the Royal Court, she jumped off and walked quickly across Sloane Square. The First Church of Christ, built with American money and up-kept with £5 of her own, was like a sandstone ship that had lost its moorings and become wedged behind shops off Sloane Street. The door was open, the main hall was empty, it was lunchtime and no one needed prayers except her. She knelt on the floor amidst the chairs. The parquet floor was hard and dusty. She closed her eyes, but found she had nothing to say to God and God had nothing to say to her.

Finetta arrived by taxicab three days later, a suitcase in her small hand. The cabbie said, "I was told to make sure she got in safe," and left her on the doorstep with Enid at the door, looking down at her. She took her up to the sitting room and sat her at the tea table. She put her suitcase in Ian's room. She said to Ian, "Your sister's here." They didn't say much when they saw each other, nothing at all — except Ian, who said, "Moppet," and then shut his mouth, as if her name had fallen out by mistake. She told Peel to clean the other bedroom, and went out to buy sheets.

In that evening's post was a letter and a bill from Shoreham.

To Miss Enid Campbell,

Term fees are usually paid in advance but I'm afraid these are in arrears as I was not notified of any change until now and these have not been paid. I understand you will meet the balance forthwith.

Fagus is doing very well and I look forward to welcoming you to our little school.

My warmest regards,

Miss L Barnes

Headmistress

The next morning a wire came from Crowther.

Courts deciding residency in the interim. Have motioned he reside with you. C

She hadn't been to court. How was it they could decide anything? She left the children with Peel and went to see him.

"The wheels are in motion," Crowther said.

"How long before we go before a judge?"

He laughed and puffed out his cheeks. "A while yet, madam. These things are very slow."

"She's sent my daughter to me."

"Isn't that a good thing?"

"And a bill from my son's headmistress."

"It sounds like she's handing them over."

"Then why hasn't she cancelled the fight?"

"She's not after all of them," said Crowther, "is she."

It wasn't a question.

Another wire arrived three weeks later, weeks in which she'd stared at her children and they'd stared at the table, and all had silently agreed that it was rather better if they spent most of their time in their rooms; either one, though they seemed to prefer Ian's. Finetta's was smaller and darker, the window was to the back. Enid moved in a daze. She woke and thought, this can't really be happening, can it? and then would hear Peel getting the children their breakfast, and remember. Sometimes she couldn't manage her post. She left it piling on the hall table, but Peel had received the wire and handed it right to her with her tea. It said: *Ian to reside with you in the interim. Visitation set out. C*

She took the bus.

"Why?"

"Why is he to remain with you?" said Crowther.

"I didn't expect him to."

"I hesitate to say, madam, that you know nothing about the law."

Why should she? She knew nothing about anything — bank accounts and bills, light bulbs and clocks, children. Douglas used to do the former, paid and changed and wound; Everett and Mary the latter. Peel had her hands full; running the kitchen, shopping and meals were all she could manage. That's what she said, anyway.

"So he's to stay with me until we go before a judge?"

"And hopefully after, if I've understood your point correctly," said Crowther.

"And she is allowed to visit?"

"He is set to visit his aunt at regular intervals. See here," he turned the document so she could see it, "the third Saturday in each month. They've asked that he stay at least three nights on each visit."

"Fine," she replied.

She wished she hadn't. The first time he went, she sat at the kitchen table unable to move until he came back. Of course she went to bed and got up again; of course she didn't only sit at the table, but it felt like it — it felt as if, if she held her breath, he'd be home by the time she breathed out. What if she keeps him? she'd said to Crowther. Then our case will be stronger, he'd replied, and she hadn't known whether to laugh or cry.

He came back, not in the clothes she'd sent him in but back, nevertheless, a little boy on her doorstep, dropped off by the Rolls, his teddy under his arm. This time his nanny had to give him a push, and it was she who hurried away as soon as Enid held him.

The next time the third Saturday in the month rolled around, she decided to send Finetta with him. They hadn't asked for her, and she didn't ask Crowther, but having her there in the house while Ian was gone had felt like torture — if she did leave the kitchen table and breathe out, Finetta was there making her hold her breath again, reminding her, not letting her forget.

So she sent her and waited, and tried to make a holiday of it — three days without children, what could she do? She could do anything. She could give Peel the time off and stay in bed all day. She could go to the First Church of Christ and pretend to be a woman in shock, so that all healing hands would be put upon her, or she could go to the park and see the first blossom come out, undisturbed by little hands saying *hurry up*, or *I'm cold*.

She didn't do any of those things. She lay in the bath for as long as possible. She lay in bed listening to the radio. She ate her tea in a cafe on the King's Road, sausages at six o'clock, like a child. The children came back, no nanny this time, dropped off in the Rolls that pulled quietly away, the driver impassive at the wheel, not looking round.

"Did you have a nice time?" she said to Finetta, who held Ian's hand up the steps.

"Very nice, thank you," said Finetta.

The next morning, Crowther was inundated with letters from Joan's lawyers about child welfare and bathing, what constituted an adequate diet and the threat of further court orders if the children were left to play alone in public gardens. They weren't public gardens, they were private, open to residents of Evelyn Gardens and they weren't left alone — she always kept an eye on them from the sitting-room window — but that didn't seem to make any difference to Joan. Anyway, she'd learnt. Messages got through. Finetta must have spent the whole time blabbing. She didn't send her again, and Joan didn't ask to see her, so there it was.

He went, he came back, he went, he came back, on and on it went, into 1927, rolling through spring into summer. As May took hold of London, an infection took hold in his eyes, those eyes of his that still wouldn't look at her. She tried to delay his visit, but Joan threatened her with another court order. Crowther said, "Every row is an expense, madam. I advise you to stick to the arrangements."

"But he has an infection," she replied.

"Is it your fault?"

"She'll say it is," Enid said, picking up her purse, knowing she was beaten.

She packed him off to Joan. She tried to fix his eyes before he went, but they looked terrible.

29

.....

Joan, 1927

THE CAR DREW up and Joan rushed outside. "There you are!" She lifted him from the rich interior of the Rolls. "What's wrong with his eyes?"

Duncan hurried after him. "It looks like an infection, ma'am."

They were red and puffed. Joan held his face to the light from the hall chandelier. He looked like he'd been in a fight. The rims were caked with dry, sore skin and the left eye was hardly open, almost stuck shut. "Call a doctor," she picked him up in her arms, "and McKinley," she headed for the stairs, "and Douglas."

She sat him on her knee, her arms around him. The first time he'd come back she hadn't been able to let go of him at all. Now his visits were dropping into the familiarity of habit; it gnawed at her, she didn't want to get used to it. She held him and kissed his head while the doctor leaned and inspected.

"Pink Eye." The doctor took off his glasses.

"How long will it take to go down?"

"A week, perhaps. It's an infection, not serious, but certainly jolly uncomfortable."

"I know what Pink Eye is. Where would he have caught it?"

"From another child, I should imagine; perhaps playing in the park, some unsavoury bugs on a football, or —"

"Do you still go to the gardens, Ian?" Joan said.

"With Peel." His voice was small.

"And does this Peel play football?" said the doctor.

"Peel is a housekeeper, my sister's. It doesn't matter."

They bathed his eyes in a calming solution and he looked a little better, as if he'd been crying for days, but not as if he'd been punched. She read to him while Nanny Duncan unpacked his case and threw away any clothes they didn't recognise. Peter Rabbit was his favourite of all the stories. He liked it when she said *soporific*, the bunnies so full of lettuce they fell asleep. Sometimes they'd say it at each other till they laughed, but today he was dozing off too, snug against her, warm, safe. She closed the book. She always skipped the part when the bunnies were trapped in the sack.

"Duncan," she said softly, "use these pads again tomorrow, first thing and make sure he keeps his hands nice and clean." She kissed him and tipped him off her knee into Nanny Duncan's arms.

Pat and Douglas were in the drawing room.

"What are we going to do?" Joan lit a cigarette. Pat handed her a gin.

Douglas said, "We're not up till November."

She'd never known the courts would be so slow. A month to agree visitation, six months to get a hearing date and it had just been put back again. "He can't go back like this. I won't have it."

"How could she send him?" said Pat.

"She had no choice," said Douglas.

"And I'm jolly glad," said Joan. "Imagine if she were allowed to hide him away?"

"Make sure you put that report on file," said Pat, reclining on the sofa.

"Can we apply to have him stay till he's better?" said Joan.

"Worth a try," said Douglas. He refilled his drink and plonked himself in the armchair that used to be her mother's. Sybil's retreat to Scotland had lasted; she'd said that she might never come back.

Joan took the armchair on the other side of the hearth. A gin in her hand, she rested her head back, her eyes on the cornicing that ran around the ceiling. This was home forever now — all dreams of flats were gone. Ideas of independence from her family had left with Enid. For a year she'd plunged about in the meeting of the waves; her mother a force to her right, Pat a force to her left, the children the ship she sailed in, as if trying to round the Cape of Good Hope, but being caught in the currents and locked in one place, prevented from sailing anywhere. Her mother's retreat to Scotland had been a blessing. Pat had moved in for good. *Hang the servants,* she'd said when Joan had worried. *Let them talk,* but if they had, Joan hadn't heard it. The chatter of children had blotted out everything. Perhaps when they were old, and this was over, when Ian was safely on his way into adult life, she'd sell this place and take up residence in the apartments on Cumberland Place. They'd have proper privacy there. Who needed an enormous house and far too many staff to manage? Tradesmen saw the address and doubled their prices. But none of this could be dealt with until Enid was dealt with.

It took up every waking hour, and most of her nights too. When she couldn't sleep, she plotted — undoing and rearranging problems in her mind, worrying the padlock that kept her shut out from having it over with. Why couldn't the courts hurry up? Should she try writing to her? What if she tried the same trick and refused to send him back? Then morning would come and Pat would tell her to see sense. Over breakfast she'd give her a million reasons why rational and sanity were the weapons in her hands, that she mustn't throw them away, do something rash, regret it.

She sighed, took a slug of her gin and said, "I'll wire McKinley."

"He should stay at least a week," said Pat.

"Until he's better," said Douglas.

Why was everything up to her? These two in her drawing room — one she loved, the other she tolerated, but both looking to her to do whatever it was that needed doing: hire servants, run the house, manage court, get Ian back — since when was she mother superior? Since she'd welcomed them into the hall all those years ago, that's when. Since she'd stood about with

Douglas, while Fagus held a chair, and Finetta played hop scotch on the tiles, and Mary held Ian. Since Douglas said *can you have them?* and she'd said, *yes.*

"Perhaps we should insist on monthly medical reports," said Pat.

"Force her hand?" said Joan.

"Make her show her colours."

"But then she'll only go and find some quack," said Joan.

"All the better." Pat reached behind her for the ashtray.

"Not for Ian." Joan rested her head again on the back of the armchair.

Douglas sighed, brushed down his trousers and stood up. "All right if I pop up and see him before I go?"

Was this what he'd been like at that ghastly villa, all nonchalance and absence? When he'd handed them over all those years ago, after she'd said yes, and stood in the hall, and Finetta had played hop scotch on the tiles, he'd said *I know you'll take care of them,* as if he knew anything.

She closed her eyes. "Of course, go on up. Although he mayn't be ready. Nanny is bathing him." None of them understood. Pat always said she was too involved and Douglas said hardly anything at all.

30

.....

Enid, 1927

S HE'D BEEN IGNORING the letters from Miss Barnes; the first one, and all the ones after that, the bills that kept dropping through her door with increasingly frank notes saying we really must have this met, and so on. But another three days of waiting yawned ahead of her, and she'd done every other errand, every shopping list and gas bill, every inventory of the linen cupboard and bulbs that had blown. There was nothing left on the list she kept on the kitchen counter; the one she updated and crossed out every day, she'd done everything except see Fagus.

So she had three days. Plenty of time. She could go down, sort out this ridiculous bill, get away, recover. She took a train to Shoreham, and a taxi cab to Castlemere School. The driver knew where it was; he said he often brought parents down, loaded with trunks and sweets. Enid said, "Can you wait?" and rang the bell.

It was more of a house than a school: not very old, white,

pitched-roofed: it looked more like a vicarage. A small woman with neat, bobbed brown hair opened the door.

"I have an appointment with Miss Barnes," said Enid.

"I'm Miss Barnes," said the woman, holding out her hand.

She led Enid into the hall, the air of a school — chalk and ink and desks that tilted up, corridors and the echoing of footsteps. Enid heard chatter and shrieks, a master saying "Quiet" as she passed a door to her right.

They arrived in Miss Barnes' office. "Can I get you refreshment? I understand you've come from London. I do hope your journey wasn't troublesome."

"No trouble at all, thank you." Enid sat down.

The office was neat, like Miss Barnes. A pot plant on the windowsill, a small tidy desk, a wall hung with a green baize board — elastic zigzagging over it, and timetables pinned up. Miss Barnes opened a door to her left and popped her head through. Enid heard her say, "We'll have that coffee now, Miss Pettifore."

"No, no," Enid held up her hand, "I'm quite all right."

"I expect you're eager to see Fagus. He's terribly keen to see you. He's waiting in the library. I can have coffee sent down there if you like."

"He knows I'm here?" Hadn't she expressly said not to get him worked up? Had she not underlined the word *sensitive*? She'd only managed the journey by holding on tight to the thought that he didn't know she was coming, that she could move upon him slowly, perhaps see him first, across a lawn or in a classroom, before she spoke.

Miss Barnes sat down and pushed her glasses up. "I'm told you've been abroad for some years. Miss Campbell —"

"My sister?"

"Indeed. She said you were terribly pleased to be back."

"Did she." Enid studied the blotter: smashes of blue ink on white, half hidden beneath a folder.

"I thought we might deal with housekeeping before you see him. Better to get these things out of the way. Your sister was always most prompt in paying. In the past we sent terms fees to —" she opened the folder, "a Mr. McKinley, Bircham & Co, 46 Parliament Street. Would you like to arrange the same?"

"No," said Enid.

"You'll settle by cheque?"

"If you insist," said Enid, forgetting herself. Why take it out on this woman? This neat and mousey Miss Barnes who knew nothing. Who had Fagus in her care.

The thing was, she'd shut him out. The thing was, she'd pushed him to the furthest, darkest recesses of her mind, hoping she'd forget. Three children to care for. This wasn't what she'd wanted. Well, only for a minute, but that minute, those moments, had passed. Three children to care for, and she couldn't.

She got her cheque book out of her purse.

"Thank you," said Miss Barnes, blotting it and putting it away. She held the door. "Shall we?"

Enid got out of her chair. The library was back along the same corridor, past shrieks and chatter and masters saying "Quiet."

Through the hall, and along another passage. Miss Barnes left her at the door.

It was more of a room with books. Not a library; not something head-to-toe in spines, with ladders and deep armchairs and pipes. Fagus sat at a table. His legs were too long to swing now. His toes were tucked under; he held the table edge, he sniffed the air like a dog.

"Fagus." Her voice came out wrong, like an arrow fired when her arm wasn't ready.

"Mummy?"

She couldn't move.

"They said you were coming."

He was grown so big; she'd missed it all over again. He was a youth in uniform, whose body had taken over. It strained at the seams of his blazer, his shorts drew up from his knees, his socks fell down.

She wiped her nose and went over to him. She drew up a chair beside him. "I've come to see you."

"I knew you would." He smiled.

She took his hands in hers. "Do they treat you well here?"

"Oh yes, frightfully well."

"And you've a comfortable bed?" Why had she asked that? What difference did it make?

"Oh yes. We sing songs."

"In bed?" He needed a haircut. His fringe fell almost to his eyes.

"In the dorm. At night. Mary sits with me."

"Mary?"

"She's one of the housemaids. She's frightfully nice. She puts me to bed."

She thought he'd been talking about Mary at Cherry Trees. "Why does she put you to bed?"

"None of the others are blind, Mamma —"

He hadn't called her that since he was little.

"Only me and Mary takes care of me."

She let go of him. She'd never heard him say *blind*, either.

"Miss Barnes says you'll take me for luncheon. Mondays is left overs, so I'm glad. Mary says there's a place the other boys go with their parents. What'll you have? I'd like chops and rice pudding. Can I have that?"

The taxicab was still waiting outside. She'd forgotten. "Hang on a minute, Fagus, my driver, I just have to —"

She ran outside. She could get in and tell him to head for the station. She could. What good had she ever done? She could drive away. Fagus would remember it as some strange interlude in his half-lit life, someone would explain it to him as another erratic move from his strange, half-crazed mother. She leaned in at the driver's window. "Do you know a place for lunch? Near here? The other boys go there."

"The Grenadiers."

"Can you wait?"

She ran back inside. Fagus hadn't moved.

"Jolly good. Shall we go? Where shall I find your coat?"

"I think Mary left it over there." He pointed toward another chair.

She got him into the cab in slow, precise movements. The hall, the doorways, the steps, each of these with her arm through his.

The Grenadiers was exactly the kind of place a mother took her son for lunch, or a man his mistress — as she guided Fagus in, they passed a couple shielding their mouths in a corner. Douglas had got it right. Take a mistress, lose the wife, loan the children. The best of every world. Had he been down to see Fagus? She had no idea.

"There's chops," said Enid, reading the menu.

"I'll have chops and mash and jam roly-poly," said Fagus.

"I'll have the soup," said Enid to the waitress.

While they waited she poured them both some water. "Here, Fagus." She held it out to him. His hand wavered over the table until he found it.

"Thank you, Mamma."

He sipped and put it down, but his fork was in the way. It tipped — she only just caught it. She put it beside the little vase of flowers set between them. "Put your napkin on your lap."

He felt for his napkin and slid it carefully towards him.

"And what do you do at school?" she said, as if they'd been talking merrily all along.

"Lots of things."

"I hear you study French."

"Madame Santiere left, and the new master prefers book work. He says, when am I going to France anyway. Shall I go to France, Mamma? I should like to. *Demain, dès l'aube, à l'heure où blanchit la campagne, je partirai. Vois-tu, je sais que tu m'attends.*"

"Stop it, Fagus."

"It's by Victor Hugo, Mamma. I know it by heart. *J'irai par la forêt, j'irai par la montagne. Je ne puis demeurer loin de toi plus longtemps.*"

"That's enough, Fagus."

"It's called 'Tomorrow at Dawn.' *Je marcherai les yeux fixés sur mes pensées, Sans rien voir au dehors, sans entendre aucun bruit, seul, inconnu, le dos courbé, les mains croisées, triste, et le jour pour moi sera comme la nuit.*"

"Why don't you tell it to me after lunch?"

"Madame Santiere said I had a beautiful speaking voice. She said I made her cry. *Je ne regarderai ni l'or du soir qui tombe, ni les voiles au loin descendant vers Harfleur, et quand j'arriverai, je mettrai sur ta tombe un bouquet de houx vert et de bruyère en fleur.*"

"I said, that's enough," said Enid.

"That's the end, anyway. Shall I translate it for you?"

"I know what it's about."

"It's about Victor Hugo going to his daughter's grave."

"I know what it's about," said Enid again. Every child learnt it. She'd learnt it with her own governess.

"Do you speak French, Mamma?"

"Everyone speaks French, Fagus."

"Oh."

"Not as well as you."

"Oh."

"Your chops are here. Move your hands."

His plate was put in front of him. He felt for his cutlery.

"How many are there?"

"Don't poke them."

"Shall I cut here?"

"That's the bone."

He sawed, his knife got stuck; he pushed and it shot out, sending a potato onto the tablecloth.

"Wait." She put her soup aside and picked up his plate. "There." She passed it back to him.

"Have you cut it up into pieces?" He swapped his fork to his other hand.

"Try to use both hands."

The waitress came over. "Can I get you anything else?"

"Another napkin," said Enid. Hers was messed with lamb chop, her fingers sticky. She tried her soup. A thick mushroom broth.

Fagus chewed slowly. "Can I pick up the bones?"

"I should think not." It was hard to eat while watching him, his elbows and arms, the edge of the plate, gravy and spuds, his glass of water too near.

"They won't let me use my hands at school either." He felt for his glass. His fingernails knocked against it.

"Put your knife down while you drink." She held it steady until he'd grasped it.

She tried her soup again. Revolting. She must breathe. "And have you seen Papa?"

"Oh yes," said Fagus. "He comes to see me quite a lot. At least once a term. We normally have tea in the library. He brought a friend with him last time. She gave me a whole bag of sweets."

He lowered the glass, but it was too near the plate. She thought he was going to let go of it. "Fagus," she cried.

He jumped. Water splashed onto his hand. He swung his arm one way and knocked the vase of flowers; then the other, and the bottom of his glass caught the edge of his plate and went flying over it, water everywhere. The crash made everyone look. Enid leapt up — Fagus felt for the edge of the table but found his plate instead, too late to not pull, and his lunch, his chops and gravy and boiled potatoes, went piling off the table onto his lap.

Waitresses came running with cloths.

"I'm sorry, Mamma."

"No, no." She couldn't stop shaking.

They mopped him up, and Enid wiped his face.

"Mary usually helps me."

"She sounds nice."

"She's terribly nice, Mamma." He was covered in gravy stains and damp. "Are we going?"

She held his hand. "I'll come and see you again very soon."

"But we haven't had pudding."

"We'll have pudding next time."

"Papa usually comes at Christmas too."

"With his lady friend?" said Enid. They reached the doors. Someone had gone to get them a cab.

"He usually brings me something."

"And Aunt Joan?" It had just come out, falling like the water and the plate.

"Oh yes, Dodo comes all the time, too. During the holidays, mostly."

"So you've lots of visitors." It was a statement, not a question.

"Quite a lot," said Fagus.

A cab drew up and they went out to meet it. Enid spoke to the driver: "Can you take him to Castlemere School? They'll pay the fare."

"Shall you not come with me?" said Fagus at the open window.

"I have to catch my train." She leant in and kissed him quickly, her cheek against his while the cab chugged vapours into the warm May air.

31

.....

Enid, 1928

Dear Dodo,

On Sunday Nanny came for Ian. "Enid the brute" happened to be having a bath, so I saw Nanny she said she was dressing my dolly; After, she had gone when I was tidying my cupboard I wanted so much to see you, that I cryed! It seems babyish to say that but I did.

Once when Peel didn't want to take us to church and, "Enid the brute" was not going, she went down and had a lot of talk with Peel, came up again and put me strait to bed for the rest of the day and i was in bed from 11'oc till the next morning.

Will you pay for the stamp's of the letters I send because I dere not buy stamp's 'cos I might get into trouble. I am sorry it is such a short letter but I must get up now. Don't write back or I will get into trouble.

Love from your always loving
Moppet
xoxoxoxoxo

Enid folded the letter and stuffed it into the pocket of her skirt. The Rolls was waiting in the street with Ian in it. It was lucky she'd checked his suitcase. She'd found notes like this before. She clipped it shut and called down the hall, "Peel? Come and get his things."

From the sitting-room window she watched Peel hand the suitcase to Duncan. Over a year had passed since Ian arrived — that's what she called it now, *arrived* — as if he'd come in a cab with a suitcase too.

She looked in on Finetta, little spy that she was. She'd thought she'd stopped the messages in their tracks until she'd started finding notes hidden in Ian's suitcase. How many had got through that she wasn't aware of? How many had been posted in secret?

Finetta was busy with her bird book, bent over it, sticking in pictures. She didn't look up. Tape and scissors lay on the floor beside her. Joan had sent it to her for Christmas; it was enormous, with hard covers in green fabric and large empty green paper pages, waiting for things to be stuck in it. Finetta had chosen birds, which was lucky, because when Enid had seen it she'd said *a scrap book, you could stick* — and then hadn't been able to think of anything. For Ian, Joan had sent a mass of little things, all wrapped individually — little tin cars and trains and soldiers. He kept them under the bed, she'd seen them there. Finetta said he was opening one package at a time, one every week or something. Nothing had come from Scotland; or perhaps her mother had sent packages to Bryanston Square for him to open there. She didn't know. She didn't want to know.

Just as she had at Didlington, she'd written a number of times to her mother, and a number of times torn the letters up. What could she say? Help me? If her mother cared, she'd have held her hand while she cried in the window seat at Cherry Trees, a clean dress on, her hair brushed for the first time in days, Ian on show in the cot, Finetta held by Mary. She wouldn't have smiled and clapped her hands and turned her face the other way. She wouldn't have given everything to Joan when she knew Enid had nothing. She'd have come to Didlington Hall. She'd have come to Evelyn Gardens. She'd have tried to comfort her.

But she hadn't. Nothing had come from her mother, no attempt at correspondence, not even letters of rage. The silence was like a wall that she couldn't stop looking at.

"Come and have tea, Finetta."

"Yes, Mamma." Finetta closed her book and got up. She followed Enid to the sitting room where Peel had put the tea things — a large pot, two cups, a plate of herring sandwiches.

"Would you like to pour?"

Finetta had her hair in pigtails; she'd learnt to do it all herself. She must have read it in a book somewhere, a girls' annual or something. Peel took them to the library sometimes, a concept that Enid had needed explaining. *Whose library?* she'd said. *The public library, ma'am. Oh,* Enid had replied. Well, if she wouldn't take them to church, then it would have to do.

Crowther had told her to play down the whole *Christian Science fancy,* find some other church to take the children to and other friends to meet, ones that were *less conspicuous.* Those were the words he'd chosen, as if Ruby and her religion stuck out like the sandstone ship off Sloane Street. Other friends? She didn't have any. The community in Norfolk were the only people she had. She'd taken the children to Didlington Hall three times in the past year and it had been rather jolly, at least for Ruby who'd gone simply mad over both of them, but especially Ian. Enid had kept the details vague when she'd written the first time. *Children with me after all. Shall we come for a few days' visit?* If Ruby had had her way they'd have moved in for good; as it was, they'd stayed a week longer than planned. It had been early summer, and Ruby had asked Ian to pick a winner from the runners and riders at the next race meet. He'd picked three in a row. Enid had never seen him so animated. He melted into Ruby as if she was his mother. Ruby had said he must have the most simply marvellous magical powers, and exclaimed she wanted to keep him forever. Enid had replied *you'll have to get past Joan first,* and Ruby had touched her arm and smiled her try-to-be-brave smile. As far as Ruby knew now, Joan had started it, which she sort of had if you went back far enough, which Enid did whenever her thoughts threatened to madden her. But anyway, Crowther put a stop to her going to Didlington, advised her to be *less conspicuous,* so she'd written to Ruby that they'd have to hold fire for a while. She'd found a church in Fulham instead, a *normal* church full of *normal people*, where she stuck out instead. Peel wasn't keen on it either. Peel turned out to be a Seventh Day Adventist, which didn't help anyone.

Finetta picked up the pot. It was almost as big as her. Not quite, thought Enid, brushing the ridiculous thought away. But Finetta had to hold it with both hands and pour very carefully; it took all her concentration, like the bird book.

"That's plenty," said Enid, watching the tea rise in the cup. Finetta put the pot down. "Come and sit. Have a sandwich."

They sat together, mother and daughter, one playing with the ring on her finger, the other taking a tiny nibble at a sandwich.

Enid's gaze drifted around the room. She'd brought the armchairs from Cherry Trees and the tea table and drinks bureau. Her sitting room in Fulham looked like the one in Cherry Trees had been picked up and squashed and suspended three flights above the earth. Only one of the rugs had fitted, and even it didn't fit terribly well: it flipped up against the far wall. Douglas would have done something about it. He was always rather good at fixing things. He'd have filled the drinks bureau too. She'd got as far as buying sherry.

He'd agreed to a divorce on her terms. She'd heard from him not long ago. She hadn't been able to understand it. She'd taken the paperwork to Crowther. "Does this mean there's no row?"

"The petition is from your sister."

"But if I sign this I have custody?"

"As I say —"

"But why is he doing this? Doesn't he want them?"

"I suspect he wants a divorce more."

"Then she won't have a case."

"She's petitioning for custody only of her heir. It is a different case entirely to that of your marriage, madam."

"I thought he was joint petitioner."

"He is — in other words, he is supporting your sister's case while extracting himself from the firing line."

That was Douglas all over, but she'd been shocked at how she'd felt the day the decree absolute dropped through her letter box. She hadn't loved him, she hadn't wanted him; he certainly didn't want her, and yet she'd wavered in the hall, the envelope discarded, the papers in her hand. She'd looked at it and felt small. At least he'd changed the names on their bank accounts. Her allowance, the allowance that used to run Cherry Trees, all £41 a month, still arrived at Coutts & Co, but it was hers.

"May I get down, Mamma?" Finetta had eaten half a sandwich.

"Yes." Enid crossed her legs the other way and touched the letter in the pocket of her skirt. Nothing on Finetta's face betrayed it. Enid the Brute. Enid the Brute. "You can go to your room." Of course she was doing it to pally up to Joan, but still, these thoughts were like seeds, planted and growing in her daughter's mind, with no way of plucking them out. All she could do was keep Finetta here and hope they died away. She wasn't a brute; she was desperate. She didn't know what to do with any of them. If you didn't know what to do with a child, everyone knew you sent it to its room.

Finetta closed the door behind her, and Enid relaxed a little. She poured herself another cup of tea; this one a little tepid and a little strong, but it would do. Here she was, on her own at the table again: same old room, same old second cup of tea while the mantel clock ticked. Every day was like this — a long drag into the unknown that turned out to be familiar and relentless. She'd started going to the Chelsea Arts Club to fill the time — at least everyone there seemed as misfit as her. No one took any notice of a lone woman with a book in the garden, and exhibitions were so packed with extraordinary-looking people that Enid felt quite plain. She wasn't, of course. Even now, even ageing, someone would stop her and say *you must sit for me, you have such eyes,* or some such thing. She hadn't said yes to anyone yet. It felt too carefree a thing to do when it was all she could manage to stay upright each day. She had to save her concentration for the silent teas and endless suppers — more than once she'd gone to bed and left Peel to it, kitchen and everything. What had she done with the children before? She couldn't remember. She'd had Everett and Mary, a villa, a husband who came and went and a family somewhere, silent but behind her.

Life at Cherry Trees looked strange now. A comfort, a glow, soft days and ham hock bubbling in the kitchen; a life of rarely getting dressed, of occasional doctors come to check on her, occasional rows with Douglas and bleak promises to get up. None of the roar and dirt of London; none of the dark, narrow corridors and dark, narrow stairs of a tall house in Fulham. No sense that any child was waiting for her. In this house she couldn't escape the feeling that they knew she was there, in the next room or downstairs, that they held their breath when she came upon them, that they only half played. What did other mothers do? Perhaps she should send them to school. But Ian was too young, and Finetta had already learnt to read and write — that was clear from her notes. Joan must have taught her.

At some point, with all the money she didn't have, she would have to find Finetta a governess; some organised woman who'd teach her French and piano, some German too, although unremarkably it had gone out of fashion. She'd have to do something with her anyway, at least until she was old enough to be sent on her own tour of Italian churches. Except who would go with her? There was no aunt to get her skirts caught in a gig. There was only Joan who'd teach her to smoke and play blackjack, if she taught her anything more at all. Joan — who'd as likely not want her either.

At least Finetta was resourceful and contained. Ian threw a presence about him as if Joan were behind his eyes, seeing into the room, the living, breathing mass of her; the gin and Turkish smokes, the careless abandon that made Enid mad. There was always something different about him when he came home: a missing coat or a new toy, his hair cut or a sudden refusal to eat tongue. Crowther told her not to get lost in detail.

Three days to wait until he came back. She could go to see Fagus again. She always meant to. Each time a thousand letters from Joan resulted in dates they could both tolerate, she thought *I shall go to Castlemere. It will pass the time admirably.* She had such plans. But then the trains failed, or her nerves failed. It was too cold, too icy, a terrible winter storm, and worries she'd never get home again. The summer holidays had come and she didn't want to bump into Joan. Christmas had come, and she'd reassured herself that Douglas always went at Christmas. Bills came, and she thought *I can't afford the train fare.* Her little boy was being shut out of her heart, and she thought *I mustn't disturb him with my worries. He has his nice housemaid who puts him to bed and sings with him at lights out.*

He'd brought her back from Norfolk. His birthday had jogged her senses into being, for one brief summer of watching other mothers play, and thinking she could do it. But her one brief visit had scared her. He wasn't a child swinging his legs on a bench anymore or a huddled mass beneath the covers of his bed. He was the living breathing embodiment of everything she'd done wrong. He was the child who had made her heart sing, the handshake with the devil that had cracked her apart and then him. Fagus. Her boy. She couldn't stand it.

In the comfort of her armchair, the tea things left on the table for Peel, Enid told herself for the hundredth time that disturbing him was selfish, that he was better cocooned in the known black world of Castlemere, that she would only make him cry.

32

.....

Joan, 1929

MCKINLEY WATCHED THE clock and gathered statements, Ian came and went, and Joan stared down the date of her first court appearance as if it was birth — unstoppable, inexorable, something she had no choice but to get through.

It came at last, and she wore blue. A dark belted dress, a fur wrap, a hat that sat low on her eyes, chosen by Pat who strode, chin up, beside her. On the pavement outside the chancery division of the High Court, a few members of the press were gathered; flash bulbs went off as Pat and Joan hurried in.

McKinley greeted them in the hall. "We're first up."

The narrow glass doors to Court 14 were open, and McKinley stood aside to let Joan pass before him. She squeezed along a bench in the high-walled coffin of books and robes. Green velvet curtains hung over the entire wall behind the perch where the judge would sit.

"We've got Merrivale," said McKinley quietly.

"Is he good?" said Pat.

"Very hot on tradition," said McKinley.

Joan didn't know if that was good or bad. She couldn't speak. She leant forward and looked along the row of knees to Enid, half-obscured by the belly of her counsel.

Two years had told Joan nothing new about her. Ian still arrived nervous and thin, and still left miserable. She'd won him for a stay in Scotland so that he could see his grandmother, but Sybil, dampened by rain and the ruin of her family, had been ill. She'd spent most of his visit cocooned in her bed, wrapped to the eyeballs in eiderdown.

The curtains shifted, a gap opened up, and from a small hidden door came the judge. Everybody got to their feet. Lord Merrivale climbed to his perch and settled, his robes flapping and his eyes old and narrow above beaked nose and ermine collar.

Douglas was first to the stand. His shoes squeaked across the parquet floor.

Their barrister was called Smithson. McKinley had recommended him. Joan thought he looked like a child, not old enough to carry the weight of her future anywhere. He smiled at Douglas, and they got through the preliminaries while Joan unwrapped a boiled sweet. She wished she could have some water. They'd got drunk last night, in horrid anticipation, and she hadn't been able to stomach more than a coffee for breakfast. Now she felt sick. Her mouth was dry, her belly wailed for food.

Douglas rested his hands on the sill of the witness box as if he was on the deck of a ship looking out to sea, the waters decidedly choppy.

Smithson said, "In your affidavit, you state that, during your marriage, your wife was reluctant to fulfil her duties. Could you expand on this?"

"She spent very little time with our children, very little time with their care in mind," said Douglas. "She was unresponsive, un-naturally gloomy; she took to her bed as often as possible, not like a normal mother at all. She shunned society altogether, mine and that of our children and her wider family. She closed down, often refusing to get dressed at all."

"And what was the effect on the children of this abnormal behaviour?"

"They were very ill-affected by it." His voice was flat. "My daughter was extremely shy, my eldest became a cripple, and, although my youngest was very young when she left, since she snatched him he has developed an extremely nervous disposition. I see no reason to believe she has changed her ways. Our medic called it Mother's Blues. He said she'd likely snap out of it."

"And did she?"

"She took off."

"Leaving her children."

"Yes."

"A crippled son, a daughter — and Ian."

"Yes."

"Did she attempt to see any of her children for the years she was gone?"

"She did not."

Joan looked along the line. Her statue-sister had not moved an inch from her position. Eyes front, mouth shut, shoulders back.

Smithson said, "How did the crippling of your eldest son come about?"

"He fell down the stairs when he was four years old."

"These were stairs at the home of Lady George Campbell. Was he left to go up unaccompanied?"

"I believe so."

"Had he not a nanny?"

"She was with my daughter. Enid was supposed to be with him."

"But she wasn't."

"No."

"And what was her response to this tragedy? I expect, as any normal mother would be, she was distraught and felt terribly guilty."

"She was distraught, all right. I don't know about guilt. She got it into her head that it was something to do with sin. She'd dabbled in unusual spiritual practices when she was young, before I'd met her, but I thought she'd given them up. When Fagus fell she took up with the Christian Scientists."

"And they are?"

"A sect, from America. A cult who think illness is a sin which can only be cured by prayer. They've been over here preaching their nonsense for a while, so I understand. The main thing is that they don't believe in medicine. I discovered my former wife was throwing our son's prescriptions away and tying him to a chair. She believed her prayers would bring back his sight, the strength in his limbs —" He held the rail.

"You stopped her?"

"I stopped her immediately, of course. He made some recovery quite quickly. It was a while ago. He can walk steadily enough, but his eyesight is not recovered."

"He's blind."

"Yes."

"And is your former wife still a member of the Christian Scientists?"

"I believe she is."

They'd had her followed.

Smithson cleared his throat. "Tell me, sir — what in your opinion are the qualities which make up a woman's fitness to be a mother?"

Joan bit her lip. Please God, let him say it right.

"Love, tenderness, patience, a firm hand, solid Christian morals, and most necessarily, a sound mind."

Lord Merrivale leaned from his perch. "And in your opinion, sir, does Miss Enid Campbell possess these qualities?"

Knocked by the voice from above, Douglas shifted to see him. "No, my Lord, I believe she possesses none of them."

Smithson sat down and Enid's council stood up. A man called Crowther. McKinley had said *never heard of him*.

"Mr. Anstruther," her man Crowther curled one hand in the other, "what proof do you have that Miss Enid Campbell is a Christian Scientist?"

"She spent two years living with them. I understand she visits a church in Chelsea. She tied our eldest son to a chair, and read the Christian Science manual over him. Isn't that enough?"

"Enough proof? No, I'm afraid it is not. Did you not think she was searching for solace? That her son had suffered a terrible injury, and that she was carrying another child, a child forced on her under threat of losing an inheritance promised to her?"

"Promised to him."

"Promised to her immediate family."

"She wasn't under threat."

"As a result of his injuries, Lady George Campbell saw fit to disinherit him, leaving her fortune — hanging —" The pause filled the courtroom. He smiled and turned to Lord Merrivale. "My Lord, Miss Enid Campbell is not a Christian Scientist. She has joined no church; she subscribes to no doctrine, other than that of the good and honest Presbyterian beliefs of her mother, Lady George. Her behaviour immediately following her son's accident *was* erratic and ill-thought-out, but here was a mother distraught — suffering not only the loss of her eldest son's faculties but the loss of a security — a security promised to her on the death of her brother. Yes, she fled to friends in Norfolk who dabbled in unusual practices but where else —" he looked at Douglas again, "do you suggest she might have gone? Did she not give you another son? Did she not put aside everything to provide her mother with an heir? Is she not allowed friends?"

Douglas said nothing. Crowther lowered his eyebrows and carried on. "Mother's Blues. Had you ever heard of such a thing before you were married?"

"No," said Douglas.

"Grief?"

"Of course."

"Exhaustion?"

"This is ridiculous," said Douglas.

"What about fidelity? Is that ridiculous too?"

Douglas opened his mouth and shut it again.

Crowther said, "Would you not consider that a lack of fidelity on your part, preceded by the loss of her father and brother, and coupled by the strain of childbirth thrice over, mayn't have contributed to the state of sadness and listlessness, the *not getting out of bed and joining society,*" he read from his notes, "that you accuse her of?"

"Everybody lost someone —"

"I was unaware that number of sufferers softens the impact of grief."

"— and I was perfectly faithful until she ceased to fulfil her side of the bargain."

"I'm so glad we've established your infidelity as her fault," said Crowther.

"I fulfilled my role, and I expected her to do the same. Plenty of women cope perfectly well without going off their heads."

"Or so you think. Perhaps your own mother cried in the night when you could not hear her. Perhaps your own father saw fit to earn enough income to make his wife independent of her family."

"I couldn't possibly make Enid independent of her family," snapped Douglas.

"And luckily for us all, that issue is not up for debate," said Crowther. He bowed quickly to Merrivale, and Joan breathed out.

33

.....

Enid, 1929

JOAN'S FACE LOOKED out of control, as if she couldn't decide whether to scream or go to sleep. She'd never seen her sister so discomposed. Not dishevelled; she'd none of the lounger, head back, arm raised to shield an aching head from the sun, about her. She was clipped into her suit like a soldier, but her face — she looked scared. Enid watched her take the stand.

Their man was bent over his file, talking in whispers to McKinley. Enid recognised him from the drawing room at Bryanston Square all those years ago, when their mother would call him in to discuss her Will in vaguely threatening tones.

"Miss Campbell," their man began, "how long was your nephew in your care?"

"Two years," replied Joan. She gripped the rail as Douglas had.

"On what arrangement?"

"When my sister deserted her children, their father brought them to me. We had no reason to believe she would come back, and this was why no formal arrangement was made."

"Do you believe that your sister is fit to be a mother?"

"No."

"And your feelings for your nephew?"

"He is extremely dear to me."

"And sole heir to your estate?"

"Yes."

"No matter who he resides with?"

"That is correct."

"I am told by his nanny, a Miss Duncan, that you are equally dear to him. We shall hear from her in due course. In the meantime, madam, would you care to outline to this court why you feel it is imperative that he be returned to you?"

"Certainly. My nephew is set to inherit a substantial fortune."

It could be their mother up there.

"So being, he will become an influential member of society."

They looked so alike.

"He will need adequate training — not merely in education, which, under my guidance, he will receive at Eton, but daily example of good behaviour, acceptable religious morals, and the highest social connections. None of these are available to him under the doubtful guardianship of his mother. My sister is an outcast from normal society —"

She couldn't stop staring at Joan's hands, so still, so rigid, clasped on the edge of the stand, the words tumbling over them.

"— She lacks any maternal instinct, and is wholly incapable of meeting any needs other than her own. With me, my nephew will receive the best of everything; with me, he will be properly equipped for the life that awaits him on my death. He inherits not only a fortune, but a name — it is for society's good, not my own, that he must be taught to carry the twin burdens of our blood. An inheritance steeped in ancestry — what is the good of one without the other? What is the good of either, if a child lacks instruction? I think not only of him, but of his children and grandchildren. We are but guardians; all we do is pass it on. Without my hand to guide my nephew, his fortune will be frittered or stolen, and society will lose a useful member; worse, the damage his mother has wrought will be felt for generations to come."

Would she never stop? Would she never shut up? Enid wanted to scream *I am here, you know* — but of course she knew. She even looked at her for a moment.

"Thank you, Miss Campbell," said their man. A child. All of twenty. "Most eloquent. Most eloquent indeed."

There was a pain along the centre of Enid's back. She dropped her head and stretched her neck. She heard it click. When she raised her head again, Crowther was already standing. She couldn't afford a solicitor *and* a barrister. Crowther had said he was quite used to doing both.

He smiled at Joan, who didn't smile back. "Thank you, Miss Campbell. What a fine speech, and may I say how generous it is of you to temporarily desert the grandeur of your life, to stand in this simple court room, and declare your sister unfit to raise an heir but not, I understand, a pauper cripple, or his equally poor sister, who —" he raised his hand as if Joan had been about to interrupt him, but she hadn't. Joan was staring open-mouthed but nothing was coming out of it. Crowther carried on, "— are as dear to her. You say you had no reason to believe she would come back; yet she did — at which point you refused to return her children to her."

It was Crowther who'd advised her. She'd told him she was going to agree custody, but he'd said, *did you sign?*

"That is a lie." Joan banged her hand on the rail. "She never asked for any of them. She invited Ian for tea and snatched him. Finetta she didn't ask to see at all."

"My Lord, Miss Enid Campbell will be called to speak under oath. She will tell the court that she did not give custody to her husband in the matter of their divorce. In point of fact, custody was given to her. It was when she asked to see them that she learnt they had already been given to their aunt. Following on from this shock, she demanded that at least her son be sent for tea. Her actions, although wholly regrettable, must be seen in context."

"In context of a total fabrication," exclaimed Joan.

"Then can you explain why you went on to send her daughter after him? I also understand you notified the headmistress of your eldest nephew's school —" Crowther paused to address Lord Merrivale. "The eldest nephew is the cripple, my Lord."

Lord Merrivale nodded.

Crowther continued, "— that Miss Enid Campbell would now

be paying the bills. In other words, although you claim she didn't want them, you allowed them all to go."

"I believed she should have *some* responsibility for her off-spring."

"But not all," said Crowther. "Only the ones you didn't want." He smiled again. "Let us return to the subject of your fine speech. I must say that it is somewhat unusual to hear a spinster aunt divulge the secrets of motherhood. Do tell me more, Miss Campbell. Childbirth, for example. Does social standing make a difference to how that is conducted? I have shocked you, madam. I do apologise, but this is a court of law and questions must be asked."

"I'm perfectly aware of what this is," said Joan.

Crowther rubbed his palms together. "Jolly good. Excellent. We are off to a flying start, are we not? Then do tell me, as we are all aware of where we are, why your youngest nephew deserves your superior care while your crippled eldest nephew and his sister do not?"

"Neither of them are my heir."

"Is this all a question of money, madam? Have you not said that your sister is unfit to be a mother?"

"It was never my intention to strip her of her children. Fagus and Finetta were old enough to know her when she left and remember her when she came back. Ian was not. He had no memory of her at all. As far as he was concerned, I was his mother."

"But you are not, and nor shall you ever be. Your sister, Miss

Enid Campbell, is. Now, either she is fit to be a mother to all her children, or she is not. Fortunately, we have our learned judge —" he waved his hand at Lord Merrivale, who scowled into his ermine collar, "— to answer that most perplexing of questions. I understand you have never married, Miss Campbell."

The sudden turn of questioning caught Joan by surprise. Enid could see it in the way she moved her head, as if a tennis ball had gone whizzing past her nose, missing it by a whisker. When she found her voice she said, "That is correct."

Crowther said, "But you have a companion, a Miss Dansey."

Enid was tempted to look along the line, but she didn't. Why shouldn't they use it? Crowther had said not to hold back. He'd said he'd seen families rip each other to shreds in these court rooms. He'd said they'd use everything too.

Joan said nothing. Crowther carried on. "I understand she is great pals with Mrs. Nicholson and Mrs. Trefusis."

"Relevance," shouted Lord Merrivale.

"Forgive me." Crowther bent obsequiously to Lord Merrivale. "I am so easily side-tracked. I should have said that I understand she is great pals with women in general. Will she also be taking part in the raising of this special boy, should he be so fortunate as to be ripped from his mother?"

"My Lord!" Their man was on his feet.

"Get to the point, Crowther," shouted Lord Merrivale.

"Newspapers are so scurrilous, are they not?" continued Crowther. "It must have been frightful to have been mentioned so — so often, and with such — innuendo. I have looked, but have failed to find any such — such scandalous material surrounding the friends of Miss Enid Campbell; friends you've done your best to imply are not of the sort to be anywhere near such a child as your nephew. Divorce, yes, that is unsavoury; a brief dalliance with unusual spiritual practices in a time of great upset — in the context we can all see how this may have come about — but can we be sure that a spinster aunt and her —" he coughed. "I'm so sorry. Might I have a glass of water? I seem to have something stuck in my throat."

A clerk ran off while they waited. When he returned, glass of water in hand, Crowther drank it slowly. He put the empty glass down. "Forgive me. Where was I? Ah, yes, the relationship between you and Miss Dansey. Is the household of a spinster aunt, and her *friend*, one in which a young man can safely gain a proper understanding of the natural world?"

Enid never knew how the meaning of a word could be changed mid-sentence, but Crowther had done it; he'd leant on the word *friend*, as if he were doing Joan a favour, as if he were being nice. Joan looked faint. Crowther said, "May I get you a chair?"

"No."

"Very well. Do you believe it is your right to have the child?"

"Yes."

"As it is your right to be sole beneficiary of your mother's estate?"

"Yes."

"Despite the fact that had your brother lived it would have been his, and you and your sister left equally at his mercy?"

"But my brother did not live, and my mother decided she could no longer sail the ship alone. She wished to be rid of it long before my sister absconded; that act only shored up her mind. She wished it to be in safe hands, and as her heir was only two years old, and his mother vanished, she gave it to me. I am merely a caretaker."

"And what a caretaker you are."

"No ship can be sailed by two captains."

"But must the lucky captain throw her sister overboard?"

"I didn't throw her. She jumped."

"So it's her fault that she's destitute and fighting for her son?"

"Yes."

"Despite providing your family with a much-needed heir, an heir which you failed to provide yourself? Would it be fair to say that you have always wanted a son, but finding yourself disinclined to the company of men, unearthed the perfect alternative?"

"How dare you!"

"If Miss Enid would agree to be seen by a medic, and that medic to declare her fit, would you be content to drop your petition?"

"She is not to be trusted."

"That does not answer my question, madam."

"You don't know her. She'll ruin him."

"I believe a medic is the correct person to assess her, don't you?"

"She'll lie, she'll pretend to be absolutely perfect and the next minute be flinging chairs across rooms."

"Or children downstairs?"

"Precisely." Joan banged her palm on the edge of the stand.

"However, she did not fling her child downstairs. He fell. Yet she was made to feel that his fall, blindness and crippling were her fault. Have you been jealous of your sister from the nursery?"

"Crowther," barked Lord Merrivale.

"I do apologise." Crowther backed away, his hand shielding his face as if Lord Merrivale were about to swoop and peck his eyes out. "Relationships between siblings can be so fraught. I imagine it is the same for Miss Finetta and Master Ian. Perhaps it is better they remain separated from each other — one in the shabby environs of Fulham, the other in the sumptuous surrounds of Bryanston Square. Let us hope the young lady is able to marry out of her poverty and that the young man shows mercy to their crippled brother. His fortune will certainly be enough for all three of them, should he learn the generosity of spirit so vital in a gentleman of power. No, I cannot see a way out of it — my Lord, give the boy to his aunt. The rest of his family must be left to rot without him."

Lord Merrivale sighed. "Is that it, Crowther?"

Crowther bowed, and returned to his desk, while a clerk helped Joan from the stand.

34

.....

Enid, 1964

S HE CAME TO in the prayer room. Mandy sat beside her.
The room was hardly used; at least, Enid hardly used it.
Chairs in a circle, a stack of books on a table by the wall. A
teasmade and tray of cups, a vase of flowers. There were weekly
prayers, and an occasional guest speaker, just like the old days
at Didlington; but she didn't need prayers now. She needed Ian.

Not for the same reason she'd needed him then. That was over.
Done.

"Do you need anything, Enid?" said Mandy, squeezing her
hand.

She wanted to laugh.

"It's just gone three. We thought you might like to change
into something clean. Your dress is back."

"Did you telephone her?"

Mandy sighed. "Now look here, Enid. We tried her at home

again, but there was no answer, see? Your Finetta must have gone out early. We didn't have the number."

Not if she was meeting Ian. If she was meeting Ian, she'd have — Enid didn't know what Finetta would have done. Set her hair? Gone for lunch? A brother and sister together — she didn't even know if they saw each other. Were they bosom pals, or had she not seen him for twenty-five years either? No. That was impossible; they'd lived together for so long. Finetta must have planned it. That's what she'd done. Some mismatched effort at forgiveness, his forgiveness of her for keeping him away so long. It was clear to her now. Ian had always wanted to see her, but Finetta had said she was dreadful, cowardly, a *brute*. He'd got his way, but only because she wanted to prove it. And she had.

"Let's get you changed," said Mandy.

They left the prayer room and headed for the bathroom down the hall.

She'd proved that Enid was a brute. She'd sprung it upon her, knowing the shock would be too much. It wasn't on, it wasn't fair, it couldn't be this way. There was so much that Finetta didn't know; so much that she didn't understand. In the large tiled bathroom with extra handles and a handheld shower, Enid let Mandy move about her quietly, washing her neck and stripping off her clothes. She hung on to Mandy's back. Finetta was the brute, the silent creature — she always had been. Scheming away with that bird book of hers, writing secret notes, never saying a thing. Being so pretty.

"There," said Mandy. She did up the clip at the back of the

blue dress with the scalloped collar. "That's better. Ready to go? Do you need the lav?"

Not with you in the room, thought Enid. She could keep herself buttoned up for hours if she needed to. "Where are we going?"

"Well we can't stay here," said Mandy. She led her out of the bathroom.

"My stick," said Enid. Mandy handed it to her. "I told you she was difficult."

"Your Finetta?" said Mandy, taking her arm. "Anyone'd be grateful to have such a daughter. Prompt as anything, always bringing something."

But there was so much Finetta didn't understand.

"You told her it was perfectly all right?" said Enid.

"I told you, Enid. She wasn't there. But she'll be here any minute. You can ask her then."

"It will be too late by then."

"Do you want to wait in your room? The fire's lit."

"If he doesn't come, I'll never know."

"Perhaps your Finetta can tell you."

"She doesn't know. She doesn't know anything." Enid stumbled on the step to the next corridor.

"Perhaps you'd be best waiting in the office with us. We can keep an eye on you."

In the office, Enid was placed in the same chair, near the window, side-on to the end of the desk that was scattered with cups and paper clips. Dawn crossed one fat leg over the other as she wrote something down in a file. Mandy flicked through a desk diary.

"You have to call." She tapped the plastic wood with her finger-nail. "He's the only one who knows."

He'd know because his father would have told him. Douglas would have handed over files, perfect explanations of events that included plot numbers. Dawn's chair squeaked and the girl with the poor complexion came in. "Can you help with the tea? They're clamouring."

Is that how these girls thought of them, the inmates in this brick prison of failed prayers — just stupid animals clamouring for distraction? Didn't they know they would be old one day too?

"I'll sit with you," said Mandy, as Dawn got up to the sigh and slow rise of her office chair.

Finetta had stayed home in that house of narrow corridors, *the shabby environs of Fulham*, locked with her bird book and Peel — who'd doubled as a reluctant governess for a few pennies more, and taught her house-keeping, while Ian went to and fro across London. All those years — could they have known it would go on so long? Affidavits and witness stands, letters, endless letters, arranging this and arguing that. Douglas had married his mistress and had a daughter. Ian was sent to school. Fagus had carried on, unvisited and unseeing, put to bed in a dorm and sung to by a housemaid, and through those years Ian had shrunk from her and grown into a young man, while Finetta had bloomed and wilted. Enid stared at the office floor. She saw her feet in neat brown shoes, her hands unfolding in her lap, her rise to the witness stand.

35

.....

Enid, 1930

THOSE TERRIBLE BENCHES, the green velvet drapes, the panelled room like a high-walled coffin. When she got up to speak, she tripped and jarred her thigh on the corner of a table. She wore gloves, knowing how her hands would be seen, and Crowther had said, might I suggest that you leave that fabulous bauble at home, madam? We don't want to give the wrong impression, so she'd put the ring in a drawer, locked it and pocketed the key in her purse.

Joan and Pat stared at her as if she were a painting. Their man Smithson approached her. "Miss Enid Campbell, you claim to have wanted, and in fact asked for, all of your children — a claim, my Lord, that Miss Campbell disputes — yet," he turned back to Enid, "you took only Ian. Why was that?"

"I panicked." No, that was not the right answer. She tried again. "I knew she wouldn't agree. I thought if I got Ian, Finetta would follow and she did. I knew Ian was the one Joan wanted."

"How did you know that?"

"Because she'd made him her heir."

"I was under the impression your mother had made him heir."

"She did; to her, not to Joan."

"Were you party to the conversations that took place between Lady George and Miss Campbell in the succession of her estate?"

"Of course I wasn't."

"Then how do you know what was said?"

"I don't. I'm just saying that Ian was mother's heir, and then he became Joan's after Joan inherited my mother's estate."

"In actuality, madam, your mother, Lady George, insisted her grandson remain heir despite the act of her stepping down. Who else, after all, was there? Your son is, was and always will be heir, regardless of to whom. Might I add, my Lord, that Miss Campbell wholeheartedly agreed to this. Her inheritance was an act of caretaking, as she has pointed out, and changed nothing of the facts of Ian's position. In which case," he returned to Enid, "his position as heir to Miss Campbell was no indication of partiality of feelings — it was simply a fact. That you choose this to bring to our attention points more at your own inclination to single him out than it does hers. You kidnapped him —"

"I didn't, I —"

"— directly following the disclosure from your former husband that your sister had become an extremely wealthy woman. You were, in fact, previous to this, about to agree to give full custody of all your children to Mr. Anstruther."

"I hadn't agreed to anything. I met him to discuss things and found he'd already given them away."

"And your sister was an heiress."

"That had nothing to do with it."

"Really, madam? Do you expect us to believe that the new position of your sister, with whom you have never been friendly, had no effect on you at all?"

"Of course it had an effect on me. I didn't see why she should have my children."

"As well as the family fortune."

"I had no control over that."

"No? Would it not be fair to say that by kidnapping her heir you thereby wrested control of it?"

"No, I had no choice." Stop. Crowther had said not to say that. He'd said, *be active, madam. Make everything a choice, a mother returned, a mother desperate.* "I had to act. I —"

"And what," he interrupted her, "are we doing here, if not in direct consequence of those actions? A wresting of control by the only means available: the taking of a child who knew nothing of the storms that raged above him, who neither caused them nor stirred them. The boy has been heir since his birth. This didn't seem to prevent you deserting him. What changed on your return? To whom he was heir. That was the only difference — and yet you claim this had no bearing on you. You claim to have suddenly wanted your children, all of them; yet kidnapped only him. What sense can we make of this? There is but one explanation: jealousy and spite, madam. A total disregard for the well-being of your children in an effort to wring punishment about the ears of your sister. These human emotions are not foreign to this court. Indeed, our learned judge will be all too familiar with such behaviour. Reason and rational, the facts, rarely play a part in the actions that bring people to these rooms. Jealousy, spite, revenge, the wish to cause harm — these are the motivations, more often than not, and they were the motivations that drove you, that day, to demand to see the child you had deserted, to snatch him and to refuse to give him back. You are not fit to be a mother to anyone, let alone a child of such vital importance who has known his aunt for a great deal of his life, who could not have remembered you at all, who would have continued to live a life free of confusion and upset had you not snatched him. You are not fit to be a mother, madam. Your actions have shown that. What mother ties her crippled son to a chair? What mother kidnaps a child and refuses to give him back?"

"She took everything," cried Enid.

"No, madam. She was *given* everything. It is you who are trying to take."

"My Lord." Crowther was out of his chair. "Such attacks cannot be tolerated. See, Miss Enid Campbell; My Lord, this assassination cannot go on. These are not facts, these are accusations."

"Sit down, Crowther," barked Lord Merrivale, "and Mr. Smithson, contain yourself. Someone get Miss Enid Campbell a hankie."

She thought she'd put one in her pocket. She must have left it on the hall table. She couldn't see. Her hands were shaking. Someone passed her a lilac-coloured handkerchief, just like the ones her mother used to use.

36

......

Enid, 1931

S PRING BECAME SUMMER, became autumn and winter again. Month upon month of her character destroyed out loud. Her mother wrote once, to McKinley, who forwarded it to Crowther, who gave it to Enid.

"She says she won't be attending. Her heart's bad," he'd said, handing it over.

I'll say, Enid had thought, struck for a moment by the familiarity of the writing, as if she'd forgotten her past was real. It had been a ridiculous notion to think her mother would speak for her, anyway. Crowther had said they ought to try, at least. Well, she had.

Joan had succeeded in dragging all kinds of assassins over to her side. Dr. Glendower said Enid was *unusual* and *should have been monitored.* Her parochial medic from the days at Cherry Trees said she was *terribly gloomy and unresponsive, most worrisome and failed to provide enough proper natural sustenance to her infants.* Everett hobbled in and said she *hadn't been surprised when she'd taken off.* She was *terribly sorry about it. It had upset the eldest one greatly.* Friends Enid hadn't seen for years turned out to be not friends at all, as, one after the other, they spoke of Douglas' efforts and Joan's natural instinct for mothering, the fine household she kept in Bryanston Square and the splendour of Strachur in Scotland. Mrs. McManners turned up in an enormous hat and went over the story of her knitting group, how she'd *tried so terribly to get her involved,* and how rude she'd been *in not returning her calls.*

Crowther had asked, "Who shall speak for you?" — but she'd only come up with Ruby. Silly, ringletted Ruby, who giggled when Smithson helped her to the stand.

Smithson said, "Have you known Miss Enid long?"

"Oh, I'll say, years and years. She's a wonderful person. Anyone who knows her can tell you that."

"And where did you make her acquaintance?"

"At home. Didlington."

"The house in Norfolk to which she ran when she left her family?"

"That's right."

"The house that holds itself up as some sort of Mecca for the Christian Science community."

"I don't know about Mecca. That's Islam, isn't it? We believe we are one before Christ."

"I think this court has some notion of your beliefs."

"But I've only just stood up," said Ruby.

"Not yours personally, Miss Smith. Those of your church."

"Oh, gosh, yes. Sorry."

"But while we're on the subject, do educate me further. You believe that illness must be prayed away; that the use of medicine shows a lack of faith?"

"Christian Science reveals incontrovertibly that Mind is All-in-all, that the only realities are the divine Mind and idea," said Ruby.

Smithson smiled. "Fascinating, Miss Smith. Fascinating."

"Isn't it?" said Ruby.

"I'll say," said Smithson. "Why don't you tell us more?"

"Certainly," said Ruby, despite Enid mouthing, *no.* "Christian Science is natural, but not physical. Mind governs the body, not partially but wholly. There is no pain in Truth and no truth in pain. Sick and sinful humanity is Mortal Mind. When subordinate to the divine Spirit, man cannot be controlled by sin or death. Christian Science brings to the body the sunlight of Truth, which invigorates and purifies. Christian Science acts as an alternative, neutralising error with Truth. It changes the secretions, expels humours, dissolves tumours, relaxes rigid muscles, restores carious bones to soundness —"

"That's enough," said Lord Merrivale.

Ruby tilted her head to see him, and her ringlets bobbed against her shoulders. "Don't you want to know how it does it?"

"No," said Lord Merrivale.

"I think we've all got the gist," said Smithson.

When it was Crowther's turn he managed to get her onto the topic of Enid's fine character again, but it all felt a little too late.

Another Christmas, another attempt at joviality gone wrong. She'd won him for the day, and immediately, as the day dawned, regretted it. Stockings that had failed to match up to Joan's, a goose none of them could eat, and presents that fell flat. Finetta had smiled and said thank you Mummy for a silk robin, and put it aside. Ian hadn't known what to do with a stamp book. Douglas had sent him a boat. At least he'd loved that. It was over. That was the best she could say. She'd taken them to a Christmas fair, bought them each a square of fudge, and avoided any post that didn't look Christmassy; an absurd amount of invitations to join Ruby at Didlington Hall and a card from Crowther's office — that had been the sum of it. Everything else was piled on the table in the hall. The High Courts were shut until well into the new year, and so was she.

Could it really have been six years? She'd have a sherry, that's what she'd do. Celebrate the arrival of 1932 and her survival of six years of slaughter. She poured herself a glass. They hadn't got her yet, though, had they? She was still standing, or sitting anyway — in her chair by the fire, her son playing with his boat in his bedroom. She could hear him and Finetta sailing over choppy waters through the wall. She leaned her head back. The sherry melted into her limbs. She closed her eyes. It wasn't so bad, the assassination. She'd got used to the feeling of dogs at her throat. They hadn't killed her yet. They kept getting side-tracked by doctor's reports, and applications to extend his visits. Crowther had suggested they put his time on tick. They'd agreed before school broke up — that's how he'd put it; as if the legal system was a term at Eton — that they'd *apply to have her costs seen* — get Joan to pay a loan until judgement. "Won't it delay things?" she'd replied. She was meeting his costs but only just. Her allowance was emptied every month. Twice Coutts & Co had given her a loan, but Crowther hadn't seemed so keen on getting to the end when the last bill went unpaid. He'd leaned his fat stomach into his desk and said, "We cannot ignore the housekeeping, madam." Just like Miss Barnes.

The bell rang. She got up and went to the window. No one in the street. The portico obscured the front door — if someone was standing up close she couldn't have seen them. She went downstairs. The bell rang again. She checked her face in the hall mirror, her hair, the shawl slung over her shoulders. She noticed as she turned the latch that her feet were bare.

"May I introduce myself, madam, the finest winda' cleaners and chimney sweepers in Fulham —"

"Oh." A man in overalls, a cart loaded with ladders, a boy on the seat wrapped in overcoat, horse stamping in the snow. Not anything else. Not police or post boys with telegrams; not fight and defence and panic.

"Sackler & Potts." He handed her a card. "May I ask if you have anyone engaged? Charming house."

"Thank you."

"We'd be ready to start right away."

"Would you?" Douglas used to organise the men — the windows of her house had got so black she'd forgotten what clean was.

"I take it you have that chimney swept regular."

She'd never had it done at all.

"Perhaps you'd like me to speak to the gentleman?"

"There isn't one," said Enid. "But I suppose it needs doing."

"I'll say it needs doing, madam."

Sackler, or perhaps Potts, shifted on his feet. His cart horse snorted plumes of hot breath, and the boy huddled deeper into his coat.

"Will you come back next week?" She couldn't deal with it now.

"I'll say I will," said Sackler or Potts. "Be delighted."

She shut the door. You see? she said to herself, as she switched the light off in the hall. You are handling yourself. You are coping. It's all going to be all right.

As she passed the hall table, a car back fired in the street and she jumped, knocking the table edge. The pile of letters, balanced in a wide wicker basket, overflowing and only just kept in check by luck, found its luck had run out and fell in a waterfall of correspondence to the floor.

Damn it. She bent to pick them up. Gathered in her hands, there seemed no point in putting them back. She took them upstairs to the sitting room, her sherry, the fire. They sprawled on the little table beside her chair.

The first was a bill, the second a bill, and the third a letter from Ruby. She put them all aside. She couldn't face any of them. The fourth was post-marked Hatfield — where Douglas lived. Douglas' writing on the envelope. She opened it. There was nothing in it but a telegram.

> *Please come at once. Regret to inform you of the death of your son, Fagus. Our deepest condolences and regret. Un-avoidable circumstances.*
> Miss L. Barnes

She read it again.

> *Regret to inform you*
> *death of your son*
> *Fagus*

What happened next wasn't under her control. It reminded her of packing up Cherry Trees.

She put her head round the door of Ian's bedroom. He was sitting on the floor, Finetta beside him. They were throwing soldiers off the boat into the wild and choppy ocean.

"Your brother's dead."

They both looked up. She waited to see if they wanted to say anything, but they didn't. They looked at her and after a moment, a pause, she couldn't tell how long, they went on with their boat, so she shut the door. She shut the door, went to her chair by the fire and closed her eyes.

37

.....

Enid, 1964

THE GHOST THAT she couldn't get rid of.

The phrase span like so much flotsam, caught in the eddies of her mind.

The ghost that she couldn't get rid of.

Dawn's chair squeaked. The telephone rang. Mandy said, "I think that's your Finetta."

Enid opened her eyes. "Well, answer it."

"Not the telephone." Mandy pointed at the window. "Outside."

She looked. Finetta, all right. Getting out of that car. On her own.

Enid closed her eyes again and the phrase span and span, twirling her back to the fire, the sitting room, Evelyn Gardens. At some point, somewhere in the time it had taken her to do nothing, she'd moved from her armchair by the fire, snow on the ground outside, Ian and Finetta playing in the room next door.

She'd got up and done something. She must have. She must have carried on living, or how else could she be here? A package had arrived a while later, forwarded again by Douglas — Fagus' belongings, the coroner's report, another scribble from Miss Barnes.

"Mother."

A file, papers, his things. She'd put them away. She'd put them on a shelf.

"Mother?"

Seven years after Fagus' death, on the eve of another war, a bookend to the first, which wrapped the collapse of her family in the hands of something greater, she'd stood in Court 14 of the chancery division for the last time.

Finetta was already gone: to Vienna, to a finishing school far away, where she'd stayed even after school was done. Ian was in his last year at Eton; he was grown into a young man alive with the prospect of life; a man unrecognisable from the little boy who'd hidden beneath the bed and made her knuckles bleed. She hardly saw him; only when she could, when tea at school was a court order and he sat not eating, lounging in his chair in whatever tea rooms she'd insisted on, smoking while she asked, *shall I be mother?*

God knows what she'd done in the years between; how she'd lived, who she'd been, what little silly, daily trinkets had filled her waking hours. Washing, eating, reading books; she must have done all those things. She'd sat for Augustus John — she knew that had happened, because she had the picture to prove it: her head half-turned, her hand in mid-gesture as if she'd been saying something, though she could never remember what, nor how she got there, or what she'd done after or before. The before and after, the months and years of life were a blur of dark rooms and emptiness. They were loss. All of them, except the day of the final court hearing.

That day was not a blur to her at all; that day she remembered with clarity. The weather — it had been fine, she'd worn a cotton dress with forget-me-nots printed on it, and a scarf, draped over her shoulders because she knew the courtroom was cold. The smell of that room — ever musty with a tang of sweat. The look of the benches lined against the back wall: narrow, cramped, uncomfortable. The chairs and tables set on the parquet floor at the front, for Smithson and Crowther to cough over, rest their files upon and look through their papers for the very last time.

Everyone had agreed that Enid was an unfit mother, and Joan, Ian's rightful guardian. Everyone had agreed that Enid was mad, unsafe, a liability; all except Lord Merrivale, who, twelve years after it had begun, coughed, rustled his papers, and said, *I find for Miss Enid Campbell. Her son shall stay with her.*

Joan had screamed, and Pat had covered her face with her hands.

"Mother, it's me."

She'd gone home to her house of narrow corridors and thought: *now what?*

"You don't need to worry."

Her £41 a month had ceased long ago to meet her bills — Crowther, the house, Peel. She was in debt, and she was penniless.

"I told him not to come."

She'd written to Joan. That's right. It had been that way round. She'd written to Joan: *Pay off my debts and you can have him. £500 should do it. Here are Crowther's bills. Send the rest to me.*

"He isn't coming. Can she not hear me?"

Again, in her mind, she saw Ian driving away, the back of his head in the back of her sister's Rolls as the car eased out of Evelyn Gardens onto the Fulham Road and turned left. After he'd gone, Joan had cut her off. The Augustus John portrait and the files from Castlemere, they'd moved with her as she'd moved in ever-decreasing circles, from Evelyn Gardens to a smaller house in Chelsea, and a smaller one still in Pimlico, and then out of London for good; to Warminster, a workman's cottage on a dreary cobbled lane, that had had the benefit of being both easy to heat and walking distance to the local First Church of Christ.

"Mother." The touch on her shoulder made her jolt. She opened her eyes. Finetta was standing over her, smiling, leaning toward her, looking for all the world as if she was doing good.

"What are you doing here?" said Enid. Her eyes and nose watered but her mouth was dry.

"I've come for tea, mother," said Finetta. She held a tin of shortbreads.

"Without Ian?"

"Without him, yes."

"Why?"

"Why? You told me not to bring him."

"I did nothing of the sort."

"But Mother, you telephoned," said Finetta.

"I did not."

"She's been like this all day," said Mandy.

"Go and get him," said Enid.

"I can't," said Finetta.

"Go and get him this instant."

"I can't," said Finetta again, shaking her head like a mule that didn't understand plain English.

"I said, get him!" shouted Enid, but it came out weak, the volume broken.

"Enid," said Mandy.

"Let's get her to her room," said Dawn.

38

.....

Enid, 1964

A SLOW ACHE up the stairs, Mandy's steadying grip on her arm; Enid was led to her bedroom.

"I'll sit with her," said Finetta.

"Take me over there." Enid pointed at her bed.

She unlocked the Formica cupboard and drew out the portrait. Under it was a file. She put the portrait on the bed beside her, and the file on her lap. When she opened it, she was careful not to let anything slip. The top sheet was a typed document.

FREDERICK EDWARD TILLYARD M.B. *on oath saith:—*

I am a Registered Medical Practitioner and reside at 4 Brooklyn Chambers, Brooklyn Road, Worthing.

I was called at 8:30 a.m. on 2nd January 1932 to see a child at Castlemere. The child was dead when I arrived, but

I think he had only been dead for a few minutes before. From the evidence of a fall downstairs and the appearance of the deceased, it would appear likely that death was due to a fracture of the skull.

I made a post mortem examination of the body on the Sunday the 3rd instant. There were no external marks of injury that I saw. The internal organs appeared to be healthy but there was a condition of hydrocephalus present and the skull was very thin; there was a long fracture of the skull about four inches long extending down the temporal bone to the base; beneath the fracture and between the skull and the brain there was a large clot of blood occupying about two-thirds of the side of the skull. Death was due to coma following compression of the brain from the clot, the result of the fracture.

(signed) FREDERICK E. TILLYARD M.B.

Clipped to it was the scribble from Miss Barnes.

To whom it may concern
As there were no family members in attendance and no instruction given, I took it upon myself to arrange a simple ceremony for Fagus.

She'd only stayed away because of Joan.

Please find the cemetery address and plot number enclosed.

A grave was no place for a reunion but it wouldn't have been. It would have been just her.

There was no piece of paper with address and plot number; not when she'd opened it the first time, on the 5th of January 1932, or now. No address or plot number had fluttered out from between his school reports and notes from the coroner, and although she'd written, although she'd tried, although she'd thought about it, she'd never found a way. She'd meant to. She'd wanted to. She almost had.

There was a knock on the door.

"That must be tea," said Finetta, getting to her feet.

When Finetta opened it and stood back, Enid thought, by some stroke of incredible fortune, that it was Ivar come to see her — an older Ivar who hadn't died, who'd lived and taken care of them all. But then Finetta said, "Ian," and the spell was broken.

He spoke to Dawn who clattered in after him with a tea trolley. "Let me." He lifted an end off the rucked corner of the rug and wheeled it to a stop beside the armchairs. The cups clinked, the teapot spilled a drop from its spout, and Dawn giggled like a schoolgirl.

Finetta said, "You came."

Like a statement from an imbecile. Of course he'd come. She'd asked him to.

"I decided I should. Hello, Mother." He came over to her.

"Shall I put that aside for you?" Finetta reached for the file on Enid's lap.

"Have you come to tell me?" Enid said to Ian.

Finetta handed Enid her stick. "Come and have tea."

"Is that the Augustus John?" Ian took Enid's arm as if he'd seen her yesterday. Ivar's height and slim build. He smelled of expensive soap and lavender; his hands were soft.

Finetta fussed about, being mother, handing out cups. He looked around for a third chair, took the one from the window and put it beside the tea things, then sat in the other armchair and rested his ankle on his knee. Douglas but blonder, her eyes, Ivar's nose.

Enid crossed her ankles carefully to one side, her stick, propped beside her. "And are you keen on art?"

"Very."

"Do you collect?"

"Just started."

She couldn't take her eyes from him. "I don't suppose it's of worth." He was a mirage, another ghost.

He went over to her bed and picked it up. "I'd say that would fetch at least £500. Wouldn't you, Mop?"

Finetta opened the shortbreads. "I wouldn't know."

"I heard you kept it in a cupboard." He sat again, looking at Enid, the portrait on his lap.

Enid balanced the cup and saucer carefully on her knee. Finetta held out the plate of biscuits. Enid took one and put it down on the side of her saucer where it threatened to fall, so she put the whole lot on the table. She had to lean forward. It took all her strength.

Ian said, "I might have it."

Enid replied, "I don't have it."

"He's talking about the portrait, Mother," said Finetta.

"The portrait?"

Ian said, "If you don't mind."

Enid said, "I don't mind about the portrait."

"Well I don't want it," said Finetta, helping Ian to milk.

"You're very welcome to it," said Enid. "Please do have it." She played her hand over her ring, then slipped it from her finger. "This was your grandmother's." She put it on the table.

"Are you giving that to Ian, too?" said Finetta.

"If he wants it," said Enid.

Ian stood up, took the ring, and put it in his pocket. "I shan't keep you any longer."

Finetta had just topped up her own cup with milk, but she swung the milk jug away too quickly, without looking properly, and the lip caught the edge of the cup, sending it clattering sideways onto its saucer, and a cascade of tea onto the biscuits. She went into a commotion of catching crockery with both hands while Ian stood silently by, but all Enid could hear was the closed file, screaming at her from the bed.

She looked up at Ian and didn't understand. "You're going? Haven't you come to tell me?"

Finetta seemed to suddenly run out of steam. She left the sodden biscuits and the saucer, her tea half drunk, half spilled. She stood up too. "Tell you what, mother?"

"The address." Enid struggled to her feet. "The plot. Where he's buried. Your father had it. He knew. And it's no good accusing. Do you see? We all —"

Finetta said, "You're getting tired, Mother."

"I wanted to go, but she'd have been there. I didn't know who would have been there."

"Shall I bring you more shortbreads next week?" Finetta went over to the wardrobe and inspected the dresses.

"A funeral's no place for a reunion," said Enid. But they were leaving. They were leaving with their judgement intact and she hadn't had a chance.

Finetta closed the wardrobe door. "If there's anything else you need, you can leave a note in the office."

Enid looked down at her feet, so old, so worn out, squashed into unpleasant shoes. "You can't come here and accuse. I won't be accused."

"Shall we say goodbye?" said Ian.

"I couldn't go. Do you see? I tried but I simply couldn't. Joan put him there. Not me."

"I don't want to talk about Fagus," said Ian.

But Enid carried on regardless, set on a path, a desperate scramble up the hill, the boulder toppling in her hands. "Nobody could have stopped what happened. It was an accident. It didn't make any difference to anything. I had to keep fighting. I had nothing." She stared at her son and daughter, but all she saw was fear and shame shaped in the colour of their eyes. "She offered me a way out. I didn't know I'd never see you."

Ian took one step towards her. "She didn't offer it you. You *sold* me. Did you ever think I'd want to see you again?"

Why had it not occurred to her that Joan would tell him? It had. She'd shut it out.

Ian said, "I got on the train that term, my last year at school. Joan told me on the platform as I was leaving. I'd joked with her, we always had this joke between us — *not long now,* and we both knew I wasn't talking about Eton, but she'd hugged me and said, *Oh no, darling. It's over. She offered me a price.* It was only when I pressed that she told me. £500. I sat on that train and thought *at least I know what I'm worth.*"

Of course she'd told him. Of course she had.

"You stayed away," said Enid.

"You couldn't have expected me to do different. What mother sells her child? What mother kidnaps? What mother pops her head round the door and says, *your brother's dead.* Those were your exact words —" he looked quickly at Finetta "— weren't they, Mop? *Your brother's dead* and then you shut the door again and carried on parcelling me about for another seven years."

Finetta said, "We should leave."

Ian swapped the portrait to his other hand. "Do you know what Joan said before she died? She said, *I'm sorry we made such a hash of it,* a hash. As if we, me, all of us, were just a bit of a mistake."

Enid gripped her stick with both hands. "She's dead?"

He looked from Finetta to Enid. "Of course she is. Four years ago."

Finetta said, "I didn't think she needed to know."

Enid thumped her stick on the carpet. "I needed to know."

"And now you do. I didn't come here to accuse you. I don't want anything to do with you at all. I just came for this."

"The portrait?" said Enid.

"And in any case," he put his other hand in his pocket, "what can I accuse you of that you don't already know yourself? I'm glad I got away. At least Joan loved me."

"I loved you."

"You didn't love anyone."

"I loved Fagus," Enid cried.

"And he died and no one went to his funeral."

"I want to see it."

"His grave?"

"Of course, his grave."

"Well you can't."

"You don't know where it is?"

"Oh, I know where it is. I've got the plot number; only it's not there any more. It was built over. Flats apparently. Joan told me."

"Flats?"

"Years ago." He tucked the portrait under his arm. "I'm glad you kept hold of this. Perhaps I've doubled in value since then too."

Finetta opened the door. "Ian."

He hadn't taken his eyes from Enid. He stood before her, this life blood of hers; she needed only one word, or two, to make her cry, to make her breakdown, but instead he said, "I shan't see you again."

They shut the door behind them. She stood for a while longer in the middle of the room, staring at the door, listening as their footsteps grew faint. Then she walked slowly to the chairs still grouped around the tea tray. She hauled and dragged her chair back to the window. It took her ages; she had to stop twice and sit down on it, halted at a peculiar angle on the rug. When she finally got it into place, she dropped her stick in the effort to squeeze between the chair and the window. She'd pushed it too close, her legs were cramped, but she squashed in anyway, sat down and left her stick lying there on the carpet out of reach. It didn't matter. She wasn't planning on getting up.

39

.....

Finetta, 1964

T HE GENERATIONS OF sculpting that had refined her
marble beauty to perfection remained intact and unmoved
as she followed Ian away from their mother's room. She kissed
him goodbye in the foyer. "That's that then."

"See you for lunch. Let's make it twice yearly, shall we?"

"Let's."

"And I'll look into that house in Newbury."

"I'd like that."

She watched him walk across the car park to his Aston Martin,
his back straight, his suit well-cut, the keys jangling in his hands.
Then she went along to the office and popped her head around
the door. "I've got to get something from my car — I won't be a
minute. I'll call you when we've finished our tea."

"Is she feeling better?" said Mandy.

"Oh, much better," said Finetta.

When she was sure Ian had driven away, she went out to her car and got the quilt from the passenger seat. The tissue paper crunched as she held it snug against her chest. She carried it along the hall, past the office, up the three twisting stairs and along the corridor to her mother's room. Enid had managed to move her chair back to the window. God, the strength of that woman when she needed it.

She seemed to be sleeping. She didn't move as Finetta crossed the room; she was completely still. Her stick was on the floor again — Finetta picked it up, and hooked it over the end of the bed. The file was still there where she'd left it, closed and put aside. She shut it away in the bedside cupboard. Built over by flats. She hadn't known that either. Ian had never said. She'd never asked. They never talked about him. That was the most they'd talked about him since it happened.

She hardly remembered him. His was a name followed by silence, if it was ever spoken at all, and it had only been spoken by Joan; occasionally and only when he was alive. She remembered a summer at Strachur, the summer before her mother came back when she and Ian had been up visiting their grandmother. They'd been bouncing a ball down the stairs when their grandmother had come upon them and snapped at them so loud to *stop it immediately* that she'd made Finetta cry. They were sent outside to play on the lawn. Finetta thought it was the ball that had been the problem — so many precious things, so much that was breakable — but Joan had said *no, darling, Fagus* — and left it at that, her sentence unfinished. Built over by flats. Why had she never asked? Why had Ian never said? Because that was what her family did, wasn't it. They never said. They never asked. They just buried everything and built over it with flats, said there was nothing they could do, said *sorry we made such a hash of it.*

She'd been there when Joan had said that. She'd gone round to the flat in Cumberland Place. She wasn't sure when the house in Bryanston Square was sold, perhaps during the war, perhaps after. It had survived the bombing — she'd gone to look at it quickly before tea with her aunt, had stood for a moment on the corner of Bryanston Square staring up — she hardly remembered it, really. Black and white tiled hall, large, curving staircase, drawing room with French windows — those snap-shot images were all she had. The flat wasn't like that. It was crowded with heavy patterns and smoke, Joan with her legs up on a soft footstool, tan stockings, her feet bulging out of slippers; Pat reading the paper, grey-haired, refined, still thin, an air of completion about both of them that left little room for anything else. Finetta hadn't known where to sit, so she'd made the tea instead, in the little galley kitchen. *I'm sorry we made such a hash of it.* She'd peeked around the doorway while the kettle boiled and seen Ian sitting close to Joan; he'd pulled his chair up, Joan held his hand. She'd thought *she must be dying. No one ever says things like that unless they're dying* and turned off the gas. She'd been right, too. It was the last time either of them had seen her.

Finetta stood quietly behind her mother and watched the dropped face, completely still, nearly dead, not dead enough but almost; her reflection ghost-like in the glass. Her hands lay one over the other in her lap; no ring against that mud-spattered skin. Her finger looked empty without it.

She gripped the back of the chair, but her mother didn't move. The ring that was supposed to be hers was barrelling away from her; she could feel it as she pictured Ian relaxed at the wheel, the emerald, the diamonds and gold mildly heavy in his pocket. It was speeding away in the warm, closed world of the Aston, being taken to a place unreachable. That was a wall she couldn't climb, a chasm she couldn't jump; Ian did as he liked, she couldn't ask for it back, it was not what one did. It would be gone and not mentioned, not allowed to be mentioned by anyone but him. The way he'd picked it up, the way he'd squirrelled it away with the kind of command that men call self-possession. How he'd stood by as the milk crashed and the tea went flying. Those seconds of fated action — what if she'd spoken then, if she'd made a scene, if she'd said all the things she'd been bottling up all these years? But no. Women laid traps. Women laid in wait, and if they came home empty handed, it was nobody's fault but their own.

Not for a moment had she thought she wouldn't have it; those precious stones that had defined her mother's bones, had defined Finetta too. She'd imagined putting it on, seeing it on her finger for the first time and feeling, like magic, herself step into line with the generations of women behind her; the ring, an emblem of belonging unrealised. She hadn't known she'd always be without, that her mother's endless hatred really would have no end. But it was gone. It was speeding away from her, already out of reach, and her mother appeared to be sleeping.

She unwrapped the quilt and put it on a chair while she straightened and refolded the tissue paper — she'd use it again. There was no need to waste it. It would do for Christmas wrapping to her daughter. She'd bought her a necklace that she'd found at a Christmas fair. She was going to mail it, but perhaps if Ian was going out there he could take it. With the ring. Would he give it to his niece, right the ship that had listed badly, set the line straight again? It had crossed her mind more than once that her own daughter didn't deserve it, wouldn't value it, would likely not get married anyway, that she'd feel far safer leaving it to her son, but more often than not she'd ended up thinking *I shall probably have to*. Not now, though. Not now. Her mother had once again and with spectacular dismissal, broken something Finetta thought could never be broken.

She picked up the quilt. With two corners pinched between her thumbs and forefingers, she flapped it open. It flowed over the bed, a perfect map of discarded pieces made to look whole, a pretence that worked, a patchwork of mistakes hidden beneath calico — it fitted perfectly.

Epilogue

I'D KNOWN THIS story in potted facts since I was a child — my father was sold to his aunt for five hundred pounds, his mother was mad and awful, he'd had a lucky escape. What I didn't know, and will never know, were the emotions that went with it. I knew his but not those of Enid or Joan, Sybil or Douglas. None of them were alive when I was born, and although Finetta — Mop, as we knew her — used to make fudge for us, I was too young to think her connected, and never asked her anything, so these, the feelings in this book are my imaginings; a tracing of the facts over my interpretation of their inner lives.

My father gave me access to his archive of letters, court papers, medical reports and photographs, and permission to write this story. He wanted to talk about it, and told me much of what has ended up here — being pulled across the door by his mother when she kidnapped him leaving Nanny Duncan on the other side, playing with his boat when his mother told him Fagus was dead, how on the train back to Eton for his last year of school he'd thought *at least I know what I'm worth.* I asked him, if his mother were here now, what he'd say to her. He said *read my books,* and that was the birth of it really, the first clear glimpse into the nature of the hearts who made, and suffered, these decisions. It was the first sign that he cared.

It's easy to demonise and make cut-outs of characters never met, it's easy to say Enid was bad and Joan good and Douglas hopeless, but it wouldn't be the truth, and letting them live here again, giving them voice, has allowed that black and white picture to colour. They were like us — flawed, vulnerable to circumstance, well-intentioned sometimes, trying and failing and trying again to live with themselves. He was a child and damaged by it; they were adults and should have known better, yet the failure was there in the apple unbitten in the palm — their course was set through circumstance and luck, or lack of it: a war, favouritism, wealth and mental health — that Enid suffered depression became clear to me in the writing. I set out to vindicate her — a way of giving my father a version of her that wasn't so awful, excusing her in some way that would allow him to love her — and gave it up when the facts revealed an impossible to comprehend network of choices. Yet I find now that I do understand, without needing to say what she did was acceptable. It was not, and yet she had no one. Both of these are true, and both have weight. She wasn't made for children. They were forced upon her, and everyone suffered as a consequence. She suffered post-natal depression — a heightening of the grief she already felt from life itself. She was pinpointed as mad and unacceptable, she was vilified and left alone, she became someone cold.

And then there was Fagus, born with hydrocephalus, diagnosed with Sleeping Sickness, tied to a chair and sent to a home on the south coast. He is at the centre of this book. It was his death that brought home the neglect. The boy shoved out, the brother my father talked about, the body whose grave was gone. When my father told me it had been built over by flats, I took the address and plot number and went in search. I found it, not inaccessible, but as an unmarked mound among hundreds of gravestones in a cemetery in Eastbourne. I had a headstone made, and before my father died, I took him there to see it.

Acknowledgements

I've been dreaming of writing these acknowledgements for a decade. Now here I am, and as with so many aspects of becoming published for the first time, I can't quite believe it. Yet here goes . . .

My thanks to Dr. Sally Cline, who was there at the beginning, who I met on a flight to Colorado, a ticket bought to get away from the book I thought I couldn't write, that landed me in the seat beside her, and nine hours later, a place on her mentoring scheme for emerging writers. You taught me so much, Sal, not least, how to murder my darlings. Tor Udall, who got me and my work out of the house — I'd still be whining at the kitchen table if it wasn't for you. Andrew Wille, editor extraordinaire, who took a novella, saw it was a novel, and kept saying it until I listened. The early readers and champions of this book: Sara Nunan,

Acknowledgements

Dr. Harriet Mahood, Victoria Ogilvy, Andrew Cooke, Jacqueline Gerrard and Ysenda Maxtone Graham. Thank you for your endless encouragement when all I had was doubt. My gratitude to Clare Griffin, who keeps my head straight. A million thanks to my wonderful agent, Jenny Savill, who continues to hold my hand, and is patient, and whose belief in this novel changed my life. Jen and Chris Hamilton-Emery at Salt — the work you do keeps us literary fiction writers alive, not just in print but in conviction. I can't thank you enough for choosing to publish this book. My publicists, Emma Dowson and Sophie Ransom — I'd be lost without you. My friends and family, particularly Jacobi and Blake (pity the children of writers . . .) for putting up with my absences, my terrible moods, and obsessive, determined nature. And lastly, although he really should come first, my thanks to my father, for giving me this story in the first place, and his blessing to write it.